I ATE THE SHERIFF

Mallory Caine, Zombie-At-Law Thriller #3

JAMES SCOTT BELL

Print version:

ISBN 10: 0-910355-45-2

ISBN 13: 978-0-910355-45-2

Cover art by Josh Kenfield

Published by
Compendium Press
Woodland Hills, CA

PART ONE

I guess being dead gives you a whole new perspective on life.
    — Harry Dresden, legendary wizard

CHAPTER ONE

"HELLO, my name is Mallory, and I'm a zombie."

"Hi, Mallory."

"It's been twenty days since I ate a human brain."

Applause.

"It hasn't been easy. In fact, it's been the hardest thing I've ever done. I love me some brain. Don't deny it. I love how it makes me feel, how it strengthens me. I'm sorry, but cow brains just don't do it. My skin is sallow and I feel weak all the time. I think I could live with dolphin brain, but then of course I'd be beheaded by PETA."

Laughter. It was a bit uncomfortable, for we were all recovering zombies and losing our heads was a major concern of our everyday lives.

But nevertheless here we were, in the fellowship room at a Catholic church in Hollywood. The Zombies Anonymous group was started by Father Clemente, my friend and confidante, who finally got around to convincing me I needed help, that eating human beings was not something God wanted me to do.

Whatever. I still have issues with the Big Kahuna. I know I'm supposed to acknowledge a "higher power" here. But I've been pretty much on my own my whole life and I'm not ready to give myself up to anyone or anything.

But I am trying to do the right thing by Father Clemente. I owe him that much. He's been one of my few allies in this town. It's also for my own good. I'm hoping some sort of karmic balance will get me my soul back if I at least try to do the right thing.

"Now I know we're not supposed to be about excuses here. I get that. We're not playing the victim card. In fact, we eat victims for lunch."

Again, laughter filled the room. A little too much for Father Clemente's taste. He was wincing in the corner and shaking his gray head. I couldn't help that. I was on a roll.

"But I have to say, I didn't want this gig. Who among us did? How I got here is that the jerk I was in love with killed me. And then somebody who I trusted brought me back to life. And now I'm walking around like this, like we all are. So is this world some big cosmic playground with invisible hands moving the pieces? Maybe so. Father Clemente over there can tell you all about that. He may even tell you it's a good thing. But that doesn't erase the fact that I am really hacked off right now. And when I get to feeling this way I want to eat a law professor's brain, or maybe a nuclear physicist's. I want to find the smartest person in the room and remove their head and suck out their cerebellum. I admit that. I admit that's what's going on inside me. And I am trying very hard not to go on antidepressants. Are there antidepressants for zombies? Maybe. Maybe eating surfer brains would mellow us out."

More laughter.

"Well, here's the deal. It's about taking responsibility. It's about living with courage. I'm not going to be bossed around. Not by God, or the church, not by the devil, not by anybody."

Applause. Father Clemente started to say something. I'm sure he wanted to stop me from going on. But he let it go. Maybe he wanted this to be like my confession. Okay, I would let him have it with both barrels.

"And now if you'll excuse me, I want to sit down and listen to somebody else, because I'm starting to get a flashback. I'm starting to remember the very first brain I ate. It was from the head of a UCLA PhD candidate. In biology. Man, it was some of the best eating I've ever had. And I'm truly sorry. Except for the UCLA part."

I sat down. My head was pounding with thoughts of chewy doctorates. I tried to concentrate on the next zombie to speak. I'd not seen him at the meetings before. But new ones were trickling in. There were more zombies in L.A. than I'd realized. But that's L.A. for you. We take in all kinds.

"Hi, my name is Reuben, and I'm a zombie."

"Hi, Reuben."

"I ate a human brain yesterday but not today."

In unison several zombies said, "One day at a time!"

"Thanks," Reuben said. He was maybe in his mid-fifties, rough-hewn face like an old cowboy. "I reckon that's the thing I got to remember. I come from New Mexico, and we sure had some good eatin' down there. I don't know what it is with our friends south of the border, but the brains are spicy and always have a little kick."

That was it. I loved Mexican food when I was truly alive, and to be given this in my condition was just too much. I got up and, without so much as a glance at Father Clemente, went out the front doors of the church.

OUTSIDE IN THE NIGHT AIR, SAL, MY ALT-ROCK-BAND-LEADING zombie friend, said, "I can't do this anymore!"

"I know how you feel, Sal. Believe me, I know. But you've only been clean a week."

"Don't even call it clean! I feel dirty and shriveled—"

"Yeah—"

"I want an accountant. I've been lusting after accountant all day."

"Easy, Sal." Sal is in his early twenties and has lustrous nut-colored hair and, if not for the zombie part, would make a good catch for any woman. But being in the L.A. rock scene as he is, he tends toward fashionable dark angst anyway. He didn't need the zombie thing on top of all that.

"I can't go on trying to be something I'm not," Sal said.

I put my arm around him. "What do you say we go play some music and eat some cow brain and wash it down with Jack Daniels? We'll get stink roaring drunk. If they want us to stay sober when it comes to human flesh, we'll get hammered and laugh about it. What do you say?"

He looked at the ground. We were now at the corner of Hollywood Boulevard and Cherokee. The street was packed with what some called the night crowd, but what zombies called a buffet. It was like a recovering sex addict going into a strip club, or a dieter with a hundred pounds to lose walking into an all-you-can-eat joint with a gift card.

I could feel Sal tensing, big time.

"How about we get a hot dog," I said, "and pretend it's James Gandolfini's finger?"

Sal didn't laugh.

We stood there for a moment and watched. People wandering around looking for ways to distract themselves from troubling questions about life and death.

That was not a luxury for me, as I was in a netherworld of undead existence, unable to die lest my soul be consigned to a place I knew not of. Like what Hamlet said. Roughly translating his famous soliloquy: "Dude, why go through all this trouble in life when you can end the suffering by killing yourself? You can go into a restful sleep. But wait a minute, that kind of sleep, maybe you'll end up in a bad dream on the other side ... so you probably better stick around with what you know than speed to a place you don't know. Man, this is driving me nuts!"

For a zombie, this is deeply meaningful. We're cursed and don't know where the hell we're going, but it may be hell itself.

CHAPTER TWO

THE NEXT MORNING I prepared for the office. I'm a working lawyer, and nobody is going to take that away from me. There is still a world out there that needs help, and the one thing I know how to do is practice law. I can kick butt in court, and I can also figure out what people need from the system. I was very happy practicing with the public defender's office before Aaron Argula shot me down.

Now, with the all-cow-brain diet, my skin was more problematic than ever. I use a special cream made of shark cartilage to keep it supple, keep it from flaking off. The flaking was getting worse. If I didn't watch it, chunks of my skin would fall off like tiles from a Spanish-style roof. I shudder to think (yes, zombies shudder when they think, at least zombie lawyers can, though some debate the point) that this is a sign I am on the way out, so to speak. Dying and staying dead.

So I go through my morning routine, which involves rubbing my entire body with the stuff, lots of it.

And that body still looked pretty good, thank you very much. Considering I was undead, of course. I still have desires. Not just for the physical, but I so wanted to have a family. I wanted to settle down with one man and have a couple of kids and practice

law and watch my kids grow up and go to school and find something they love to do and watch them do it.

Not an option now.

So I took my usual half-hour slather in my loft apartment in
the middle of downtown, then walked the couple blocks to my
office on Broadway.

My office is above the combination tobacco store and novelty
shop. I call it the Smoke 'n Joke. A large woman I have named
LoGo—easier on the tongue than Lolita Maria Sofia Consuelo
Hidalgo—is the manager. She is a substantially built remnant of
the Latino entertainment heyday of the 1970s. She always bugs
me about the rent. I usually get it to her late. This is no joke
to her.

"Morning, Lo," I said.

"Is time for my money," she said. She was sitting behind her
glass counter, as usual, the one filled with various toys and tricks
and cigarette packs.

"Of course it is," I said.

"You got client?"

"I've got people dying to be my client," I said.

She threw back her head dismissively. "Five hundred. Now."

Think, Mallory. "When are you going to fix the door?"

"Eh?"

I gestured toward the interior door that leads to the hallway
that leads to the elevator that takes several days to go one floor.
"The security lock hasn't worked for months," I said. "Any Tom,
Dick or Harry can waltz right in."

"Who Harry?"

"I'll get back to you."

"Five hundred! "

I went and pushed open the security door with one hand. I
could have also used my breath to open it

Upstairs is my modest cell. I had a few legal matters to take
care of off the bat. For one thing, my father was still in jail awaiting
retrial for killing a cop. The cop was a zombie and it was clearly

self-defense. But when you cut off a cop's head, even if they are undead, the district attorney's office takes it seriously.

So I was going over the transcript of the first trial, for which Aaron Argula was the prosecutor, when somebody scratched my door.

That's right, scratched.

Unsure what that meant, I simply said, "Come in."

He was about six feet tall, with thick black hair, long eyelashes, luminescent blue eyes. His broad shoulders radiated strength. The first button of his shirt was undone, revealing a luxuriant swatch of chest hair. I would've taken him for a Mediterranean import if not for his slight Texas twang.

"Are you Mallory Caine?" he said.

"If this was a Western, I'd say, Who's asking?"

He shut the door behind him. Then put his hand over his eyes. "I'm sorry. I scratched your door, didn't I?"

"And you are?"

"May I sit down?"

I motioned to one of my client chairs.

He sat and took a deep breath. "I'm told that you're a lawyer who'll understand what I'm about to tell you."

"That remains to be seen," I said. "There are a lot of things I don't understand. But I can assure you, anything you tell me will remain completely confidential."

He nodded. "I appreciate that. But the most important thing to me is I want you to believe me."

"Well, that all depends on what you tell me. People have been known to lie to their lawyers."

"I guess that's probably so."

"And it's the worst thing you can do," I said. "So I'll make you this deal. You never lie to me, I will never lie to you. And we'll keep things on that basis."

"Done," he said, with a small smile. The smile bit me. "My name is Steve Ravener. I used to be an architect."

"Here in town?"

He shook his head. "In Houston. I started with a firm but went out on my own, and was doing pretty well. I was bringing home six figures and had a steady stream of clients coming to me. And then I gave it all away."

"What do you mean by that?"

"I don't know how to explain it, except to say that I wanted more. Just more. I was addicted to the rush. Unfortunately I got into coke, Oxy. And still I wanted more. And that's when I met a group of guys in a bar who were talking about an ultimate high. And they were successful guys, too. A lawyer, a dentist, and a local talk show host. I fell in a conversation with 'em and that's where it started. I joined them one night out in the big lonely. They met a guy out there and we had a keg."

"Beer?"

"Yeah. Just kicking back having some brew, and this guy starts talking and says, 'Are you ready to try it?' And I'm all, Try what?' But the next thing I know he's singing a nonsense song, like he's some five-year-old. But then everybody starts laughing, and one of the guys elbows me in the ribs and says to join in, it's part of it. Like an initiation."

"Do you remember any of the words?"

He shook his head. "They were just noise to me, but I went along with it, and the next thing I know it starts to happen, the change."

He stopped then and looked at me, like he was afraid to go on.

"Mr. Ravener," I said, "there isn't anything you can tell me that's going to jolt me. I've been around L.A. enough that nothing is going to shock."

"You sure?"

"I wouldn't say it if I wasn't."

"I'm a werewolf."

I was shocked.

I've been around vampires and ghosts and shape-shifters and angels and goddesses and demons, and some other things I cannot name, and they're all pretty rational, even when they're doing bad things. They have the power of reflection.

But werewolves are another matter. Totally unpredictable and vicious. A werewolf once attacked one of my clients right as she sat on the witness stand in court. I had to grab his leg and bite it. Not something most lawyers are trained to do.

"Yeah," Steve Ravener said, "I see your reaction. I don't blame you."

"I don't mean anything by it," I said.

"You're afraid I might turn and come after you."

"Been known to happen."

"Sometimes I can control it. Sometimes it controls me. But there is no way out. That's what I am now."

"I don't believe in no way out," I said. "I think the minute we start to think that way is the minute we start to die, truly die."

"You sound like you know what you're talking about."

"I did pass the bar."

"I mean more than that. Like you're dealing with something, too."

"Let's keep this professional, Mr. Ravener. Tell me why you have come to see me."

He sighed and sat back in his chair. "About seven years ago I came to L.A. I figured I could blend in better here."

"Excellent call," I said.

"I found a pack and started to run with them. Then I met a woman. Thought she was the one, you know? Beautiful. Teaches Pilates in Beverly Hills. We got married."

"Did you tell her of your, um, condition?"

He looked at the floor and shook his head.

"Don't you think you might have mentioned that little item?" I said.

"I know, I know. I was trying to fight it. I thought I could find a way to get out of it."

"And have you?"

"I don't know if it's possible."

"How did she not find out?"

He said, "I turned into a pretty good liar, I guess, and then there were the kids."

The despair was evident in his voice, and in my own body, too. I knew exactly how he felt. "Go on," I said.

"We had two kids, a boy and a girl. Greatest kids in the world. I wanted more than anything to stop wolfing so I could be a good father. But then Pat found out what I was."

"Pat's your wife?"

"That's right. And now she wants to take them away from me for good."

"Are they with you now?"

"No, she has them and says she'll call the police if I try to see them." I thought I saw mist in his eyes then, but he blinked it away. "Is there anything I can do?"

I took in a long, professional breath. "It all depends on the facts," I said. "California custody law is based on the best interests of the children. You are going to have to be able to show that being a werewolf is not harmful to your kids."

"That sounds hard, doesn't it?"

"Hard. Not impossible."

"You mean there's a chance?"

"With me, there's always a chance." Why not say it? I'm good at what I do. Does Yo-Yo Ma think he's all thumbs?

Steve Ravener's face broke into a slightly relieved smile. I felt that trembling inside me again.

No, I told myself. You already are attracted to an L.A. cop named Strobert. You've had to push him away. The last thing you need is to get involved with a wolf. What's wrong with you?

"I don't have much money," Steve said. "I'm just a musician."

"No kidding. What kind?"

"Ballads. With guitar."

"Where do you play?"

"I have a regular gig in a hotel. I snag some money here and there. I also pick up work as a freelance cage fighter."

I cleared my throat. "Did you say cage fighter?"

He nodded. "I haven't clawed anyone to death yet, but it helps pay the bills."

"Are you talking about legitimate MMA-type stuff?"

"No."

"Care to explain?"

"Do I have to?"

"Mr. Ravener," I said, "do you want my help or not? If you go after custody of your cubs—I mean kids—the other side is going to tear into your life, you'll pardon the expression. So I need to know what they may uncover."

"All right," he said. "You ever heard of what old-time boxers used to call club smokers?"

I shook my head.

"It was when private clubs would put together a fight, so their members could come into a small atmosphere, like an Elks Club hall, and see two guys going at it. They were called smokers because the place'd be encased in cigar and cigarette smoke. The members would bet, pool some money to pay the fighters, and a good time was had by all."

"Sounds like it. What better way to spend an evening than closely watching two guys with gloves pound each other?"

"Yeah, well, they were outlawed way back when, but it's just gone underground. They do it in cages now. If you're on the circuit and you can hold your own, you do okay."

"Okay, this case may indeed take a little bit longer. Werewolf, musician scraping by and now an illegal cage fighter. Is there anything else you need to tell me, Mr. Ravener? Anything at all?"

"I just want to see my kids," he said.

The way he said it, the longing in his eyes, humanized him. If there was any thought that his lycanthropy had taken that away, it was gone now. I saw a man who simply loved his children and was afraid he might lose them.

Being a zombie, I have a weakness for cases involving creatures who are considered outsiders. We both certainly qualified.

But I am also a lawyer, and that means a certain practicality. Especially with a landlord breathing down your neck. "Mr. Ravener, I can begin to make some inquiries, but I will need a thousand dollars as a retainer. After that, I'll bill you on an ongoing basis." A little part of me was hoping he'd decline. A wolf man, after all. But another part of me was hoping for that *ongoing* thing.

"I can do that," he said. "I'll just have to schedule a few more fights."

"I don't think that's—"

He took out a checkbook and slapped it on my desk.

CHAPTER THREE

AFTER STEVE RAVENER left I summoned Nick to my office.

Nikos Papadoukis is my diminutive investigator, a Kallikantzaros from Greece. That means he is gnomelike and cursed. According to legend, the Kallikantzaroi create havoc for twelve days after Christmas, sometimes even stealing children. Nick says this is definitely not true and can get quite passionate about it.

Just like he does about werewolves.

He has a small office—naturally—across from mine. When he came in, I said, "Got us a new client."

"I saw him leaving. Hub hub." He bobbed his bushy eyebrows at me.

"It's *hubba hubba,* and don't bob your bushy eyebrows at me. He's just another client."

"You don't fool me, doll."

I closed my eyes and wished a water balloon would land on his head. Nick had recently taken to reading old detective novels, trying to up his skills. The archaic language was an unfortunate consequence.

"What's he in Dutch for, sister?" Nick asked.

"Don't you dare call me *doll* or *sister* again, or I'll give you cement shoes and take you for a ride."

"Hey, I know what that means! "

"It means it's time for you to do some work. On a family law matter."

"With the good lookin' guy?"

"That's why I'm talking to you. I need to know the background. The number-one thing is, he's a werewolf."

Nick pounded my desk with his fist. "No! You cannot get into this with a werewolf. They are mean, nasty, killing machines. I have seen them at work in the old country. Oh, you do not want to be near, in any way, a werewolf."

"He came to me for help, not to eat me."

"Someday he will try to bite your arm off. He cannot control himself."

"I know a little bit about that," I said. "And you know I've been controlling myself."

Nick shook his elfin head. "This is different! This is wolf! You are undead, but you can still think, you have a will. Not him. Wolves do not have will. They are all instinct. I fear for your life if you get involved with one of these creatures."

"Why don't we take it one step at a time? Are you willing to look into this for me?"

"No!"

"You are afraid then?"

"You are tooting I am afraid! I do not want anything to do with werewolves."

"Fine," I said, loudly slamming a desk drawer closed. "Why don't you open up a tea shop? Or take up knitting? I don't need a timid runt fouling up my investigations."

He drew himself up to his full four feet and puffed out his chest. "You think you can talk that way to me? And get away with it?"

"I'm paying your bills."

"Okay," he said quietly. "Will I need a roscoe in case I run into a mug?"

CHAPTER FOUR

I WALKED over to the county jail to see my father, Harry Clovis.

"I've had a vision!" he said, the moment he was shackled to the interview table. He still had his big white beard but was looking a little thinner than normal.

"Another one?" I said.

My dad was one for visions. It had been through a vision in Mexico, when he was an on-the-run biker outlaw, that he got word from the Lord, or so he said, to take a big sword and start lopping off the heads of zombies. He almost got me before he discovered I was his daughter. Then he took off the head of a dirty cop named Bracamonte, and that was the subject of his first murder trial. I got him a hung jury. I am so good, it's a shame I'm undead. I could have had my own firm by now. I could've been a sixtieth-floor lawyer, instead of one of the denizens of the underbelly of society.

"The Lord showed me that you would be healed," my dad said. "That you would never need to eat another human's flesh."

"You sure that wasn't just a slide show?"

"It's true!"

What it really was, was just a father showing concern for his daughter, the walking dead. That warmed me. "Dad, I want you to know I've been sober for weeks."

"You haven't eaten anyone?"

"Nope. I'm on the wagon."

"The Lord be praised!"

"I thought you'd like that. Now you don't have to have those dreams about cutting off my head and stuffing my mouth with salt anymore."

"I would like to be through with such dreams."

"Now we need to talk about your retrial."

"How's your mother?"

"Well, Dad, she's ... she hasn't changed much." My father and mother were not together in any sense of the term. Both were inhabiting planes of existence that were, to put it mildly, incompatible.

"Look after her," my father said.

"I try, but she's got a strong will."

"Just like her daughter."

"Hey, I'm *your* daughter, too."

"And I'm glad."

Silence.

Dad said, "Don't worry about me. I'm content."

"Content?"

He nodded. "To be here, to be fed, to have time to think and pray and have my visions. I am recording them. I want them to be published."

Yes, everybody in L.A. wants to be a writer. "But we need to strategize about the trial."

"The Lord will see to it."

"Now hold on just a gosh darn minute," I said, using the deferential epithet so as not to upset him. "God, if he's interested in anything down here, isn't doing the legal legwork. I am. I'm the one who is defending you—"

"With the Lord's help—"

"With Nick's help."

"No, daughter. We are not alone. The sooner you realize that—"

"What I realize is that we have to get some things straight," I said. "First of all, I don't want you saying anything in court. Not a thing."

"But what if I want to pray?"

"Keep it in your head."

"What if I need to use the bathroom?"

I rolled my eyes, even though they felt a little loose in my sockets. "Dad, listen to me. It's really simple. If you need something, write a note and slip it to me. I don't want you saying anything out loud in court, understood?"

He gave me a direct look. "What if the judge asks me a question?"

"Then I will stand up and tell the judge not to talk to you unless you are on the witness stand. I am your voice, Dad."

My father said, "Thank you for loving me."

My heart fairly burst then. If only I'd been able to hear those words when I was growing up. I babbled something about our next court appearance, then got out of there. My head was light from lack of eats and I didn't want to faint in his presence.

CHAPTER FIVE

I WALKED BACK toward my office, fighting the urges. I went down Main Street then up Broadway, past the normalcy of life, past people eating at the Mexican places and the Subway shop off the first floor of the Bradbury Building. That's an odd and disquieting sight. A great old brick architectural gem from the city's heyday befouled by a fast food franchise. There's a metaphor in there somewhere, but I was too hungry to think one up.

I continued walking up to First Street, then cut over to Spring. That got me walking past City Hall, the lair of Mayor Ronaldo Garza. I always get a little tremolo of anger when I am near this tower of corruption, this monument to man's ability to find every possible way to gather power.

The history of Los Angeles is one of layer upon layer of corrupt officials greasing palms and eliminating opponents. It's no wonder that Father Clemente believes Los Angeles is the war headquarters of Lucifer. Father C thinks in global terms. He says there is going to be a new assault on heaven and earth led by Lucifer and his armies. And that they are gathering here in the aptly named City of Angels.

There is evidence to support this theory.

I've had run-ins with fallen angels, with the spirits of the wicked dead, with ancient territorial gods who go by names like Marduk and Dagon. They seem to be in town for some sort of Shriners convention of the dark world.

Tough. I have enough problems of my own. Let the two super powers battle it out, if that's what's really going on. Just keep me out of hell, thank you very much.

A clutch of reporters and TV news vans were assembled around the steps of the venerable building. A bunch of men and women in suits and smug countenances were there, too. I recognized a few. The city council and their staffs.

What was going on? It wasn't campaign season yet. And I hadn't heard about any major pieces of city business to be announced. Usually this sort of thing was reserved for kick-offs or crises.

The fellow standing at the microphone knot was someone I was not familiar with. He had the young, lean, and hungry look of the ambitious pol. Full of himself, which I guess is what you have to be these days to be a politician. Heaven strike us down if anybody humble ever ran for anything.

As he started speaking I made my way to the outskirts of the small crowd. A blue uniform told me I'd gone far enough.

"I just want to listen," I said.

"You can hear from here," he said.

"Do I look like a troublemaker to you?"

"Yes."

"Good call," I said.

The guy at the mikes said, "Ladies and gentlemen, members of the press, thank you for being here today for this momentous, indeed city-changing, announcement. And now it gives me pleasure to introduce to you the leader of our fair city, the man who worked his way up from the barrio to the mayor's office, the mayor himself, Ronaldo Garza!"

Out he came from the grand doors of City Hall. It was an entrance. To a press conference yet. The diminutive pol with the gleaming white teeth and a smile as sincere as Uriah Heep's. He stepped up to the microphones and smiled for a moment, letting the cameras capture his denticle splendor.

Then he spoke. "On behalf of myself, the city council, and all people who love this city, I announce today the formation of a new initiative of civic pride. The City Angels of Los Angeles will be an all-volunteer army of good-minded folks dedicated to bringing this city all the way back to its place of prominence in the country. As you know, my administration has been a huge success in saving the city of Los Angeles from the brink of ruin. Now we need to finish the job, together. So, for the next six months, all those who sign up to be a City Angel will receive a T-shirt and a special booklet of coupons good for discounts at some of our finest businesses here in the city, as well as deals on tickets to Clippers, Lakers, Kings, and Dodger games. All we ask is that you be ready, willing, and able to help our city when the time comes, and we all know those times will come. We have challenges ahead, but together, we will continue to be the leading light and a cultural beacon not just to the Pacific Rim, but the whole world."

He paused, smiled, and said, "I will now answer a few questions."

He called on a reporter, who said, "How many do you expect to sign up for this?"

"I would like to make it the entire city! Really, there is no reason for anyone to skip this, if he or she cares about our beloved Los Angeles."

Another reporter shouted, "Is this the most innovative initiative ever in the city of Los Angeles?"

Wow. Tough one.

"It most certainly is," Mayor Garza said. "But I believe in bold strokes when it comes to the well being of my town."

Barf.

Mayor Ronaldo Garza believed only in stroking what was good for his own ambitions, and that included being in league with the dark side.

So I found myself yelling a question. "Who's running this town,

Mr. Mayor? Who calls your shots?" The whole assemblage turned around and faced me. "Well, well," the mayor said. "If it isn't one of our esteemed lawyers, Ms. Mallory Caine."

"So answer my question," I said.

"Ladies and gentlemen, Ms. Caine here has long been a thorn in the side of the city. One of those local agitators. We would appeal to her as we would to all citizens, to come on board and join us as a City Angel."

One of the hack reporters shouted at me, "Yeah, why don't you, Ms. Caine?"

"Why don't you quit being told what to do?" I said. At this, the mayor—still smiling, by the way—nodded to a uniformed policeman. The policeman started down the steps toward me.

I can take a hint. I walked toward Temple Street and just kept going.

CHAPTER SIX

I CONTINUED ALONG past the federal courthouse and crossed over the freeway. It's almost as if that artery of traffic is the border of a time warp, for on the other side is the Plaza of old Los Angeles. This was the center of town back in the late 1800s, directly across from the train depot. Here you will find little Olvera Street, now a bit of a tourist attraction, where descendants of the authentic Angelenos, Mexicans who were here first, sell their wares.

There is one very authentic shop at the end. This is where I buy what I have determined to eat.

Cow brains are the cottage cheese of the undead. You know how a dieter trying to be strict will eat that awful dairy product with lumps in it, maybe put it on a lettuce leaf or something. No one looks forward to that meal. You sort of die a little inside every time you sit down to eat it, as if one of the great pleasures of life has been removed from you forever.

I love to eat human brains. That's part of my nature. It's not a part that I want. I did not choose to be this way. I was murdered and then brought back to life. If that's how the Grand Designer wants to play things out, I think it's a pretty ghastly idea.

The old man who runs the shop greeted me with his usual smile. His name is Garcia. He has the deep, dark skin of the indigenous people, now pretty much quartered in this section of the city. He is honest and knows exactly what I need. I have never told him I'm a zombie, but I have a sense that he knows it and thankfully does not inquire further.

"Ah, Señorita Caine," he said as I approached his shop, which is merely a booth with an open window.

"How are you, Señor Garcia?"

"I am better than most, not so good as some," he said.

"Consider yourself lucky," I said. I was on the opposite end of that spectrum. "I'll take the usual."

"I have it all ready for you," he said. He went to the very back of his space, where he has a refrigerator. He opened it and removed a paper bowl covered with plastic wrap. He brought it to me and placed it on the little counter.

"I have something for you to try," Garcia said. "I have seen your face when I give you this, and I think you do not like the taste."

"You are astute, my good man."

He smiled. "I have here the secret." He reached under the counter and brought up a large red bowl. In the bowl was a deeper red sauce.

"Hot sauce?" I said.

"Not just any," he said. "I have made this myself from the family recipe. It is made from the *guajillo* chile, the *chile negro*, and the dried chile pods of the Guatemalan desert."

"It sounds more like a witch's brew."

"Eh?"

"How hot is it?"

"It is not for the *gringo* tongue," he said. "But you are a tough one, Señorita Caine. And I think it will help this to go down."

"At this point I'm willing to try anything."

He happily nodded and took the plastic wrap off the calves' brains. Then he spooned two dollops of the red sauce onto the off-white bovine grub. Then he stirred the confection around until the whole thing was pinkish.

"Looks marvelous," I lied.

"You will trust your old friend Garcia, eh?"

"Give me a water to go with it," I said. Garcia fetched a purely Americanized bottled water and I paid him for the whole deal.

I FOUND AN EMPTY BENCH IN THE OLD ROUND PLAZA AND SAT down for my not so sumptuous lunch. I did my best to concentrate on the food and not the heads of the people walking by. Imagine an alcoholic sipping soda water in front of a fully stocked bar. You don't think he'd feel the bottles calling to him?

So I trembled as I watched the tourists and young families. Like this couple right out of a soap ad, with their child in a stroller, and I felt that old tug, that old wish, that old desire that shall not be fulfilled. My womb was as dead as I was.

No Norman Rockwell paintings for me. No warm family gathering around the Thanksgiving table while my husband carves the turkey and I smile at the kids. No, my Thanksgiving painting would be me, alone, with a platter of gray matter.

I took a bite of my lunch and forced it down. Today it tasted tough and greasy.

What a picture I must have been. Undead woman eating a sloppy meal by herself. Just a block away was a place I used to go to when I was human. French dip sandwiches was their specialty. Washing those down with a beer on a hot day after a court recess, that was the limit.

I forced myself to keep eating. I needed my strength. It was halfway through my repast when a voice behind me said, "Nice day."

The sheriff of Los Angeles County, the big cheese himself, Geronimo Novakovich. That's right. A Native American mother and Russian father, and had stunning good looks as a result. High cheekbones, almond skin, jet black hair. He looked perfect, as always, in his crisp sheriffs uniform. He was in his early forties and could have been modeling briefs.

"It *was* a nice day," I said.

"Now, counselor, there is no need to be adversarial. No call for any unpleasantness between us."

"You misunderstand the order of the universe," I said. "Between criminal defense lawyers and law enforcement there is very little common ground."

"Unless there is a way for each side to get something that they want. It's called negotiation." He sat next to me. "That was quite a little earful you gave to the mayor."

"You heard that?"

"I hear everything, Ms. Caine. That's part of my job."

"Uh-huh. But the job you really want is to be the next mayor of Los Angeles."

"That's not really a secret. People know I'm ambitious."

"And I suspect being mayor is only a stepping stone to statewide office. Maybe a national run."

"All of this is premature," he said. "What I am interested in now is doing my job, and my job is to arrest people for bad things."

"And that's the ecosystem. You arrest some slob, the DA tries him, and I put them back out on the street where they belong."

"I don't happen to find that amusing," Novakovich said. "My job is very important to me. The safety of the people of the city and County of Los Angeles, that's important to me. And when there's a mass murder, even of the dregs of society like a motor-cycle gang, that's a crime on my watch. I can't just let it go."

"Well, have you put anyone away yet? Maybe I should go down and pay a visit to the jail. Maybe I've got a potential client down there."

"If you pay a visit to the jail, I intend to see that you never get out."

A Latino man in work clothes stopped in front of the bench, smiled, and shook the sheriffs hand. "I like you, Sheriff Geronimo! Doing a great job!"

"Thank you, friend," Novakovich said.

"Isn't he doing a great job?" the man said to me.

"He is a piece of work all right," I said.

"You keep on doing what you do," the man said, and waved good-bye.

Novakovich said, "You see? I have spent a long time building up a good reputation and I don't intend to lose it."

"Excuse me, but before that little campaign speech, didn't you say something about me being in jail?"

"Oh, yes, that."

"Sheriff, it sounds an awful lot like you're gunning for me. Like Wyatt Earp or Tommy Lee Jones."

"I know you had something to do with it, Ms. Caine."

"With what, pray tell?"

"You know exactly what I'm talking about."

I did, but I wasn't going to let on that I knew. He was talking about the biker gang massacre in Sunland. A year ago I'd staked out an outlaw group that was a supplier to an underage prostitution ring. I didn't know that at the time. I was just looking for a good supply of criminal brains for my freezer. It was my way of justifying the killing and eating of human flesh. Eating those who deserved to die. Call it my *Dexter* reasoning.

Well, the sheriff ended up with eight headless bodies strewn on a dusty, undeveloped plot of ground. The public wanted to know who was responsible.

"I am sure I don't know what you're referring to, Sheriff. But if you had any evidence of wrongdoing on my part you'd have me locked up right now."

"Don't tempt me." Geronimo Novakovich paused, crossed his legs. Confrontational relaxation.

"Well," I said, "it's been lovely—"

"I'm here to offer you a way out," he said.

"A way out of what?"

"A way out of town."

I kept my cool, which is something I like to keep. "Now that's a little too Wild West even for you, Sheriff. You don't run people out of town anymore. The next thing you'll say is I have until sundown."

"I'm willing to give you a week to get your affairs in order."

I turned to face him. "You're serious."

"I've never been anything but serious with you, Ms. Caine. I want you out. Gone. I don't care where you go, just as long it is out of my jurisdiction. May I suggest that you actually leave the state? I'm sure you will find lots of places where you can set up your little shop of horrors. I mean law office."

"Okay," I said, "now I'm getting mad. You interrupt my lunch to give me this cheesy threat? You don't have the clout to do this. I know the law myself and maybe you should take a refresher course."

He remained unflappable. "Your mother is a drug addict. Your father is a cop killer. The apple doesn't fall far from the tree."

"Leave my family out of this."

"They are very much a part of the discussion. I can make their lives miserable. And that little runt who does your investigating, whatever his name is. And that boy who breathes fire. I'm telling you, you're not just going to be hurting yourself but a lot of other people."

I don't know exactly what it was, the lousy food in my stomach or the lousy company on my bench, or the cheap threats that he could, unfortunately, carry out. Maybe it was just a combination of everything, but I did something I hadn't done in years. I threw up. And all over the sheriff's nice, crisp uniform.

CHAPTER SEVEN

SHERIFF NOVAKOVICH YELLED something unprintable and stood up and looked at himself. Looked at his clothes in horror. This guy was more vain than whoever Carly Simon's song was about. I don't think he was as upset about the indignity of a zombie vomiting on him as he was that he just plain didn't look good right now.

He cursed me again and told me if he ever saw my face in the city or county he would make up some excuse to blow my brains out. I didn't have the heart to tell him that wouldn't kill me, though it sure wouldn't do much for my looks. He stormed off.

I sat there feeling empty. Maybe getting out of Los Angeles would be a good idea after all. Why was I here? Why was I continuing to let events unfold around me that I had no interest in resolving? I'm talking about that big apocalyptic battle Father Clemente keeps mentioning.

Who needed it?

I realized I wasn't as alone as I thought. I did have my father and I did have my mother and despite their being screwballs I cared about them. I had Nick, and Jaime, the boy who could breathe fire. More on him later.

And then there was the city itself. I don't know. Los Angeles gets into you.

It's a city for dreamers and I have dreams. Someday I want to open a cemetery right next to the 5 Freeway as it heads north toward the Newhall Pass. I want to put a big sign up so all the commuters can see it: *If You Were Dead You'd Be Home By Now.*

Yes, dreams. Crazy ones and any other kind you want to have. That's L.A., and I was not going to let some tinhorn sheriff (I just love saying *tinhorn sheriff)* run me out like I was some saloon floozy cheating cowboys at cards.

BACK AT MY OFFICE, NICK WAS READY WITH A PRELIMINARY report on the Ravener matter. "The wife, she works for a radio station. I found a story on her, talking about her kids and her new boyfriend."

"Boyfriend?"

"She has taken up with a fellow named Dwayne Dewey."

"What's he do?"

"Get this. He works for the mayor."

"He works for Garza?"

Nick nodded. "I looked him up, too. He is one of the mayor's ponies."

"Ponies?" I said.

"You know, does what he's told."

I said, "I think you mean cronies."

"Maybe," Nick said.

"So this woman, Pat Ravener, takes up with someone who works for the mayor. I don't think that would have any bearing on the custody battle, other than the fact that she is having an affair."

"Do people not care about that anymore?" Nick asked.

"The courts don't look at it the same way they used to. It's all going to come down to what is in the best interest of the children. By the way, what can you tell me about them?"

"The girl is seven and the boy is five."

"Normal kids?"

"You're asking a Kallikantzaros what's normal?" Nick jumped

into a chair. His legs dangled over. "What do you want me to do now? Put on a tail?"

"I don't think we're into the tailing thing yet," I said. I felt my forehead. A little perspiration there.

"What is it, Mallory?" Nick said.

"Huh?"

"You are feeling, what is it?"

"Oh, nothing."

"You forget, I am a—"

"Yeah, I know. *Barometer.*"

He folded his arms. "You are sick maybe."

"No."

"Hungry."

"What of it?"

"You are going to your meetings?"

"You're not my nursemaid," I said.

"But your friend, maybe."

God love the little fella. He was cranky and obsessive and clumsy sometimes, but he had a big heart. Too bad. You have too big a heart it gets broken easily.

"All right, Nick. Get me more on this Dewey fellow. And try not to worry too much about me."

He slid off the chair and winked at me. "You got it, kitten."

"Out!"

CHAPTER EIGHT

I SAT in my office until dark.

You know that old movie with Ray Milland? The Lost Week-end? It's about an alcoholic. He has these horrible visions when he's drunk, and when he's trying to get off the stuff. Well, that was booze. You have no idea what you go through trying to get off of brains.

I hope you never see it in your nightmares.

The visions I had this time had owls in them. Owls with teeth and yellow eyes, flying around taking bites out of my skin. I've had trouble with owls in the past. Lilith, the demon goddess, often appears in that guise. I never know what is behind the eyes of an owl. The only friendly owl I ever knew was Max, my guardian. He was a spirit who had done good in life and had been dispatched to do good for those of us walking around. Even though he had been a Catskills comedian, and told bad jokes, he was a good spirit and he cared about me. But he was gone now, his spirit somewhere else. He had helped me fight off a satanic attack while in owl form, and they'd gotten rid of him somehow, the rats.

I had to get out, walk around.

But if I did walk around I'd be outside with all the flesh.

Could I just get home, maybe suck on a frozen finger? I had a hand in my freezer for just such an occasion.

I thought I could do it. I could do this on my own. I could beat this thing.

When I put on my Amanda wig I should have known I was only kidding myself.

Amanda is my New Jersey streetwalker alter ego. She comes complete with wigs of different colors—I prefer brick red or purple—and has been known to pick up a john or two for dinner.

I had managed to stay off that beat for a while now.

But now I walked along the dismal, crowded, brain-buffet streets of downtown. These are not the glamour streets. Here there is real darkness dwelling, people at the edge of reality, last hopes.

Maybe if I could walk fast enough to get my mind off my hunger, I'd be all right. And I figured if I walked around downtown, as opposed, say, to the UCLA campus, I wouldn't run into an intellectually sumptuous brain.

I was wrong—oh, so wrong.

It was right outside of a bookshop that he came into my path. A used bookstore, one of the last in Los Angeles. Bookstores had been drying up faster than spit in the desert, victims of the new commerce in electronic and digital merchandise. I was sad to see that happen. Just another sign of the apocalypse—which may be on its way.

But here was one bookstore hanging on for dear life, and outside stood a man with no hair in a big black coat. And he stepped right in front of me and said, "You look like a lady who could use a good book." He was articulate and obviously charming. I just kept looking at that bald head of his, thinking of what was inside, what luscious, thick membranous goodness. I wanted to open his head right then and dip into it with a spoon. My breathing got heavy and fast. I was dizzy.

"Are you all right?" he said.

"Drift," I said.

"Now I am never one to leave a lady in distress," he said. He took my arm. I was too weak to resist. He started walking me down the street. "Let's go get something to eat."

"No eat. Can't eat. Don't want to eat. Don't say the word eat."

"Let me ask you a question."

"Terrific."

"Do you think I look like Tom Selleck?"

"That's your question?"

"Yeah."

I blinked. "Aside from the fact that you have no hair and no mustache, and aren't as handsome, yeah, you look like Tom Selleck."

"I knew it. Everybody says it."

"Are you deaf?"

"Let's get a drink."

His head suddenly looked like a casaba melon to me. I used to love casabas. This one had a brain inside it. "Get lost," I said.

"That's not a good reason. Your mouth is saying Get lost, but your eyes are saying something else."

"Yes, I want to eat your head."

"What?"

"Metaphorically."

"I like you," he said.

"Good night." I started to walk away, but he stepped in front of me. We were on a dark part of East Third, between two commercial buildings. There was still enough light from office windows across the street to cast a pale luminescence, enough to see his big, luscious head.

"Listen, darlin', we're just two people who met outside a bookstore. But it's a dark night and I've got something you don't know anything about."

My hunger pangs were like two cats fighting inside a duffel bag. "Okay, big boy, what've you got?"

He leaned over and whispered in my ear. "A very big knife."

I feigned a moment of shock.

"Now don't scream or try to run, because I used to play football and I can outrun you. You won't get five steps."

I said nothing.

"But I like you," he said. "I don't want to do you any harm at all. I'm not like that, really."

I was bursting. "You played football?"

"Huh?"

"You said you played football. Where?"

He paused. "Uh, Ohio State."

"Good school. You get in on a scholarship?"

"I was a walk-on."

"So you got in on your grades. Must be pretty smart."

"What's all this have to do with us?"

"I like a man with a good brain. He doesn't have to use a knife on me."

"What if I was kidding about the knife?"

"Were you?"

"No. But let's not let that stop us."

Ohio State. Good grades. Nice, big cranium. Smooth on the outside, like an M&M.

"Where's a nice quiet place we can have a drink?" I said.

"Why not my place?" he said.

"You're local?"

"Got a loft at the Franklin."

"Nice. What are we waiting for?"

He took my arm and we started back to the lights of the Main, and headed south.

The next three blocks was one of the hardest walks of my life. I had in my purse Emily, my hook tool that I used to shove through nasal passage or eyeball, paralyze the victim, and then draw out precious brain matter in the manner of the old Egyptians. It was everything I could do not to whip it out right there and use it on the street, even though there were people all around now, some walking dogs in the newly minted urban atmosphere. There were the drug addicts and homeless, of course. I passed at least one vampire. I had a sense of these things and knew that when someone bared their fangs at you and hissed, it was usually a vampire—or a demon who needed dental work.

I ignored it all. I just wanted to eat. I wanted to get to Bald Head's place, have my meal, and go home.

What was worse is the guy wanted to talk the whole way. And what he wanted to talk about was achieving his goals.

"I went to a Tony Robbins seminar once, and it changed my life. He said you could become whatever you want and then gave me the technology to achieve it. He said I could reinvent myself. He said first I needed to make a list of all the elements in my identity that I wanted to have. He said then you need to get excited, be like a kid again, and dream big. Then you come up with a plan of action that will help you know that you are living consistently with your new identity."

"I thought you wanted to be Tom Selleck," I said, almost fainting from lack of food.

"No, I just said I look like Tom Selleck. What I wanted to be is something entirely different. I knew that my value was power. I wanted to have power. Isn't that what most people want? I wanted power over women and power over people I did business with. Power is the thing. That's what I chose. And then I put in a plan of action to achieve it."

"How much further is it to your place?"

"Oh, right there. I just wanted to talk some more."

"No more talk. I need a drink."

"Okay," he said. "Let's go on up."

Up was to the top of the Franklin building, one of those renovated places that used to be a transient hotel. This place had the look and smell of an urban hipster, someone trying very hard to live consistent with his income. He had framed prints of Doug Webb and Warhol, sort of retro-hip cool, and an interior design out of sixties advertising culture. I guess this was a guy who loved Mad Men, designing a life around that look. Sort of like a little girl who gets theme pajamas based on the latest Disney animated feature. I wondered if he had Don Draper slippers in a closet somewhere.

"How about I make you a martini?" he said.

"Why don't we get down to business?" I said.

"Don't insult me," he said. "Why can't we just do this like civilized adults?"

I put my hand in my purse and felt around for Emily. I was going to make this short and sweet and get out of there fast.

But the guy quickly went behind the open bar. He started preparing martinis, pulling out a couple of glasses and then a bottle of Beefeater. "I didn't tell you what I wanted to be," he said. "I only told you I wanted power. Are you interested?"

"Frankly, no."

"Rude. This isn't what I thought it would be."

"I'm sorry to disappoint you."

"I've just got to share this with you. You take olives?"

"No. Eyeballs."

He laughed. But I was actually thinking of martinis with eyeballs. Sounded pretty good.

"What I decided I wanted to be was a serial killer," he said as calmly as if he were telling his grandmother about his new job as an insurance salesman.

He looked at me, no doubt waiting for some sort of reaction. When I didn't give him one, he frowned. "I'm actually serious about this. I wanted to prove that I could become something just because I chose to do it. And then, show people that I was powerful enough that they couldn't figure me out. Because every serial killer you've ever heard about has some sort of pattern that an FBI profiler can pick up, or some nonsense like that. So I thought, what if I did something along these lines that was completely random? It had no pattern. It had no profile. Just because I decided to do it. Isn't that an amazing feeling, to be able to do something that big?"

"I think I'm going to need that drink after all."

He put ice in the martini shaker but didn't cap it. "But aren't you scared now? That I'm going to make you a victim?"

"What if I scream bloody murder?"

"Oh, we get lots of noise up here. Parties and the like. You can scream if you want, but it will be the last sound you make."

"You are sounding so authoritative," I said. "Powerful. I'm shaking in my shoes. Now let's have that drink."

He seemed disconcerted. "You can pretend not to be scared," he said. "But I'm not buying it."

"Let's cut to the chase here," I said. "I'm a serial killer, too."

He said, "Come on, no way."

"Way."

"How many?"

"Too many to count."

"Ah, you're no serial killer. We keep track. I've got seventeen under my belt. I know the time and date of each one."

"Well, I'm not that careful. I just kill and eat."

"Eat? Wait a second, are you a zombie?"

"Bingo. Now do you mind offering me your face for a moment?" I took Emily out of my purse.

"You're serious!" he said.

I said nothing, just walked straight for him.

"Wait!" he said. "We could do great things together. I'm with the CA."

"The what?"

"City Angels. I can get you in."

"You're stalling."

"No! We're going to change the world. You need to—" He suddenly stopped and came around the bar. In his hand was a sword.

It wasn't as big as the one my father had wielded when he was hunting zombies, but it was plenty big enough to separate my head from my body.

I had to have a weapon bigger than Emily. She was for up-close-and-personal work on a dead or incapacitated body.

I grabbed an art deco lamp, probably facsimile. I put my hands around the smooth body of a woman in robes.

I ran around to the other side of the sofa and stripped the lamp of its shade. I pulled the cord out of the socket.

"Do you think that's really going to help you?" He said, brandishing the sword like Inigo Montoya.

"How did you happen to have a sword ready?" I said. "That's a zombie-killer weapon."

He hesitated.

"This wasn't a chance encounter at all was it?" I said. "I was supposed to bump into you. You engineered it."

"I don't know that I would use the term *engineered*. And the fact remains I am a serial killer. It's what I do for a living."

"What would it take to get you to give up whoever hired you?"

"A lot of money and we can talk."

"Will you take a check?"

He began to slowly make his way toward the edge of the sofa. I circled, keeping the sofa between us. I expected him to spring over at any moment and I was fully prepared to jam the sweet lady I was holding in his face. If I stopped him it would only be temporary. I had to get that sword out of his hands. Besides, I was feeling so weak now I was running only on zombie adrenaline. That's weaker than the human kind and runs out a lot faster.

"I really like you," he said. "I don't like to like the people that I kill."

"Why don't we postpone this, then? I'll come back tomorrow and we can discuss it further." I was eyeing the nice rug, some sort of Oriental weave. I had in mind what to do.

As soon as he stepped on the opposite end of the rug I reached down and pulled with all my might. Nothing happened. The rug didn't move, he didn't go down, and I realized I was not in a Bob Hope-Bing Crosby movie.

He lunged forward with the sword. I managed to whack it away with the art deco lamp, which turned my body slightly so his momentum carried over my hip. In my street-fighting classes, that was a move that had served me well. But even with those skills you have to have a certain amount of strength, and mine was running out.

He went to the ground and I saw one opportunity. There was a glass and wood bookcase on the wall, full of nice leather-bound volumes. They looked like they'd come from the Franklin Mint.

I jumped to the wall and pulled on the case. It didn't move. It was secured solidly to the wall.

Nothing was going right.

He was on his feet the next second.

I looked around at options. I was not going to be able to get out the front door. I could run into a room and close the door and try to hold out there, but that wouldn't be for long.

There was always the window.

No, there wasn't always the window. The window was a last resort that no one ever really tries.

Except when an egghead serial killer comes at you again with the sword.

I was getting mad now, even as I was feeling my strength leaving me.

When someone's got a blade, it's usually one momentary distraction that's going to get you any advantage. If I had something to throw in his eyes, that would give me the leverage I needed. But what?

Then I remembered the martinis. He had poured the gin and ice in the shaker, but hadn't put the top on.

I backed toward the bar.

"Tom Selleck would never do something like this," I said.

He raised the sword and started coming toward me slowly, balanced, leaving no way of getting around him.

I backed up one more step and felt my butt hit a bar chair. With my left hand I raised the art deco lamp and turned slightly so I could put my hand on the bar and partially hide what I was doing with my body.

He was four steps away from me, then three.

My hand touched the silver shaker and then wrapped around it. I'd have to make this count.

I made my move. And in the next moment the guy's face was covered with gin. I took hold of the lamp with both hands and stepped into the blow like a hitter into a pitch.

Flush across the face, and I knew he was going down. For a long time.

By that I mean, forever.

He kissed the ground and was out.

The sword came in handy. It's always better if I can remove the head, then access the brain through the basement, as it were.

I'm not going to beat around the bush here, or even around the carcass, I'm just going to tell you what a sweet savor it was. Oh, how I missed this. It was a delicious brain.

You can get drunk on brain, you know.

There's a point at which, if I have too much of a good thing, my speech starts to slur and I feel tired. Sometimes I wonder if I might black out.

As I staggered toward the door of the apartment, I was keenly aware I could be calling attention to myself. I'm pretty good at knowing how to keep blood off me, but it's not always possible. My clothing bill is the largest part of my budget.

I straightened my Amanda wig and did a quick wash up in the bathroom. Then I went to the door of the apartment, looked out on an empty corridor.

I managed to get to the street without being seen by anyone. But the street was moving and the buildings were spinning around me. I was quite aware of the looks I was getting from people walking by.

Maybe that's what finally got to me. What exactly was I now? A drunk, after a fashion. This was not what I'd seen myself doing after law school. I was going to be a great trial lawyer, help people.

Big laugh. I couldn't even help myself.

I wobbled over to a building with a big arched entrance and crumpled there.

CHAPTER NINE

SOMEHOW, some way, I woke up in my own bed.

My head was a Salvation Army drum beaten by a sumo wrestler with ADD.

They talk about fates worse than death. I was undead and still very close to something worse. This was a flesh and brain hangover, big time.

I spilled out of my bed and crawled to the bathroom. I ran cold water out of the shower and put my head under it.

What day was it? Tuesday? Or Friday?

What had happened?

Oh yeah, ate a guy. The Tom Selleck guy.

What about before that?

The sheriff. He'd threatened me.

The mayor. He'd made me ill.

My father ...

My father! We had a court appearance at 10 AM.

Clock ... I dripped out of the bathroom and checked the clock by my bed.

9:35.

Just kill me now, I pleaded with the fates.

Nope, they answered. They apparently wanted me alive and dead at the same time.

I threw on a suit and applied some shark cartilage cream to my face. Makeup on. Pulled my hair back and made it as smooth as I could. I had to look good, just had to.

Because I would be meeting the scum of the earth, the son of the devil himself, Aaron Argula.

Aaron was the man I had fallen in love with in law school. He'd dumped me and moved out of Los Angeles, but back to L.A. to work for the DA's office. Which is when I'd seen him again and felt some of the old feelings.

What I didn't know at the time was that it was Aaron himself who had killed me and brought me back to life by using a *bokor* named Ginny Finn. *Bokors* are practitioners of voodoo magic, associated with animating and controlling the dead. Ginny had been killed by a cyclops, and with her my chance at getting my soul back might've died, too. So I was not pleased with Aaron Argula, to say the least.

To top it all off, Aaron had the temerity to ask me to marry him. As the son of Lucifer, he thought he was going to be big in the new power grid in Los Angeles, and wanted me along for the ride. What he wanted was to control me. There seems to be some kind of fight over which team I'm supposed to play on. I'm like this great free agent that everybody wants on their squad. I don't like either side. I don't like the way the game is set up.

I'm a zombie without a country, a walking dead person without any allegiance.

It had been several weeks since I'd last seen Aaron on the steps of City Hall. That was his last big attempt to get me to marry him, to show me all of the things that could be happening in Los Angeles soon.

I will tell you that my throat was a little dry when I walked into the courtroom. Aaron wasn't there yet. But I felt the anticipation. There was something about him that still drew me, and I hated that. I wanted to be completely rational and do everything in my power to destroy this jerk. The best way I could do it was beat him in court. He hated to lose. I hated to lose. Something had to give, and I was going to make sure it was him.

The judge today was Toni Ishiguro, a former deputy D.A. who had done something rare—run for the office and won. In California, anyone can run for a local bench, but the voters never know anything about these people. They usually just vote for whoever is already a sitting judge.

But this time Ishiguro ran a professional campaign with a lot of money behind him. The whisper was it was coming out of the mayor's office, but no one had any evidence of it. Of course not. Mayor Garza was a master at hiding things, like the fact that he is the puppet of the dark side.

I sat at my counsel table and waited for the deputies to bring my father in. He was shackled as usual, dressed in the orange coveralls of the high-profile jail inmate. He was an accused cop murderer, so he was high-profile all right.

"How are they treating you, Pop?" I said.

"I'm going to bust out of this place," he said.

"Shut up."

"The Lord will help me, as he helped Peter in the Book of Acts."

"Don't even think about it," I said. "It can't be done, for one thing, and for another if you try it you're going to be in worse trouble than you are now. They're going to put you in a cage. Do you want that?"

"I must be about the Lord's business."

"Dad, if you're going for an insanity defense here, it's not going to work. You are not going to fake it. We are going straight to the self-defense that the first jury got hung up on. You just stay calm and don't speak until I tell you to."

"I have had a vision, Mallory. In this vision I saw rivers of blood, yea, and you were standing in it."

"Can I say Yuck now?"

"And in your hand was a shield. And with this shield you held back the blood. This is a sign from God." My father was about to go on further when the courtroom doors opened and Aaron walked in.

Our eyes met and I saw what I thought was a short flinch. But then again, my own eyes probably flickered self-doubt.

I stood right up to face him.

He gave me a curt nod. "Ms. Caine."

"Mr. Argula."

"You're looking well."

"Is it all going to be clichés now?" I said. "Is that what the son of Lucifer comes up with?"

Aaron's cheeks burned hot, and I figured that was in keeping with his eternal abode. "Don't try to pull anything in here," he said. "I will have you thrown in the slam for contempt."

"You will?"

"Just try something."

"Ah, I see. You and the judge have a little thing going on here."

"Don't try to make accusations you can't back up."

"Aaron, please, this is Mallory. Do you think you're going to put something over? After you murdered me, nothing you do will surprise me."

"If anyone hears you say that I will sue you for slander. And I will win."

"Win what? I haven't got any money and my reputation is shot to hell, if you'll pardon the word, Junior."

"Don't call me that."

"Isn't that what you are? Daddy's little boy?"

He looked like he was going to explode into sulfurous bits, then fell back into cool control. "Let's get this over with," he said, "then go somewhere to talk."

"Oh no, I'm not falling for that bit again."

"I have something to say to you."

"You can do your talking here," I said. "That's all I want to hear from you, and precious little of that."

"You're going to be very sorry," he said.

"Yeah, that's what everybody keeps telling me. But I am sorry. Sorry I ever met you, you lying piece of demon fat."

That was the end of our conversation. He turned his back on me and went to his own table. As I went back to my own I caught a glimpse of the courtroom. There were a few people sitting out there and one presence that shocked the dermis off of me. Steve Ravener, werewolf client, was sitting in the back row.

I didn't like that at all.

Since the judge was not on the bench yet, I went out to the gallery.

"What are you doing here?" I whispered.

"Came to watch you," he said.

"Why?"

"Isn't it allowed?"

"Yeah, it's allowed, but it's a little creepy."

"I wanted to see you in action." He smiled, and I was both charmed and repelled. I had a history with men who could smile like that, Aaron being one of them.

"Look, it's just a hearing today," I said.

"I don't care. Let's talk after."

"If we talk, I'm going to charge you."

"Fine with me. We'll make it official."

I shrugged and walked back to my table.

My father said, "Who was that? Another zombie?"

"No, Dad. He's not a zombie."

"Good. I don't want you mixing with that sort."

Judge Ishiguro came in. He was about forty. He ambled with the swagger of a samurai, which is ironic because it was with a samurai sword that my father had separated zombie heads from bodies.

The judge did not seem to have an ounce of humor about anything, even about irony. I thought there might be trouble, because humor and irony are two of my best traits. But then my record with judges isn't the greatest. It's an authority thing.

Judge Ishiguro called the case. He asked if there was anything to discuss before setting a new trial date.

I said, "I would like to ask for bail, your honor. There was not enough evidence to convict in the first trial, and I believe that entitles Mr. Clovis to be considered for release. Clearly, he is not a threat to the community, nor is he a flight risk." Of course, there was the little matter of his threatening to break out of jail, but I didn't take that seriously and had no duty to report that to the court. "So I request you release him to my custody and he will show up when the trial begins."

"Ha," Aaron said. "A promise from Ms. Caine. I'll let the court decide how much that is worth."

"Now, let's not squabble," the judge said. "We can all get along. This is Los Angeles, this is a new era in our city. We're all going to get along with each other, just like Rodney King wanted us to."

Oh, brother. The Rodney King case again? King was a black man who was pulled over for speeding by some white cops. He was apparently high on angel dust. When he refused to comply with the cops' order to cease resisting, he got pummeled. This was captured on videotape and became the heart of a sensational police brutality trial. Rodney King at one point said, "Can't we all just get along?" Not much, it seemed.

But I kept my mouth shut because having a judge at least give the appearance of impartiality was a rare enough thing that I was determined to enjoy it while it lasted.

Aaron, of course, opposed the bail motion and when the judge denied it I was not surprised at all. I hadn't expected this would be an option, especially in a high-profile cop-killing case. But if you're a defense lawyer you try everything.

Then the judge dropped the proverbial other shoe. A big cement one.

"There is just one more thing," the judge added as he looked at me from his imperial bench. "I've reviewed the transcripts from the first trial, and on the court's own motion I am going to rule inadmissible any evidence relating to zombies, zombie-ism, or the undead. Such evidence is highly prejudicial and that far outweighs its probative value."

Well, hit me with a rock salt hammer. "You can't do that, your honor! That is the very foundation of our defense!"

"Then you are just going to have to find a new foundation," the judge said calmly.

"I object in the most vehement terms!"

"Duly noted. Will there be anything else?"

"Why don't we just hang my father right here in the courtroom?"

"Why don't I find you in contempt of court? The fine is five hundred dollars. Will there be anything else?"

There were words I wanted to say in a torrent of protest and outrage, but they got mangled in my throat like fighting bobcats.

"Mr. Argula?"

"Nothing from me, Your Honor," Aaron said.

"Then trial is set for three weeks from today, the seventeenth. Court is adjourned."

You know how it feels to have your breath knocked out of you? You're gasping to get something into your lungs and your body fights you, clenching out of sheer panic. Without zombie evidence there was no way my father had a chance.

As the deputies came to take him back to the lockup, my father said, "Remember the vision!"

Maybe the insanity defense would be the way to go after all.

Aaron sidled over to me like a triumphant general. "That was certainly a surprise."

"Oh, I'm sure it was."

"Honest, Mallory, I didn't know anything about this. I probably would've moved for the same thing, but I didn't expect the judge to do it on his own."

"Well, congratulations. You and the judge seemed very simpatico. You're on your way, Aaron, to the top."

"Mallory, there's something I want to say to you."

"Put it in a memo and e-mail it to me."

"I'm serious. This is heartfelt."

"What does the heart of Satan's son look like?"

"Do you have to do this, Mallory?"

"Do what?" I said.

"Act like a petulant child."

"Should I act like a lying, murdering, demonic DA instead?"

"We can act like professionals."

The courtroom had emptied by now, except for one spectator. Steve Ravener still sat in the back, watching. Aaron saw my gaze.

"Who's that?" he said.

"A talent scout for Dancing With the Stars," I said. "Likes my moves."

"Same old Mallory. Want my offer?"

I swept my briefcase off the counsel table. "I can hardly wait to hear it, Aaron. Do tell."

"You want to save your father, don't you?"

"What have you got in mind?"

"I won't seek the death penalty. I can get him twenty-five to life."

"And I should take that offer why?"

"Because there is no other way to keep your father from the needle. But I need something from you in return."

"Terrific."

"I'm going to tell you something," Aaron said, his voice barely above a whisper. "The only reason you are still walking around is that you haven't taken sides."

"I'm on the side of truth and justice, and my father."

"I'm not talking about this case. I'm talking about you and the church and that meddling priest You have not taken on their cause fully, and I appreciate that."

"And I live only to gain your appreciation, Aaron."

"Listen, despite everything, despite the fact that I tried to kill you and control you by bringing you back as a zombie, despite all that, can we just bury the hatchet?"

"In a manner of speaking, right?"

"If you will just leave Los Angeles quietly. I can arrange a nice position for you in a major law firm in Houston. You will have a chance to help people there. They specialize in supernatural cases, and the best part is they are zombie friendly. Just between you and me, and you didn't hear it here, they have a supply of human brain food that is to die for."

"Nice phrase."

"I'm talking about rare delicacies, finding some of the most intelligent brains on earth. Sort of like dolphin meat. Think of it, Mallory. You could be feasting on systems analysts from India, mathematicians from Germany, National Merit Scholars from the University of Houston."

I had to admit, it did sound good. But I wasn't going to give Aaron the satisfaction of seeing that on my face.

"The answer is no," I said.

"Bravado was never a problem for you, was it?"

I smiled.

"But that was when you had a soul," he said, and walked away.

CHAPTER TEN

AH, Aaron. Thanks for the low blow, you demonic slime. It will be my pleasure to beat you in court.

If I could. Outwardly I was showing bravado, but inwardly the doubts were starting to creep up. I couldn't begin to imagine the resources he'd be able to pull together. Not just the usual government things, like investigative manpower, but also the spiritual forces awash in Los Angeles. The son of Satan surely had some pull there.

How much of my life had I wasted on Aaron Argula? How much of my love? What did any of that prove except that love was a fool's dream?

"You did good."

I turned around. Steve was at the rail. I'd forgotten he was even in court.

"What was so good about it?" I said. "I got my head handed to me." I wished I hadn't said that.

"You fought," Steve said. "You didn't just shrink."

"But I got bupkis."

"I don't think you'll get bupkis for me. I believe in you."

I shook my head. "Why are you so trusting?"

"Let's figure it out. How about a drink?"

. . .

WE REPAIRED TO THE GALLERY BAR AT THE BILTMORE. OVER martinis, Steve said, "I watched you in court, the least you could do is come hear me sing."

"I'll try to do that sometime," I said.

"I mean it. Get to know your client."

"I know enough."

A melancholy swept across his face. "I don't know if you do. I don't know if anyone does."

"Hey," I said, "there's a certain zone of privacy for all of us. I don't think that's a bad thing. I don't think our confessional, Dr. Phil culture is any the better for sharing every shred of our messed up souls to everybody in the wired world."

"But you're my lawyer," he said. "And maybe my friend."

"Lawyer is fine."

"I need you to know that I'm trying to get out of the life," he said. "I don't know that any werewolf has been successful in keeping from turning. But if he plans ahead, maybe he can keep from doing damage. Just like in that movie, *Abbott and Costello Meet Frankenstein*."

"I loved that movie as a kid," I said.

"Right? Lon Chaney, Jr. as Larry Talbot, and he tries to convince the boys to keep him locked up? That's what I'd want you to do for me."

"I don't do lockups."

"Something, anything," he said. "You're the only one I can trust."

"I find that hard to believe. Surely there are others."

"No," he said. "I'm alone in the world."

He sounded sincere, and maybe he meant it in the same way I did. I had zombie friends, like Sal, and I had Nick and a few others. But when you're a zombie there's always the feeling that people are against you from the get-go. And why not? You want to scoop out their heads.

Same with werewolves. They'll rip your lungs out, Jim. Warren Zevon told us that. We need to listen.

"Surely you can think of someone who might be able to vouch for you," I said.

"You mean like another wolf?"

"Maybe."

"Will they let a werewolf testify in court?"

"I can get virtually any witness I want to testify, if they are relevant to the cause. I've had ghosts and vampires testify before." In my father's first murder trial, the ghost of the great actor Darren McGavin gave testimony for me. Which reminded me, maybe I needed to get some ghost help on this matter. If you work with a ghost, they can get in places unseen. But they have their own way of doing things, and don't usually take direction well.

"You know," Steve said, "werewolves would make the best witnesses."

"Why's that?"

"We're completely honest. It's part of the change. A wolf doesn't hold anything back. Like how he feels." There was a little electric pop in that statement. It snapped inside me. This wasn't good.

"Let's keep the honesty thing in our back pocket for now," I said.

"You don't want me to be honest?"

"About your case, yes. That's all."

He took a sip of his drink. "Whatever you say."

"Tell me about your wife and Dwayne Dewey," I said.

Steve paused. Then: "He's a flack for Mayor Garza, and he moved in on Pat when she was the most vulnerable. We were having problems and he was there."

"How did she meet him?"

"He was a guest on her radio show. She does a program that covers local stories, sometimes politics." His voice trailed off and he looked into his drink as if it showed sad pictures.

"We don't have to talk about it now," I said.

He put his hand on mine. I took it away.

"Perhaps we better call it a night," I said.

"The night is young."

"That line is old."

"It's not a line, Mallory."

Some of me wanted him to take my hand again. But most of me was still professional and this was crossing a line. "Did I say you could call me Mallory?"

"It seems fitting."

"Not fitting," I said. "Thanks for the drink."

He stood. I made no move to get up.

"Aren't you coming?" Steve said.

"No. I'm going to have another drink."

He started to sit back down.

"Alone," I said.

He looked flummoxed for a second. Only a second. "I hope this won't hurt our working relationship."

"That's the only relationship we have," I said. "And no, it won't hurt it."

"I'm glad."

He turned and walked out of the bar. Which is when I noticed the woman at a table, looking my way, smiling. It was one of those knowing looks. I was not feeling charitable about it so I went over to the table and said, "Can I help you?"

"No," the woman said. "But I can help *you*."

She had black hair, big eyes, a come-hither look that must drive men mad. She wore a tasteful black halter dress that accentuated her shapely form. Sensing she might be a demon, I demanded to know her name. Demons have to name themselves if you ask.

She smiled. "I'm no demon. I'm a ghost. But I'll tell you my name anyway. It's Beth."

"Sure."

A cocktail waitress came by, asked if I wanted a drink. "Another Beefeater martini for me," I said. "And whatever my friend wants."

"What friend?"

The ghost smiled at me.

"Never mind," I said. "Just for me."

After the waitress left I nodded at the apparition. "Okay. I believe you. Now how can you help me?"

"I see things," she said.

"I imagine you see dead people, like Haley Joel Osment."

"I didn't like that movie at all."

"You saw it?"

"I go to movies. What, do you think I just float around all day?" She had a winning petulance about her. My kind of girl. "What do you know about the spirit realm?"

"I've had experience with it," I said. "I was just telling my client I've called a ghost as a witness in court. I've confronted demons."

"That makes sense, then."

"What makes sense?"

"The fact that they're afraid of you."

The cocktail waitress appeared with my drink. I don't usually eat the olives. I made an exception tonight. I popped both of them in my mouth and withdrew the plastic pick they were on. I dropped the pick on the table and took a nice slug of the martini. "Explain, please."

"I guess you didn't see the two demons who tried to stop you from coming in here."

That was certainly news to me. "I saw nothing."

"I was hanging out in the lobby. That's what I usually do, you know. We ghosts tend to return to the places that meant something important to us, something unresolved. I was supposed to meet somebody here on January 9, 1947, and he never showed up. I keep hoping to run into his ghost and ask him what the heck he meant by standing me up. Anyway, I saw them in their spirit form waiting in the lobby. I see this from time to time. Demons do a lot of waiting, looking for bodies to inhabit. But then you came in, with your fella."

"He's not my fella. He's a client."

"He didn't look like a client. You were having a drink with him in the bar."

"Strictly professional."

Beth smiled knowingly. "Keep telling yourself that. I used to tell myself that, too. Anyway, these two demons started at you like they were torpedoes from a submarine. But just before they reached the two of you it was like they hit a brick wall. An invisible barrier of some kind. It actually knocked them backwards. And then they screamed and wailed. I hate that sound, the sound of demons screaming. Then they took off as fast as they could. They swept right by me. I saw fear on their faces."

"So you're saying you think they're afraid of me because of that?"

"Or of something about you. I don't think they were afraid of your friend. I mean client. You're not a human being, are you? I mean in the normal sense of the term."

I struggled with whether to tell her about me. But then, what could a ghost do? And I didn't think she was going to be able to use anything I told her against me. The demons of Los Angeles were already well informed of my condition.

"I'm a zombie," I said.

"I thought so," Beth said.

"It shows?"

"I've been following you and I see how you sometimes get nervous around people. It isn't because of your profession. You're a very competent lawyer. So I thought it had to be something else. A flesh eater was one of the possibilities. And I know that's been happening a lot more lately."

"Why were you following me?"

She pushed back her ghostly black hair. "I heard that you were a lawyer who could be trusted with things like this."

"Like what?"

"I'm only half a ghost," she said. "Don't look under the table, but the lower half of me is missing. It all goes back to my murder."

"Murder?"

"Ever heard of the Black Dahlia?"

Of course I had. The most famous unsolved murder in Los Angeles history. Elizabeth Short. She'd been surgically bisected, the two parts of her body left in a vacant lot. No one had ever been brought to trial. "You are the Black Dahlia?"

"I never liked that. It's not who I was. They just made up a name to sell papers."

"But, well, you obviously know who killed you."

"Not just killed. Tortured."

Oh, yes. I remembered that now.

"It was a sadistic surgeon here in town," she said. "He was questioned as a suspect a few years after my murder, but they didn't arrest him. Shortly after that he left the country. He got away with it. I'm just left here as half a ghost."

"Why is that?"

"I have to help solve a murder in return," Beth said. "Then I'll be whole again."

"Really?"

"I want to help you solve a murder."

I took a sip of Beefeater. I needed it. "I don't really have any unsolved murders on my plate."

"I think you will."

"Um, why?"

"I don't know, but the demons don't like you."

This I wanted to know more about. "All right, be specific. Tell me exactly what you think you know."

She looked at my drink. "That looks so good. I miss them."

"Focus," I said.

"Sorry," she said. "Okay, it's like this. I was hanging out here at the bar, no one able to see me of course, when I overheard a couple of demons talking. They were in the bodies of two Holly-wood producers, so it was hard to tell. Anyway, one mentions your name to the other, and then says it's part of the prophecy."

"What prophecy?"

"Well..." she started to say, then her face froze. I mean, dead froze like it was suddenly transformed into a photograph. And then I watched as that pretty face turned into a bloody mess. The mouth slit on either side and formed a grotesque smile. Burn marks all over.

I was seeing her death mask.

And then a good portion of hell broke loose.

A black cloud swept into the bar, separating into several clouds, trailing a wake of wind. Bottles and glasses shattered behind the bar. The bartender went "Hey!" and the cocktail waitress screamed.

Beth Short's horrible mouth opened. The whole lower half of her face unhinged.

"Help me!" she wailed.

I was picked up and thrown to the floor. *Wham!* My head thwacked the hard surface and it stunned me.

The sound of keening pierced my ears. The sound of demonic delight.

I rolled over and got up, staggering like a boxer.

The black clouds were retreating as fast as they'd come in.

And Beth Short's gory torso was in their grip.

She looked at me one last time before disappearing completely.

Just like she had in 1947.

Which left me to deal with the angry barkeep and hotel manager.

"Who's going to pay for all this?" the manager said.

"Insurance," I said.

"It was *your* friends."

"Are you kidding me?" I said. "I'm minding my own business, I don't know who that was."

"She was talking to someone," the bartender said.

"Who was it?" the manager said.

"Did you see anybody sitting here?" I said. "Besides me?"

"Something was going on," the barkeep insisted.

I said, "You got demonized. I'm sorry to tell you that. But if you let ghosts in here you never know what's going to happen."

When I tried to leave, the manager grabbed my arm. I yanked out of his grasp. "Don't try it."

I had half a mind to eat him. Instead, I walked out, went through the dining area that used to be the hotel lobby, and out the door onto Olive Street.

The same way Beth Short had the night she disappeared.

CHAPTER ELEVEN

I HEADED DOWN Olive until I hit Seventh, turned left, and walked until I came to an old building that held some specialized offices.

I hit the buzzer and waited. Nobody came so I punched it again. Finally I heard footsteps. It was late and I figured the only people in the building now would be the ones I wanted to see. Or, rather, the one.

The door opened and a very large man with a face like a can of knuckles said, "We're closed for business."

"How you doing, Chester?"

"Like I said, we're closed."

"Tell him I'm here."

"But—"

"Just tell him. It'll all work out better if you do." He waited a second and thought about it. It looked like it took a tremendous strain on him. Then he said, "Wait here," and shut the door.

I was here to see one Meyer Harris Cohen, better known as Mickey. Cohen was one of L.A.'s most notorious mobsters, back in the fifties. Everyone thought he died in 1976, but he actually became a zombie. Until someone cut off his head. A zombie hunter named Harry Clovis.

Yep, my dad. I had not told Mickey this.

I actually called Mickey Cohen's head as a witness in my father's first trial. You use what you can when you're a criminal defense lawyer. You can read about that and a whole lot more in my journal, *The Year of Eating Dangerously*.

Mickey's old hideout was just a warehouse guarded by his two main thugs. He had taken a bold step in setting up shop downtown.

Five minutes went by. I thought maybe they'd decided to ignore me. That's not a healthy thing to do. But the door opened and Chester told me to follow him.

We walked down a long, echoey corridor, then through a door that had a staircase. Down one flight to a level without windows. At the end was another door, and this one Chester knocked on three times quick.

It unlatched. Another of Mickey's men was inside. When the door closed I heard Mickey Cohen's voice. "Mallory Caine. To what do I owe the pleasure?"

Mickey's head rested on a pillow on some metal shelving. He could have been a Halloween mask.

"Hi, Mickey. How you feeling?"

"Still waiting for a body," Mickey said. He had asked this of me before. He needed a zombie body—one where the head was cut clean off. A regular human body would just atrophy. It was one big problem for the Mick.

"Sorry, Mickey, I'm not in the body procuring business."

"Then why am I listening to you?"

"I need a favor."

"In my day, favors were given after favors were paid. Otherwise something is owed. Which will it be for you?"

"I can offer you legal advice when you need it. I'm always happy to do a small favor like that."

"Not good enough. I want to be a body again. I want to be able to walk around and go to nightclubs."

"Nightclubs are not the way they used to be back in the fifties," I said.

"That's what's wrong with this town. It doesn't know its history. It doesn't know what quality is anymore. Kids today."

I said nothing.

"What is it you want?" Mickey said.

"I want to know about a guy named Dwayne Dewey."

"And I should know him why?"

"Because he works for Mayor Garza. And he does things that aren't exactly on the up and up. Gee, sort of like you used to, Mickey."

"Don't flatter me now," he said. "Again, why should I help you if you can't get me what I want?"

"Why don't your boys do the dirty work?" I nodded to his thugs, one very large (I call him Disney Hall) and the other a younger guy with two days' growth of beard. I call him, imaginatively, Beard.

"I can't jeopardize their standing," Mickey said. "I need them with me, not in jail for procuring."

"Why do you think I can do it?" I said.

"Come on, Miss Caine. You know what you are. You know where you can get a headless, walking dead body. Or make one."

"You want me to turn on my own kind?"

"I learned a long time ago that sometimes that's just the way it's gotta be."

"Not in my world, Mickey."

"Oh come off it. Your world is a living hell, like mine, with a lust for brains that don't quit."

"I'm kicking that habit," I said.

"Oh yeah?"

I wanted to lie to him, but knew he wouldn't buy it.

"So where does that leave us?" I said.

"Certainly not shoulder-to-shoulder," Mickey Cohen's head said.

"Maybe you should just help me out of the goodness of your heart," I said.

"Heart? Where would I put it?"

His thugs laughed.

"I'll see what I can do about a body," I said. "Is that good enough?"

"Come see me when you've got something. And try to make it snappy."

"What about Dewey?"

"He lost to Truman," Mickey Cohen said.

There was no talking to the man when he got this way. He was just a head, but he still liked to throw his weight around.

CHAPTER TWELVE

ON TUESDAY I was in my office early, trying to concentrate on work.

But in my world, that never seems to last too long.

I had to figure out a way around the judge's ruling on zombie evidence. How was I going to get around *that*? It would be the subject of an appeal for sure, but I don't like appeals. I want to win at trial and go home.

There had to be a way.

But just as I was about to dig into some law someone knocked softly on my door.

I didn't want company, but it could always be a client. "Come in," I said.

And in came Jaime Gonzalez, closing the door quickly behind him, like he was afraid.

I got up and started toward him, but he rushed to me first. He threw his arms around me and buried his head in my stomach.

"What are you doing here?" I said. "Is your mother with you?"

He shook his head.

I gently pushed him back a little and knelt to get face to face. "How did you get here?"

He pulled something out of his back pocket. A bus ticket.

"Why?" I said.

"I am having the bad dreams," he said.

"What sort of dreams?"

Jaime looked at the floor as he spoke. "They scare me. There is blood. And it is all around."

Jaime is a ten-year-old boy who breathes fire. There were some nasties who were after him, including a Rakshasa, a Hindu demon, who'd posed as Jaime's mother.

But we finally got Jaime reunited with his real mother, and located them in a safe haven outside Los Angeles county. Whatever was after him wasn't touching him out here in Temecula, but we weren't taking any chances. Father Clemente had rigged up the modest apartment Jaime and his mother were in with a crucifix and some incantations of protection.

Why? Because according to the Book of Revelation:

And I will give power unto my two witnesses, and they shall prophesy a thousand two hundred and threescore days, clothed in sackcloth. These are the two olive trees, and the two candlesticks standing before the God of the earth.

And if any man will hurt them, fire proceedeth out of their mouth, and devoureth their enemies: and if any man will hurt them, he must in this manner be killed.

Father Clemente believes that Jaime—because of his fire breathing, which only comes out at times of stress—is one of these two witnesses. And if he ever connects up with the other witness, it will be the beginning of the end.

"I've had dreams like that," I said to Jaime. "But we have to remember that dreams can't hurt us."

"You are in the dreams, too."

That chilled me. "We have to call your mother."

"I don't want to go back! I want to be with you!"

"Jaime, your mom is going to be worried."

He nodded, sadly.

And then my window shattered. My office became a swirl of papers as a rushing wind blew in. It knocked Jaime to the floor. He screamed.

I was aware of something in the room, an apparition. I shouted, "What is your name?"

A husky, female voice said, "Ishtar."

Ishtar? Yet another Mesopotamian demon-god crowding in to Los Angeles.

"If you've come for the boy," I said, "then you can save your breath. And who is going to pay for that window?"

Something resembling a woman materialized in front of the broken glass.

"You are the one I have come for," Ishtar said.

I have learned not to negotiate with demons. They cannot be trusted. You have to use strength with them. "You can make an appointment just like everyone else."

"Silence!"

"You don't have any authority here. You don't come busting into my office like this. You demons tried this before, trying to strong-arm me. And by now you should know it doesn't work. I've got some sort of protection, you know?"

Ishtar laughed. It was one of those creepy laughs that echo. "Your time is running out. Your protection is going to leave you. You have to make your choice now."

"Always with the choices. Look, Ishi, let's just agree to disagree. You're not getting me, you're not getting the boy, and you are going to pay for that window."

I didn't figure that last one would work, but I wasn't in a very forgiving mood.

Ishtar said, "On the fifth day of the fourth month of the Year of Dagon, it shall come to pass that the earth will shake and the dead will rise and the Father of all will take vengeance. There will be blood. It shall be so and remain."

I had no idea what she was spouting about. I was tired of ancient prophecies in Bible verses and omens. Just leave me alone.

And Jaime too. I wasn't going to let anything happen to him again.

"You've had your say," I said. "Now don't break anything on your way out. Be gone."

"You have had your chance," Ishtar said.

"Get out."

With another laugh, Ishtar turned back into invisible wind and went out the way she came in, with a few of my papers swirling after her.

I picked up Jaime and put my arm around him. "I'm going to call your mother. I'll bring her up here. You need to stay with Father Clemente. Things are going to get heated, and you'll need his protection."

"I just want to be near you."

"And you will be. I promise."

CHAPTER THIRTEEN

THAT NIGHT I was watching American Idol and found myself wanting to eat every contestant and all the judges.

So I went to another Zombies Anonymous meeting at Father Clemente's church.

But just as I walked in the door I kept thinking, What good was this doing me? Why was I even fighting it? Just eat flesh and let the cosmic chips fall where they may.

Then I thought, No. Fight on. There was still some sort of morality in me that hadn't been killed off. It wasn't very big, this morality. It could easily be overwhelmed when I was hungry. But there it was and I guess Father C had convinced me it needed heeding. It was the last scrap of humanity in me, and if I ever wanted my soul back, maybe I'd need it.

I don't know. I was dazed and confused when I walked into the church on Selma. It looked like a healthy crowd. Sal was there, and Reuben the Cowboy, and a zombie couple named George and Ramona Shack. Some other new faces. Where were they coming from all of a sudden?

I had a cup of coffee with Sal and Reuben. The cowboy asked me how I was doing and I told him I was doing okay.

He said, "One time, before I was re-upped, I was rodeoing, bull riding mostly. They had this one bull in Texarkana, name of Mad Max. I guess that was on account of a Mel Gibson movie. You recall that?"

"I never saw it."

"Well, this bull was aptly named, he was, and no one had been able to take him to the limit. I wanted to get ten seconds on him. That was my goal. Everybody said it was impossible. But I got on up there and told myself to believe. Got to believe."

"Did you do it?" Sal asked.

"Nah. Got thrown on my butt in three," Reuben said. "Which taught me a lesson. You have to do more'n believe. You got to have help. And that's why we're all here. We can't do this on our own."

I thought about that as the meeting went on. Ever since I was a little girl being raised by an ex-hippie mother who sometimes seemed like the real child in the room, I'd been on my own. Taking care of myself. Now even more, because demons wanted to control me, use me, kill me.

When it came around to my turn to speak, I said, "Pass."

CHAPTER FOURTEEN

NEXT MORNING I MADE MYSELF A CALVES' brain omelet and doused it with Tapatio sauce. When my taste buds were alive that would have made this concoction at least palatable. But now it was no use. I had to force it down and felt sick doing it.

But at least I made it. One day at a time, I told myself.

I got to the office a little after eight. I like to come in early and avoid Logo, who opens up shop at nine. The street is just starting to stir and it's fairly quiet. I can get some research done and work on upcoming motions.

But I was surprised by Nick pounding on my door at eight-thirty. I let him in and he said, "Give me a medal!"

"How about some coffee instead?"

He stomped around in a circle.

"Decaf," I suggested.

"I am a genius!" he said. He was carrying his SpongeBob back-pack—Nick was frugal with his money and picked this up for a buck at a shop on Broadway—and he opened it and took out some papers. These he slapped on my desk.

"Read," he said.

"All right, calm yourself," I said and went to my chair. I picked up the papers. "What have we got here?"

"Microfiche copies," he said. "I am at the library at Fuller getting these."

"Fuller?"

"The seminary, in Pasadena."

"What were you doing there?"

"Just read!"

So I did. The copies appeared to be reproductions of physical pages from an old book. The script and typesetting were pre-1800s at least. The first page held the title, *On the Restitution to Sound Mind of Diseased Intellects and Corrupted Souls*. Not exactly Nicholas Sparks. At the bottom of the page were Roman numerals: MDCXXVIII. I had to study it for a moment. Then I recalled that D stood for five hundred. That would make this a book from the year 1628.

I looked at the next page, which had a major heading: *Lycan-thropy*. On the next page was a section that Nick had circled with a red pen:

The werewolves are certayne sorcerers who, having annoynted their bodies with an oyntment which they make by the instinct of the devil, and putting same into certayne inchaunted drink, imbibe. Suche a one does not onely unto the view of others seeme as wolves, but to their owne thinking have both the shape and nature of wolves, so long as they are under the effecte. And they do dispose themselves as very wolves, in wourrying and killing most of humane creatures.

I looked at Nick. "What do you make of it?"

"Make!" he said. "Did you see that there? The instinct of the devil. What you got in a werewolf is not just mill-of-the-run night creature."

"Run of the mill," I said.

"You client belongs to the devil!"

I had to chew on that for a moment. What if he did? Were

there different kinds of belonging? Was I dealing with someone who was not to be trusted?

Nick took out another paper, this one a AAA road map. He had circled a portion of it.

"Look here," he said.

The circle was around a spot off the Pacific Coast Highway, near Malibu.

"What's there?" I said.

"Werewolves," he said. "Center of activity."

"You're saying this is where the wolves are?"

"I am a barroom ... I am a gumshoe!"

"Uh-huh. But what if you're picking up movie producers? They're wolves, too, and a lot of them live in Malibu."

He threw up his hands.

"Thanks, Nick," I said. "You're a good egg and not a Palooka."

He smiled. "I think that's good, yes?"

"Yes."

He nodded once, then said, "Get rid of that wolf client. He's not so good."

I shook my head. "Once I take a client, I rep him to the end. Unless he walks out on me."

"And if he don't chew off your arm," he said. "Watch yourself, baby." He walked out and I could have sworn he hitched up his little shoulders just like James Cagney.

Yeah, I was repping a werewolf. I knew the risks. Or thought I did. But the devil thing was bothering me.

I needed to have a word with my client.

An hour went by. I was reading the latest advance sheets from *The Daily Journal* when my door opened after a single knock.

It was LAPD Detective Mark Strobert. Mid-thirties, with green eyes out of a Scottish romance novel, Strobert was a good cop. I eat good cops for lunch. Figuratively speaking. At least most of the time. I once ate a dirty cop who was also a serial killer. It was one of my most satisfying meals. But I generally let cops continue to walk the street.

And Strobert, well, against my better judgment and eating habits, I'd let him get to me in a way I hadn't known since I'd been alive. Just a small pluck on the cold veins of my dead-but-alive heart. Not a feeling I liked.

After he closed the door I said, "Sure, come in."

"It's been too long," he said.

"That's a matter of who's keeping time," I said. "I happen to be busy."

His forehead wrinkled into a neon sign that said *Sadness Café*. It was understandable. I don't think he'd quite recovered from the time he took my alter ego, Amanda the hooker, to a Mexican restaurant. A bowl of guacamole had developed a case of rolling eyeball, moving around and staring at us.

Freaked him out. Avocado dip staring at you tends to do that, especially if it explodes. It's a wonder Strobert didn't file for stress disability after that. But it showed he had inner grit. I liked that.

"Since when does a cop walk into a lawyer's office uninvited?" I said.

"When he's investigating a murder," Strobert said.

"You ever heard of knock-notice rules?"

"I'm in a hurry," he said. "Besides, the way you've shredded me on the stand I figured you owe me a favor."

I laughed. "You got attitude, that's for sure."

"I'm investigating a murder."

"And you want to talk to me why?"

Strobert helped himself to a chair. "A guy named Floyd Bates."

I shrugged. "Got nothing for you. Never heard of him."

"He was a part-time actor. Sort of looked like Tom Selleck."

"*Magnum, PI* Tom Selleck? Or Monica's boyfriend on *Friends* Tom Selleck?"

"This isn't a joke. Floyd Bates didn't have a brain inside his head."

"Actors are that way."

"I'm serious. I'm talking somebody . . . *something* took his brain out of him."

I sat up in my creaky chair. It sounded like a cat wailing. "What does any of this have to do with me? And make it fast."

He didn't answer for a long moment. He rubbed his palms on his pants a couple of times. He looked like a boy getting ready to attempt his first front wheelie. Then he brought his gaze up to meet mine. "I need to ask you something," he said.

I waited. Never give a cop verbiage if you can help it.

"There's something going around," he said.

"Flu?" I said.

He closed his eyes. "Listen." He opened them again. "There's a lot of craziness in this town right now. You know it and I know it. So I'm asking you, just how much you know."

"About what?"

"Zombies."

He let the word float there like a black feather drifting down. I waited till it hit the floor.

"Let me see if I understand you," I said. "You came here to ask my opinion about zombies?"

"Not just any zombies," he said. And stopped there. He knew about me. That had to be it. Or thought he did. I wasn't shocked. You eat enough flesh they're going to find out, eventually. And then the cops'll try to pin every brain snack on you.

But I wasn't about to give myself up. Poker faced, I said, "Now hold on there, cop. You don't just throw that stuff around."

"Is it true?"

"I don't owe you anything," I said.

"Just asking."

"Well, don't."

"You deny it?"

"I don't have to deny anything. Now why don't—"

"Where were you on the night of—"

"Stop," I said. "Now. You want to question me, you better put me under arrest. And you better damn well have probable cause. And for your information, it isn't illegal to be a zombie. If a zombie is in recovery and on a bovine diet, there's nothing you can do about it."

"And you know this how?"

"I handle all sorts of clients. The only kind I wouldn't defend are dirty cops."

"That's a low blow," Detective Strobert said.

Yeah, it was. But I wasn't feeling civil. Not with a possible murder rap hanging over my head.

Strobert's eyes flickered, like a small green flame about to go out.

I said, "You ever consider taking a leave?"

"You think I need it?" he said.

"Let's just say you've looked better."

He stood. "I don't like what's happening in this city. I liked it better when all you had to deal with were human dirtbags."

"It's always been a crazy kind of town," I said in a bizarre attempt to comfort him.

"There's crazy and then there's flat-out M. Night Shyamalan," he said. He turned to me. "I wish things were different."

"Different how?"

"Between us."

"Why?"

"You know why."

I swallowed hard. "Now I know you need stress leave."

"I hope it's not true," he said. "I really hope you're not..."

"Leave it at that," I said.

CHAPTER FIFTEEN

EDDIE'S WAS NOT your typical biker bar. You would think the place would be all pool tables and black leather. True, there was a lot of that going on. Eddie's had one pool table and most of the male patrons wore some form of leather—jacket, vest, or chaps.

But on the walls were a series of watercolor paintings, in soft pastels. Butterflies and meadows and birds on the wing. It was as jarring as if I were to walk into Martha Stewart's home and see framed images of infamous criminals. (I shuddered thinking that there is a possibility that might be true, but I let that go.)

Later I would find out that these watercolors were the work of Eddie himself, Eddie being the biggest, baddest, most notorious biker since Sonny Barger. If he wanted to do watercolors, he got to do watercolors.

As I was taking in the atmosphere just inside the doors, I noticed several sets of eyeballs looking at me. Some were of the biker variety, some were of the biker chick variety. I was of the undead variety, so I didn't feel any sense of danger. Mostly I was going to be annoyed, I was sure, because this was going to turn into a wild goose chase.

But I had to follow up the lead.

I went to the bar and sat on the stool next to one of the fattest men I have ever seen up close. His black leather vest looked like it had to be a whale skin with armholes. He turned his face, covered with a massive red beard, and said in a high-pitched voice, "My urine is pink."

Now why would a voice like Mike Tyson's tell me that? I didn't want to know. I looked for a bartender. He was way down at the other end.

"It's been that way for a while," Gargantua said. "I'm hoping that it will clear up in time for the end of the world."

I've had many clients who didn't take their meds, others who were simply prey to the vicissitudes of mental illness in its various rainbow forms. So I wasn't really freaked out about random mutterings from a man the size of a zeppelin hangar.

"I've been to a doctor, but they just want to cut me open. I got something against being cut open. You?"

"I'm waiting for someone," I said.

"Can I buy you a beer?"

"Thanks anyway."

"I don't bite."

"I think I'll just walk around," I said. I started to get up, but he grabbed my arm. I took it away.

"People don't usually treat me so rudely," Gargantua said.

"I'm not people. I'm a lawyer. And if you touch me again I'll have you arrested."

"In here?" He laughed.

Now what?

The man put his big paws on my shoulders. "I want to buy you a beer."

I kneed him in the groin. And all of a sudden cheers broke out throughout the bar. Apparently I'd just provided an evening's entertainment.

"Look," I said to the assemblage. "Somebody wanted to talk to me. I'm Mallory Caine, lawyer. Who was it?" Seven or eight hands shot in the air.

"Very funny," I said.

Then I felt something tug my slacks. I looked down and the mini biker stood there. "Let's talk," he said. His voice was low. So was he. A bona fide little person, in vest and jeans.

"You're the one who called me?"

"You want to know about wolves, don't you?"

By this time Gargantua had regained his manhood and pushed me to the side. "I'm going to have to deal with you now."

But mini biker said, "Back off."

"This ain't your fight."

"It's a woman, idiot. You're not going to fight her. You're going to leave her alone."

"You've been riding me for a week," Gargantua said. "I'm sick of it."

All of a sudden the little one pulled out a knife from the back of his pants. The knife was as big as he was. "You want to dance?" The little biker spun the knife around in his hand as if it were a baton. Gargantua's eyes got big and round.

"Break it up." The bartender had materialized at our end. He looked like a cross between Dr. Evil and Dr. Phil.

Gargantua didn't move. The bartender reached under the bar and came out with an aluminum bat. With a fling of his arm the big biker sulked off.

I looked down at the little guy and his blade. "I'm a friend of Nick's," he said.

HIS NAME WAS ROCKY NIBBS. WE WENT TO A TABLE IN THE back corner of Eddie's to talk.

"Yeah, I know Nick," Rocky said. "I know all the little people worth knowing in L.A."

"Are you a Kallikantzaros?"

"Nah, just a Wild Thing."

I shook my head.

"Name of our club," he said.

"Now I know where the wild things are," I said. "Here at Eddie's."

"What you want to know about is wolves," he said. "Nick's nervous about it. But you don't have to be."

"How much did Nick tell you?"

Rocky Nibbs shrugged. "Enough. And he's right. You're about this far from gettin' torn up."

"Why do you know so much about it?"

"My brother. He was one of 'em. Got a silver bullet through the head." He was quiet for a long moment. "Anyway, you got one shot to get in good with 'em."

"With who?"

"The wolves."

"Okay. What do I have to do?"

CHAPTER SIXTEEN

THE HILLS ABOVE MALIBU, California, are still as untamed as they were when the Native Americans looked at them and, in their language, said, "Are you kidding me?"

Yes, there are multimillion-dollar homes facing the ocean, but once you go inland about half a mile, into the canyons, you find a scrubby veldt of manzanita and coastal sage, rock and scrub oak and snakes.

This is where the coyote roam.

And the wolves.

At least according to Rocky Nibbs it was. I was to wait here for further instructions.

I'd driven Geraldine, my yellow Volkswagen bug, up a fire road, parked at the top of a ridge. I got out and could look down at the lights of Malibu and PCH on one side, and the emptiness of the hills on the other.

And oh yes, the moon was full.

"Don't move," a voice said. It was not the deep, growly voice of a wolf man. It was lighter in tone.

"Easy," I said. "I'm not doing anything."

"You look like you're looking for somebody," the chirpy voice said. "Maybe I can help."

I started to turn.

"Don't move!" the voice commanded. I was looking at a man of modest height, his features oddly familiar in the moonlight.

And then, from the side, a shadow jumped my way. My nocturnal companion pushed me hard, and the shadow form sailed across my falling body.

"*Yidda fonda! Golga maletha!*" said the voice to the shadow. I turned slightly on the ground and was looking right into the snout of a snarling wolf.

It was looking me in the eye, but, in seeming obedience to the nonsensical language uttered by the stranger, it did not strike.

"*Wiiupr*," the stranger howled, and the wolf started backing away from me. Not looking happy about it at all. It then stood up on two legs and spoke. "You not tell me what do."

"As long as you can't speak in complete sentences, I will," the stranger said.

"Kill you some time."

"You want to take me on, Spike? You think you're ready for that?"

"Wheel spinner!"

"Get out of here," the stranger said. "You're stinking up the hill."

The wolf on two legs looked at me again. "Your neck mine," he snarled and ran off into the darkness.

I was nuts to be up here alone.

"You're nuts to be here alone," the stranger said. He helped me up and now I could see his face clearly.

"No way," I said.

"Don't tell anybody," he said.

"Yeah, I can see it would be bad for your image."

"And ratings."

"But my question is this, how did Pat Sajak gain authority over werewolves?"

Pat Sajak smiled. "I could say it was dumb luck, like a spin on my show. Or I could say it's a curse. Or I could tell you the truth."

"Why don't you start there?"

"Why should I trust you, Mallory Caine?"

"You know me?"

"And I know what you are."

"How do you know this?"

"The way you get to be king of the wolves is the same way you run a business. Information."

"I don't get that. Don't wolves just operate like animals?"

"Oh, sure. You have to become a wolf yourself."

"Are you a werewolf?"

"Is that so surprising?"

"To be honest, Pat Sajak is the last person I'd tag as a werewolf."

"Vanna got me into it. Once I was, I couldn't stop. It was back in a time when people were watching Trebek more than me. I needed a confidence boost."

"Can you control it?"

"Only for a little while. The moon is telling me it's time. But you're safe with me."

"How do I know that?"

"I'm Pat Sajak! Am I going to gnaw someone's arm off? Come on and meet the pack."

A CHILL WIND JUMPED UP FROM THE OCEAN, SMELLING OF SALT and secrecy. From where we stood there were no lights of civilization visible. No sound of cars swooshing down Pacific Coast Highway. The moon and stars cast silver shards like broken glass made of pearl.

And I was walking down a fire road with Pat freaking Sajak.

"The wolf's life is not all visceral energy and peak experience," Pat Sajak said. "You don't get anything for nothing in this world."

"Not even on Wheel of Fortune?"

"Well, there is that. But it's just a game show, and do you know how hard it is to be associated with that show?"

"How hard?"

"Not hard at all!" He laughed. Then a short wolf howl issued from his mouth, almost like a loud belch. "Oops. Excuse me. The cell tides are pressing. I'll have to let go soon."

For a moment the only sound was our feet on the dirt floor.

"What happens when you let go?" I asked.

"It's unlike anything you've ever felt in your life," he said. "Well, almost. It's like a sexual climax, only more intense."

"More?"

"Imagine that."

I didn't want to. I needed to remember my alive-self like I needed salt in my mouth.

"And then it's like a water slide down into your animal nature," he said. "And you hit it with a big splash. Then you're in the sea of your own senses, the pool of your passions, unafraid of anything. That's the best part, the mental part."

"You should write the brochure," I said.

"It's not for everybody. I wouldn't want to see Keith Olbermann out here."

"I understand."

"Here we go," he said. And he started down a path I could barely see. All I knew was that we were heading down, down, down and I was beginning to get a little nervous. If I hadn't been with Pat Sajak—who has about the most trustworthy face in the history of TV, I mean, come on!—I might have bolted back to Geraldine.

But then we came to a clearing where I could hear several trucks idling. Then, on second listening, I realized it wasn't trucks at all. It was the low growls of a wolf pack, in harmony.

"They are singing the song of the wolf," Pat said to me quietly.

"They have a song?"

"Written by Sting himself."

"Is he a wolf?"

"No, he's a songwriter. Where have you been?"

Always with the cracks, that Pat. I guess there are some things even werewolfism won't kick out of you.

The hum of the growl-song went on for another couple of minutes, getting progressively louder, until it sounded like bagpipes in the back of a cement mixer as piped through Aerosmith's old speaker system.

When I looked back at Pat in the moonlight, he was no longer recognizable.

His face was fur, his teeth visible. He had removed his shirt and was shag rug all over. He was breathing heavily, as if he'd just gone through that climactic water slide routine.

"Oh baby!" he said at last. That's when the singing stopped. And the wolves turned toward Sajak.

"What is the law?" he said.

In unison, the wolves answered, "Not to walk on all fours."

"What is the law?"

"Not to eat vegetables."

"What is the law?"

No answer. Some looks of confusion.

"You see?" Sajak said. "You do not know that law! That is why I have brought you a lawyer!"

Low hums directed toward me.

"Hey, wait a minute," I said.

"We need legal counsel," Sajak said. "Go with it." Growls.

"I came here to find out about—"

"Are we agreed?" he said to the pack.

More growls.

"She lawyer!" one of the wolves said. "Meat!"

A few others joined in a chant. "Meat! Meat! Meat!" Sajak put a hand—paw—in the air. "No! Her meat is not for us. It is undead."

Thanks a lot, pal. He may have been protecting me, but it still felt like a little slap in the face. No gal likes to be told her meat is undead.

"She is one of us," Sajak said. "She is not of the world."

"Kill her!" someone snarled.

"Shut your yap," Sajak said. "I am the lead. Do you wish to challenge me?"

Silence. I never would have thought Pat Sajak commanded that kind of respect, but here it was.

"If I may interject?" I said.

"Listen! The lawyer will address us!"

I cleared my throat. "I can certainly appreciate your fine club here—"

"Pack! Pack! Pack!" came a chorus of guttural voices. "Yes! Pack!" I said. "Excuse me. And I don't doubt that you could use some legal advice from time to time. But I have a full plate—"

"Plate! Plate! Meat!"

"I mean work. Try to focus."

"Focus! Focus!"

Sajak silenced them with a gesture.

"First off," I said, "I'm here on behalf of Steve Ravener. Any of you know him?"

Low rumblings, but no affirmations. Then a voice, "Tell her nothing!"

There was no mistaking. It was the wolf that had tried to jump me earlier.

"Silence," Sajak said.

"No silence!" the wolf said.

"Challenge?" Sajak said.

The wolf backed down.

"Listen to me," I said. "There's a wolf who came to me for help. I'm looking for character witnesses." What was I thinking? Asking werewolves to be character witnesses for another werewolf? But I was anticipating the moves of the other side. Surely it would be brought up that Steve was a werewolf and that rendered him unfit for parenting.

"Sniff test!" someone said.

I did not like the sound of that one bit. But when Pat Sajak said nothing, I asked him what was up.

"You must pass the sniff test," he said.

"No, I must not," I said.

"It is the law of the pack."

"I'm not even a wolf."

"Meat!" a wolf cried.

"Knock it off!" I said. "I don't want to hear any more about meat or sniff tests. I'm here as—"

"Our prisoner," Pat Sajak said.

"Excuse me?"

"We cannot allow you to leave, once the sniff test has been ordered."

"Well, you're just going to have to make an exception."

"There are no exceptions. You will be sniffed, or torn to shreds."

My insides started to wobble. Up to this point I'd been running on zombie adrenaline. Now I was starting to crash.

"What is the sniff test?" I asked.

Pat Sajak said, "You simply stand as each wolf, in turn, sniffs you. We seek to see if we can trust you."

"You can tell that by smell?"

"The nose of the werewolf can tell a whole lot more."

I heard what I thought were little wolf chords.

"So you're saying if I don't go through with this test of yours, I get thrown to the wolves?"

"I'm afraid so," Pat Sajak said. "And we have no lovely parting gifts, either."

Wolf smile. Oh, how I wanted to smack his snout. "What do I get in return?" I said. You have to get something out of negotiations like this, don't you? "We let you walk out of here," Sajak said.

"That's not enough."

"You are in no position to bargain!"

"I want some information, about Steve Ravener." Sajak bayed. At the moon. Then looked at me. "Sniff first, information next."

"Can I buy a vowel?"

He didn't laugh. And for the next ten minutes I suffered the indignity of getting sniffed by wolves. Have you ever been in a crowded elevator where someone stinks? If the elevator doors never opened, how would you feel?

That's what it was like to stand there and get sniff tested.

But I did it. Sajak was right. I had no choice if I wanted to keep my arms and legs.

The last one to linger on me was the one called Spike. He sniffed, then bared his teeth. They were dripping.

"Enough!" Pat Sajak said. I realized then that the wolves had all pulled back in a circle around me. Low hums came from their gullets.

"No one has bitten you," Pat Sajak said. "You can be trusted."

"I could have told you that from the start," I said.

He shook his head. "Now we talk."

Sajak waved an arm and the wolf circle dispersed, about twenty or twenty-five furry creatures ran off into the dark hills.

WHEN WE WERE ALONE PAT SAJAK SAID, "LET ME TELL YOU, watching spinning wheels and appearing letters does something to your soul. It makes you think that life is just a big, random, luck-filled cesspool. No disrespect, I know how lucky I am to make that much money cracking wise on a game show. I just wanted to know there was something I was in control of myself. And so I went wolf. Because of my wit and charm I was able to get to the leader of the pack. But this is no life. And I don't know that there's any way out of it. Once it has you, it has you. Do you have any idea what I'm talking about?"

"I do," I said. "I don't want to be the way I am, either."

"I like you. What do you want to know?"

"Do you know Steve Ravener?"

"I think I've heard the name. But he is not part of my pack."

"If I wanted to find out about his pack, what would I do?"

"Why don't you just ask him?"

"I have to make sure that there aren't any skeletons in his closet, so to speak. I'm representing him on a legal matter."

"I wish I could help you."

"I wish you could too."

"It looks like you came a long way for nothing," Pat Sajak said.

"Nothing? I got to be sniffed. Who would have missed that experience?"

"If you ever need to talk to me, call my office and just say that you are my third cousin."

"Why third cousin?"

"It's a code. It'll get you through. Now you better scurry off back to civilization. I can't always vouch for the actions of the wolves."

I was glad to get out of there in one piece.

CHAPTER SEVENTEEN

THE NEXT DAY I did my daughterly duty and visited my Mom at her bead store in Glendale. She'd just gotten back from Cabo, which is a place she could not afford to go. I knew it had something to do with her chasing down some new spiritual diet. She always did that. But this one was costing her.

The bell on the door tinkled as I walked in. Mom liked that old-fashioned sound. She said it summoned fairies.

My mother, Calista Caine, was sitting behind her glass counter. She looked up at me with the bleary eyes of the baked. She was on the hippie lettuce and had been for years.

That didn't concern me as much as her chasing after the flap-doodle of another faux guru.

One thing Los Angeles has never been short on is spiritual quacks peddling their snake oil to the naive and the wealthy. They've come here ever since the turn of the last century, when L.A. was just becoming a major city. My town has long been a vector, or hub, for spiritual hucksters. If you wanted to make easy money here, and you had a glib way about you, you could start a religion or simply gather a bunch of followers who thought you held the verbal equivalent of the tablets of Moses.

Only it wasn't the finger of God that wrote your script, but the greasy digits of the money grabber. The swamis and yogis and mind science types who find out there is no shortage of rubes or marks in this world.

You can look at the *L.A. Times* back then and see ads for phrenologists and spiritualists and all manner of swindler.

One guy used to go around peddling an electric belt. This was in 1903. He said it was a cure for men who were nervous, despondent, and "lacking in self-confidence," who felt that old age was coming on too soon because of the "dulling of their youthful fire and ambition." He wanted to help such men and said he would pay four thousand dollars in gold to any "weak man" who used his newly improved electric belt as he directed and took proper care of himself, if he could not make such a man sound and strong. "What is the use dragging yourself around among men, feeling that you are not like them, that you are not the man you ought to be, when you might as well hold up your head and feel like a real man again? I can take any man who has a spark of vitality left in his veins and fan it into a flame and make him feel like a Hercules!"

That same riff has been repeated ten thousand different ways in Los Angeles since then, and across this gullible country of ours.

My mother was a perfect mark. A former flower child who had never left the Woodstock era, even though the only stock she ever got close to were Birkenstocks.

She flitted to and from charlatans like a gnat to the next sweaty golfer.

And now, it appeared, she had found the mother lode of platitudinous perspiration, who charged big bucks for something or other in places like Cabo San Lucas.

All of Mom's income was derived from her modest store. True, she had no huge living expenses. But that, in my mind, did not excuse her profligacy. Which is what I told her.

"Oh, Mal, stop worrying so much about me," she said as she sipped herbal tea from a Janis Joplin mug that dated back to 1969. Janis's face had faded almost to invisibility after all these years.

"Mom, what are you gaining from throwing away your money like this?"

"It's not a throwaway, dear. It's called enlightened healing. Do you realize he cured my arthritis, just by looking at me?"

"Who did?"

"Father."

I closed my eyes to keep my head from exploding. "Mom, you've never had arthritis. And who is this Father?"

"You must not call him Gig Shivley."

"I didn't," I said.

"Oh my." She took a quick sip of tea.

"So who is this guy?"

"Mallory, you must not judge."

I came around the back of the bead counter. This was the only orderly thing in her life. Acrylic and glass beads were segregated by color into distinct neighborhoods, fenced off by spools of thread and flex wire. It was the one thing that kept her sane.

"Mom, don't you remember what Lilith tried to do to you?"

"I'm off Lilith now."

"But you're onto some new guy. Next week it'll be somebody else."

"Why must you do this, Mallory? Why must you pester me this way?"

Good question. It would have been easy for a zombie daughter to walk away from a stoner mother for whom rational thought was as rare as humility in Hollywood.

Before I could answer the little bell at the front door tinkled again. A wisp of a man, dressed in an overcoat and periwinkle scarf, came in. He was about thirty-five and looked like he never ate meat. Also, like he'd never been in a fight in his life except over the price of shoes.

"Hello, Oswald," my mother said.

"Hello, Mother," Oswald said.

"Mother?" I said.

Oswald gave me the cold once-over. "Who is this?"

"You can talk right to me, Oz," I said.

"This is my daughter, Mallory," Mom said.

"My name is Oswald," Oswald said.

"Got a question for you. Where do you get off calling my mom Mother?"

"It is a term of respect for one who is of the earth," Oswald said. "Your mother is a Mother."

"I have the offering," Mom said and headed toward the back of the store.

"What's going on here?" I said.

Oswald said, "Have you not been to a Gathering?"

"Of what?"

"Do you know Plato's myth of the cave?"

"The philosopher?"

He nodded. "I feel that you have an undealt-with amount of Septunes."

"Excuse me?"

"Septunes. They are like tumors on the soul."

My mother returned from the back of the store, carrying a business-sized envelope that looked packed. She held it out to Oswald, but I snatched it out of her hand. "What is this, Mom?"

"You give that back right now!"

I looked in the envelope. Greenbacks. "You're giving this man money?"

"That is between him and me."

"What's this for, Oswald?" I said.

"Is that your business?" he said.

"When it comes to my mom, yes, it is."

"No, it isn't," Mom said.

"Does he work for this Gig dude?" I said.

"I am in the service of Father," he said. "We do not refer to Father by his first name."

"Mom, come on. This whole thing is a snake oil campaign."

"You don't know anything," Mom said. "You have never been to

Gathering, you have never given it a chance. You are stuck in your own foolishness."

"Mom, you've been trying every wacky thing that's come down the pike ever since I was a kid. Has any of that ever done anything for you for any length of time?"

Oswald said, "I don't see as how we have to listen to this any longer. If you'll please give me the envelope."

I kept it in my hot little fist.

"Do you have power of attorney over your mother's financial affairs?" Oswald said.

"Did you go to law school, Oz?"

"Just hand over the offering and I'll be on my way."

"You ever heard of fraud?" I said.

"What we are doing is perfectly legal under the laws of the state of California."

"Oh yeah," I said. "You've got a point there. This is California after all." I handed him the dough. "But I want to have a meeting with the Father, if you don't mind."

"I don't think that will be possible. Not until you take a preliminary test. I can arrange that."

"Fine."

"It's only ten thousand dollars."

"Get out before I throw you out," I said.

He made a sound of disgust and walked out of the store.

I walked over to my bleary-eyed mother and I took her face in my hands. I pulled her close and gave her a kiss on the cheek. "Mom, don't run around with these people."

"I can take care of myself," she said. And then she sat once again behind her glass counter and pulled out a box of beads.

CHAPTER EIGHTEEN

THERE WAS another mother I wanted to see.

Steve Ravener's ex-wife.

Nick had located her. She lived in a craftsman-style home on Beachwood in Hollywood. Probably built around 1910. It had a low pitched, gabled roof with a wide, enclosed-eave overhang. The porch had thick, square columns. Yellow irises bloomed in the front yard. All in all, it was a comfy-looking home, and probably would sell for around one million bucks.

I went up the little steps and knocked on the front door. A dog next door started barking at me. That's nothing new—dogs tend to do that when zombies walk by. But this one had that high-pitched, annoying kind of bark that makes you want to lock the owner in a closet with the dog after you've thrown in a live snake.

From behind the door a voice said, "What is it?"

"Mrs. Ravener?"

"Who is it?"

"I'm the lawyer for your husband," I said. "Can I have a word?"

After a long pause, the voice said, "I have nothing to say to you."

"I'm only here to see if there might be some middle ground."

"You can talk to my lawyer."

"Fine, what's the name?"

"I don't have to tell you that."

Oh, brother. "I can't very well talk to your lawyer if I don't know the name."

"This is ridiculous. This shouldn't be happening." I heard the squeal of laughter, and from around the side of the house ran a little boy and girl. They ran all the way around to the front steps, the boy chasing the girl, then stopped when they saw me.

Clever zombie lass that I am, I turned to face them and said, "Well, hello."

The door flew open and Pat Ravener came out. She was of average height, with dark hair and full, Angelina Jolie lips. My stomach grumbled.

"Don't you talk to them," Pat Ravener said.

"Who are you?" the boy said.

He was beautiful. He had deep brown eyes, a face like Puck, an energy level that said *I want to find out everything about my world and have fun with it.*

It was a look that tore the heart right out of me. "My name's Mallory," I said.

"That'll be all," Pat Ravener said. "Come here, kids." The duo did as they were told, up the steps to Mom. The two children attached themselves to the mother's legs. The girl had a softer look than her brother. Intelligent, too. Her eyes were inquisitive, contemplative as she looked at me.

"Your kids are lovely," I said. Shouldn't have, of course. I was a lawyer representing a client and I needed to keep my emotions out of it. But I couldn't.

My remark took a little steam out of Pat Ravener. When she spoke next her voice was softer. "You say you're representing Steve?"

"He came to me and I agreed to help," I said. "Yes, I'm a lawyer. But that doesn't mean everything has to be played out in a court of law. I'm not here to threaten, but to listen. Maybe there's a way—"

"I don't think the kids need to hear this," she said.

"No, you're right," I said.

The boy said, "Daddy doesn't like Mommy anymore."

His words dropped on us like a bucket of black paint. I even felt the vibe that was written all over Pat's face. She was pained. And I was thrown for a proverbial loop. I shouldn't have been. I've had too much experience not to remember that your client only gives you one side, and that side is painted in all the favorable colors. I'd let a minor attraction to a wolf man hinder that.

Yes, I was his lawyer and my job was to represent him with zeal. That I could do. But I also had to get the facts first.

Pat Ravener sent the kids inside, with the boy moaning disappointment. But they went, and then she and I sat on the bench on the porch.

"I tried my best to help Steve get off the fur," she said.

"Excuse me?"

"I'm sorry. That's wolf talk for the high they feel when they turn into wolves. I found a recovery group for him. I couldn't take it anymore. When he goes wolf, it's scary bad."

"Do the children know?"

She shook her head. "They think their daddy is moody, and sometimes needs his alone time. But someday they're going to find out."

"Steve says he wants the family together. He doesn't want to lose the kids."

"Of course he says that. I know he loves the kids, but he's not a fit father. Not in that condition. It's like being married to an alcoholic, one who can go for days without a drink, but you don't trust that because at any time he can go on a binge and be dangerous. That's what it's like being married to a wolf man."

I was silent for a moment, and wondered myself what it would be like to be married to someone with a "condition" like my own. Would it be possible for two zombies to find happiness together? What about mixed marriages, like a zombie and a wolf man?

Here I was sitting in front of a nice home in Hollywood,

looking out at the tip tops of the Hollywood hills. Talking with another woman who was opening up about her marriage. Like I had a real girlfriend or something.

I so wanted to be normal then. I wanted to share recipes, without reference to brains. I wanted to talk about my own life and laugh and cry with somebody.

Shut up, I told myself, and said, "What might make it work again for you?"

"Honestly, I don't know," Pat Ravener said.

"May I ask a personal question?"

She looked at me suspiciously. "Why?"

"In the interest of what's best for the children."

There was a long pause before she answered. "I'm not sure I can trust you with anything personal." She stood up. "I think we'd better stop this right now."

I stood up, too, but before I said anything a luscious black Cadillac pulled to a stop. A man got out and started toward the house. He wore a dark blue suit with gold tie. He looked to be in his late thirties.

He had the walk of the power player. He might have been a lawyer from one of the big, downtown firms.

These are the kind of lawyers I like to spank in court. My back was up immediately.

He eyed me as he got closer. Then looked up at Pat Ravener. "Everything okay?" he said.

"This is Steve's lawyer," Pat said.

The guy came up the steps and stood next to Pat.

"And what's your name, friend?" I said.

"A name you better file away." He pulled a small silver case from his inside coat pocket, opened it. It had business cards inside. He handed me one. *DR. DWAYNE DEWEY, Consultant.*

"Doctor?" I said.

"Urban studies and comparative religion," he said.

My mouth was starting to salivate in that strange, zombie way.

I couldn't call my sponsor at Zombies Anonymous, so I kept repeating, *I don't want to eat* in my head.

Pat Ravener said, "Dwayne did his doctoral work at Harvard."

A Harvard man! I do want to eat, I do!

"May I ask about your interest in this matter?" I said.

"What matter?" he said.

"This family."

"That's none of your business. I'd advise you to leave now."

"This isn't your house, is it?"

She said, "Maybe it's best that you leave. I'm sorry you came out here for nothing. But from now on you'll have to talk through my attorney."

"You still haven't given me his name."

Dewey gave it. "Manyon. Charles Beaumont Manyon."

Manyon! I'd tangled with him before. This vampire who poses as a lawyer is very good at what he does. He tried to seduce me into his firm once, not sexually, but with offers of power.

"I think you know him," Dwayne Dewey said.

"You don't do much law in this town without running into Charles Beaumont Manyon. Interesting choice. I didn't know he did family law."

"This time he does," Dewey said.

Pat looked away, as if she didn't want anything to do with it but was letting Dewey call the shots. I wondered why.

"Conversation over," Dwayne Dewey said, and escorted Pat Ravener into the house.

I walked down the street and got in Geraldine and drove around the block. I again parked on Beachwood and waited. I was going to follow the man in the black Caddie.

As I sat there on this mini-stakeout I could see right up into the hills, where the Hollywood sign is. It was huge from this angle.

It loomed. I'd never thought of it that way before. But now I did.

Hollywood was not just a place, it was an idea. When it was cut out of orange groves over a hundred years ago, they thought they were making a nice little suburb for people to live quiet lives away from the bustle of downtown. Then the movie guys got hold of it and turned it into a capital of glitz. What was it the fellow said? If you tear away the tinsel of Hollywood you find the real tinsel underneath.

I was snapped out of my reverie when Dwayne Dewey got into his Cadillac and started up. I followed him at a pretty fair distance. When you have a yellow Volkswagen bug, it makes tailing someone a little dicier. But a big black Cadillac is easy to follow from behind, because it has a big behind itself.

Dewey turned right on Franklin, took another right just before the freeway. The road wound around and up, narrowing. The streets of old Hollywood never contemplated much traffic. The houses up here are eclectic, some from the twenties and thirties that have been preserved, others from the styled-down fifties with sharp lines and box shapes, probably like the people who live inside them. Some old streetlamps still survive, the kind that look like torches, with teardrop glass domes on top of concrete pillars. Dewey's big Cadillac had to go slowly to negotiate some of the turns, so I would lose sight of him for several seconds at a time, then catch up with him around some bend.

He was heading toward the reservoir. Hollywood has a reservoir right in the hills, a place where the precious water supply can be held in reserve, as it has since 1924, when the water magnate William Mulholland constructed it. It's a continuing reminder of the water wars that eventually made Los Angeles into a thriving community. It's all about water here. Water and glam.

Dewey drove on, up through Bronson Canyon, running parallel to the Griffith Park Observatory. That's where they shot a famous scene in *Rebel Without a Cause*. It's also a place where you can contemplate the universe, if that's your thing.

The universe was not a very hospitable place at the moment, so I pass.

I couldn't figure out where Dewey thought he was going. There is a lot of undeveloped nothingness out there, which is a rare commodity in the city. Most of it is protected park land. Hikers and bikers can find some rough territory if they so choose.

Then the road stopped. Dewey's brake lights illuminated the front of a triangular arm gate. I pulled over to the side of the road and stopped.

Dewey got out of his Caddie and locked it. A little squeak-beep echoed down toward me. Then he hopped over the gate and started walking, immediately disappearing behind a pine-treed hill.

I got out of Geraldine and followed. Right past the gate was a dirt road, and my heels dug into the surface. I thought then maybe I should just start wearing hiking boots everywhere. Even to court. I took a turn where I thought Dewey had headed up into the hills and found another path there, a hiking path of sorts. It was strange to suddenly feel like I was in the forest instead of Los Angeles. But stranger still was what a nicely dressed slickster named Dwayne Dewey was doing out here. At the very least he'd get dust on his very expensive shoes.

Was he meeting someone here? If there was something nefarious going on in the political realms relating to downtown, this wouldn't be a bad place to meet. No security cameras, no heavy foot traffic. Maybe there was a payoff, or a bag being exchanged. My mind was reeling with possibilities.

Or maybe he was meeting a clandestine lover. He looked like the kind of guy who could be juggling several women at any one time. Call that the romantic in me.

Every now and then I would stop and listen for any sound of footsteps out there in the leafy and pine needle surface of the land. Nothing. I continued to follow the path. I had Emily in my purse, at the ready in case I needed to defend myself in a close-contact fight. If I did kill Dewey I would have to make sure that I got out of there before my lust for his Ivy League brain completely consumed my willpower.

Just thinking about the possibility made my stomach rumble like a cement mixer.

Finally, after what I judged to be about a quarter-mile, the path opened up into a clearing. The hills were covered with scrub and dry grass. But right in the middle of the clearing, looking stunningly out of place, was a white square building designed to look like some sort of temple. It had four turrets on the corners connecting ten-foot-high white walls. From the middle of the grounds jutted a large dome with a decorative finial on top.

I watched from behind a tree as Dewey presented himself at what can only be described as a front gate. Something like an ancient palace might have. There were iron bars under a large arch. Dewey punched some keys on a pad and took a step back. A moment later the gates swung open and Dwayne Dewey went inside.

What was this place? Los Angeles has long been known for all manner of wacky enclaves in the less developed sections of the county. Topanga Canyon was a favorite for hippies and their assorted gurus. Box Canyon, in Chatsworth, has been the home of drifters and bikers and, for a time, the infamous Manson family.

So in one sense it wasn't surprising to find a bizarre edifice plopped down in the middle of nowhere. It's just that I hadn't run across one this style.

I took a picture of it with my phone, then called Nick and told him to do some research, see if he could track down the origins.

After I put my phone away I watched awhile. No one else went in or came out. Until a woman came around the far corner, stopped and lit a cigarette.

She was dressed like a Roman dancing girl. Off-the-shoulder toga (where did they sell *those*?), a gold brocade belt, gold coin earrings. Her hair was the color of a smoldering fire. She seemed tired as she puffed. As she was alone, I decided to talk to her.

She saw me approach and continued to smoke, as if we had a meeting set up.

"You're the new girl," she said.

I went with it. "Uh-huh."

"Have any trouble finding the place?"

"No, came right to it."

"Good. My name's Andromeda." She extended her hand. I shook it.

"Mallory," I said.

"That's not your given name, is it?"

"Yes, the one I was born with."

"No, I mean given by the high priest."

"Oh," I said. "No. I haven't been given my name yet."

"Well, that is something we've got to fix soon." She took a final drag on her cigarette, dropped it on the dirt, and crushed it out with her sandal. "Let's go inside."

"Let's," I said.

IT WAS A PLACE DECKED OUT LIKE A MOVIE SET. PILLARS AND diaphanous curtains, and on the wall a bas-relief image that pulled me up short I just stared at it. It was a weird scene of a guy about to slaughter a bull. He wore a funny-looking hat, a cap with a point that flopped a little forward. He was pulling up the bull's head by its nostrils, and with his other hand is slitting the bull's throat.

If that wasn't cozy enough, there was a dog and a snake under the bull, trying to get at the blood.

Then there was a scorpion—a scorpion, mind you—reaching up to grab the bull by the balls.

"What in the name of Jupiter is that?" I said. Andromeda said, "Mithras, of course. How much education were you given?"

"Not enough, apparently. What is it that we are supposed to do here?"

She looked at me warily. "Wait a minute. Who are you? You're not here to become a priestess."

"Priestess? Sure I am. Who wouldn't want to be? Where do I pick up an application?"

"You'd better get out. Right now. You seem like a nice enough person, but if you don't get out you could end up dead."

"Come on, that sort of thing doesn't happen anymore. People don't murder people for wandering into a weird temple."

"Okay, you've been warned."

She turned and started down the hallway. I followed her, but almost immediately from out of the shadows stepped a giant black man in a toga and holding a sword.

Are you kidding me? He looked like he could be a bouncer at a fancy Hollywood club.

"You'll come with me," he said.

"Are you serious? Are you really holding a sword? What kind of an outfit is this?"

"Private. Come on."

"I've got news for you, pal. You're not going to slice anybody with that sword. You have two seconds to put it down."

"You better just do as I say."

"I want to see the head guy."

"Oh, you will. Come with me."

"Put the sword down, nimrod."

He frowned, like thinking was on par with lifting weights. But he didn't put the sword down. Instead he held it firmer, pointed toward my torso. I walked up to him and slapped his face.

"Hey! You can't just do that," he said.

"Take me to your leader," I said.

Looking confused and a little upset, he turned around and I followed him through more hallways. This place seemed to have endless hallways, and a lot of rooms. Small ones off to the sides. It was like a little motel.

Presently, we pushed out into a courtyard, where the sun was shining bright. In the middle of the courtyard stood a man in a robe. This man had shoulder-length gray hair and was standing over something. As I got closer I could see it was a small barbecue pit. Well, okay, not really a barbecue pit, but something that had a fire going in it, as if coals were burning. He was looking up toward the sun with his arms outstretched and seemed to be speaking.

The guy with the sword put his hand out to stop me, indicating that we were to just stand there.

"What is this place?" I said.

Sword Man looked dismayed. The gray-haired guy turned toward me. "Were you invited here?"

"Not exactly," I said. "I was taking a walk through the park when—"

"You do not have to lie, my child. I'm here to help you."

"It's a great spread you got here," I said. "What is it that you do?"

"Perhaps we can discuss that over a cup of Ovaltine?"

Ovaltine?

"Laertes," the white-haired guy said, "would you prepare us two hot cups of Ovaltine? We will take it in the study." With that he raised up his toga as if it was a dress. He had bare feet. He started walking toward the building. I followed.

A few minutes later we were seated on large cushions and two hot cups of Ovaltine were placed before us on a silver tray by the man he called Laertes. After serving us, Laertes waddled back to the entrance and stood there with arms folded.

"We do not usually allow curiosity seekers," the gray-haired man said. "But in your case I am prepared to make an exception."

"You're Gig Shivley," I said.

"My real name is of no concern. I had a past life that is over. I am now simply known as the high priest of Mithras."

"And what exactly is that?"

"It is an ancient religion, with roots in Persia. It made its way to the Roman Empire before dying out around the fourth century. It was a competitor with Christianity, but Christianity did not play fair."

"How do you mean?"

"They paid off the Emperor Constantine, who declared Christianity to be the official religion of the Empire."

"Hm, I may have missed that in my Western Civ class," I said.

"It's all true," he said.

"So you say. In my world, we need facts, not just opinion."

"It's not opinion! If not for the influence peddling of priests, our ancient way of knowing would have had a fair chance in the marketplace of ideas. I am only trying to bring that chance back."

I shrugged.

He looked me up and down. "How would you like to work here?" he said.

"What exactly would I be doing?"

"The most important work any woman can do." He stopped and let his eyebrows bob and weave a little bit.

"That sounds very intriguing," I said. "Would you mind giving me the particulars?"

"It doesn't work that way. The way of faith is that you first place your trust in someone, and then you receive the secrets. This is not something we just give away. This is not free samples at Costco. The form of knowledge we are talking about is the greatest that there is, ultimately meant. But you cannot just hear about it. You have to give yourself to it."

"And you're just the magnetic sort of guy to make that happen?"

"You have no idea the power that is within these walls. It is more power than you have ever known or ever come in contact with."

"Well, it's been delightful having Ovaltine with you. I really have to be going." I stood up.

Gig remained seated. "You won't be going anytime soon," he said. "You do realize that, don't you?"

I looked over and saw Laertes grinning, holding his sword like a child's toy.

"What kind of movie did I wander into?" I said.

"I will make you as comfortable as possible. I will show you what it is you must do. Then it will be up to you. You may come along and find the one, true God. Or, you can choose to disappear from here."

"You're kidnapping me?"

"I don't like the term kidnapping. I prefer enlightening."

"Let me enlighten you on a little something. You're about to commit a major felony."

The ersatz holy man remained impassive as if the secrets of the universe were a gentle stream running between his ears.

"I want to talk to Dwayne Dewey," I said.

Gig said nothing. His left eyebrow moved slightly, like a nervous bug on a sweaty palm. But other than that he could have been playing mannequin.

"Don't bother denying it," I said. "I saw him come in here."

"This is a holy place," Gig said. "Pilgrims here are entitled to their privacy."

"You find him and bring him here to talk to me," I said. "If you don't I will raise one of the biggest stinks this town has ever seen, and that's saying a lot, considering the stinks we've had. I will make so much trouble for you you'll wish you were an atheist in a foxhole."

He ran his finger along a crease in his toga. "I have been threatened by stronger people than you."

"People who can eat your face?" I leaned in and glared at him, and it felt good to do it. I watched his eyes until a flicker of realization came into them. "You are one of the walking dead?" he said.

"You think about it, friend. Because you know what? I don't think you think. I don't even think you believe the stuff you're peddling. I think you're doing all this to get girls and make a nice living. So if you want me to leave you alone, you let me talk to this guy Dewey."

When Gig Shivley's cheeks started to turn the color of nectarines, I knew I'd finally gotten a rise out of this paragon of spirituality. As he was thinking of something to say a voice behind me said:

"I'll talk to her."

I turned and saw Dwayne Dewey walking across the courtyard.

He was wearing a white choir robe and sandals. He looked about as comfortable as a dog in a sweater.

"You do not have to talk to her," Gig said. "You have sanctuary here."

"Sanctuary?" I said. "What is this, *The Hunchback of Notre Dame?*"

With that Gig Shivley rose from his puffy pillow, straightened his toga, and walked off.

"What is it you want?" Dwayne Dewey said.

I stood up to face him. "I want you to explain to me what you're doing here."

"I don't have to explain anything to you. I don't have to talk to you or listen to you. I thought I made that clear—"

"This is about the children," I said.

"It's Steve Ravener who is dangerous to his children. You should know that by now."

"And what does the mayor's office have to do with this?"

"I keep my professional life and my personal life separate," he said. He was getting more annoyed, which is just what I wanted him to be. Annoyed people spill beans.

"I just get these feelings," I said, "that things are not disconnected in this city. And the main connection is the mayor. Call it a hunch, call it my breakfast. Call it whatever you want"

"Is that all?"

"As long as I've got you here, what is up with this City Angels business? What is the mayor's game?"

"You can read about it," Dewey said.

"I'm not interested in press releases."

"Why don't you join?" he said.

"I'm not a joiner," I said.

"Then I have nothing more to say to you."

"I have one more thing to say to you," I said. "Keep out of the family business between Steve Ravener and his children."

"I don't think I'll take your advice," he said.

"Suit yourself. But if you get anywhere near the courtroom I will make sure you feel the sting of my lash."

"What is that supposed to mean?"

"I don't know," I said. "But I like saying it." I started toward the exit. The big guy with the sword made a move to get into my path.

Dwayne Dewey said, "Let her through, Laertes. We don't want her around."

"That's the first sensible thing you've said all day," I said, and got out of there.

CHAPTER NINETEEN

I WENT BACK to my office and did some research on this Gig. I wanted to know where he was coming from so I could better protect my mom. Why I was so interested in doing this, I'm not sure. My mom had left planet Earth long ago. But she was my mother, she'd given me life, and I owed her or something. I think that commandment to honor your father and mother applies, even if they're weirdos. It's just something you do.

I wanted to find out what the guy meant by the myth of Plato's cave. I sort of remember that from college. It was in *The Republic,* and I wanted to go over it again.

As I recalled it, in the cave there were people tied up to stakes looking at a wall. They can't see anything else but what is projected on that wall. There are shadows on the wall. Caused by great light behind them. But they don't know that. All they know is these shadows. That's the only thing they know about reality. In fact, they mistake the shadows for reality itself.

So what happens if one of the prisoners escapes, turns around, and sees the source of the light? It's a fire. But it's so bright that it pains his eyes. He would rather go back to the shadows.

But there's a further revelation. At the mouth of the cave you actually get out into the open. Where the sunlight is. That's the biggest light of all. That's reality. That's enlightenment.

It's so big and so amazing, that if the former prisoner went back into the cave and started talking about what was out there, he would be castigated for disturbing the pleasant illusions that the shadows offer. They would try to kill this prisoner rather than listen to his tales of sunlight.

So it was pretty clear what this Gig guy was up to. He was the sunlight. He was enlightenment. He was the one who would bring truth to those who were brave enough to leave the cave. But he didn't expect anybody back inside the cave—meaning us—to understand him. So to be crucial of him was to be someone against the true light.

According to another website, Gig Shivley had been a used car salesman in Des Moines before gaining the ability to heal with a look and collect money without scruple.

Also, there was a website that explicitly set out to expose Shivley and claimed that he'd come up with his theory of the Septunes in a bar one night. He'd been drinking with some salesmen friends and dominating the conversation when one of the salesmen said, "What's your deal?"

And he said "I'm looking for acceptance," but so slurred was his speech that it sounded like "I'm looking for Septunes."

So one of the other guys said, "What's a Septune?" And in his drunken stupor Gig Shivley said, "The secret of selling more cars."

Since Shivley was the leading used car salesman in the area, the other drunken salesmen asked him for details, and Shivley said they'd have to pay.

And that, according to the website, was the birth of Gig Shivley and the Gathering.

Nick came storming in. "Where were you, baby doll? I'm going crazy here!"

"I was investigating," I said.

"Without me?"

"And by the way, I forgot to thank you for my wolf test."

He looked hurt. "You think I am the one that got you sniffed?"

"How do you know I was sniffed?"

Nick clammed up. He had the worst poker face of any gnome I've ever met. Of course I'd only met one—him—but his face was pretty bad.

"Why don't you just tell me face to face?" I said.

"Because you do not listen! That is your problem, you never listen. You think you can fight everybody and everything all the time by yourself. You cannot. You cannot fight God. You cannot fight Satan. You need to be on the team."

"Well, that's funny! What kind of a team are we when you don't have the guts to tell me to my face what the wolves can do?"

"I already tried. You did not listen."

He was right, of course.

"Nick, what are you and I doing in this world? We've each got a curse. We can't get out of it. Tell me, what is the purpose of it all?"

His bushy eyebrows narrowed down. I could tell I shocked him with my question. Truth be told, I sort of shocked myself.

"I believe in God," he said. "I believe that we are to help people as best we can and stop the bad. And if we do that, something will work out."

"Maybe that's enough," I said softly. "I'm sorry I snapped at you, Nick. What do you say we call it a night?"

"I will help you," he said. "I think that I'm supposed to help you the most of all."

CHAPTER TWENTY

YOU WALK DOWN the streets of L.A. at night and the ghosts of the past are with you, around you, watching you sometimes. Here on Broadway, walking home, I sense the ghost of Pantages. Alexander Pantages had been the most powerful theater owner in the 1920s. He'd also been a known womanizer. In 1929 a seventeen-year-old dancer came screaming out of his office, her dress torn, claiming she'd been raped. Pantages was defended by the man who became the most famous lawyer of his day, Jerry Giesler.

Pantages was convicted, but Giesler got it reversed on appeal. He was acquitted the second time. The supposed victim, Eunice Pringle, admitted on her death bed that it had all been a set up by a man who'd wanted to bring Pantages down and take control of his chain.

The name of the man was Joseph P. Kennedy.

So when I walk these streets at night I am never at perfect ease, even though I am already dead. It's just the collective fog of uncertainty that seems to hover over everything. And now more than ever because Lucifer is somewhere near, doing his thing.

I was a block away from Angels Flight now, on Broadway, which is not well lit. I thought I heard the sound of a Crown Vic coming my way.

If so, it might contain a detective named Strobert . . .

But it was not.

It was something in the dark, following me. I caught it darting into a building's doorway as I looked quickly behind me.

Okay, if it was a man I could let him come. I had Emily at the ready. An alcoholic can choose not to buy a bottle, but what if the bottle follows him home and clonks him over the head? Then I say he has every right to drink it. And if a brain comes at me with ill intent, then I'm justified in ingesting it. Such is the natural law according to Mallory Caine.

But there was also the chance it was a creature of the night, and my instinct told me it was probably a werewolf.

Could it be Steve Ravener? Was he following me for some strange reason of his own?

Or was it one of those wolves from the Sajak pack? One of those who'd shouted "Meat!"

If so, I didn't want any part of it. Because while he couldn't kill me, he could do some major-league ripping, and I am kind of particular about my looks. I prefer to have both arms and legs attached, thank you very much.

But I was ill equipped to fight a werewolf without some weapon or protection.

I couldn't run. A wolf would jump me in no time.

Why hadn't he?

How I wish I had Max with me now. Max, my guide, who had protected me at my birth and given me invaluable advice at crucial times in my recent existence. As annoying as his voice had been, he'd been a friend indeed.

I was only two blocks from my loft. Just two. If I could make it there . . .

Taking a step backward, I watched for movement. All I saw was the drift of some cross traffic on Third Street.

For a long moment nothing moved.

And then he came at me.

He was on two legs, pants but no shirt, his hairy body and face only slightly less dark than the encroaching night.

I had exactly one second to move.

Street fighting instinct took over.

What I did was duck the moment he leapt, then shoot my shoulder up. *Bam.* The howling thing went tail over muzzle, took one roll, and hit a wall.

In a normal street setting you'd take off running once the opponent was down. You don't stick around like some Charlie's Angel thinking you can kick butt. You get the hell out of there.

But he was up as quick as a cat, snarling.

"Enjoy this," he said.

I reached in my purse for Emily.

And I counted it a small victory that the wolf did not immediately spring again. He was thinking now, wary of me.

"That's right, wolf," I said. "You better be scared."

"Not scared!"

He came at me again, leaping from a distance of about ten feet. I anticipated this, dropped to one knee, and thrust out with Emily.

The point got him on the inside of the right thigh.

It was a nice score, but it came with a cost. He bit a chunk out of my left arm.

That made me mad. But not as mad as he was, the crybaby. He started howling like his paw was caught in a bear trap.

Jeez, what was it with werewolves?

Emily, dear Emily. I rolled in my pain and jabbed the wolfs other leg. He screamed twice as loud as before.

My arm did not bleed, as that's something I thankfully don't do, but it was going to leave an ugly scar. I have knife wounds and bullet holes in me. I was like a barroom dartboard in some places.

Anyway, I started running, hoping that my two nicely placed pokes would take away some of his own running ability.

No such luck.

I heard him snarl and chuff and come at me again.

I might've been killed, if it weren't for the woman with the killer Chihuahua.

THERE IS SOME DISPUTE ABOUT WHERE THE CHIHUAHUA CAME from. Was it Mexico? Or Europe?

Some say the dog originated on the Island of Malta. But have you ever heard of The Maltese Chihuahua? Sam Spade would not have bothered.

Most likely the Chihuahua emerged from Aztec culture, bred to be part of ritualistic sacrifices. Where the ancient Jews used lambs and doves, the Aztecs used little Chihuahuas as expiation for sins and sometimes for going along with the dead as spirit guides.

I think this one on the L.A. street had been bred from the souls of ancient warriors, because this little guy took on wolfie with an abandon that Genghis Khan would have cheered. With little barks and growls it jumped from the woman's arms to wolfie's neck and bit down. Wolfie howled and spun around and slapped at the giant rodent.

The woman, who had hot pink hair and was corpulent and dressed in clothes that were much too tight for her girth, screamed, "Carlos! Carlos! "

I would've stood there and cheered, or run away, but something about the little dog inspired me. So I went up to the distracted werewolf and kicked him right in his lupine jewels. As he doubled over, I whipped Carlos off his neck and tossed the little sausage to the woman. "Get him out of here, now!"

The woman held the killer Chihuahua at arm's length and ran off into the night.

A Hyundai was cruising to the corner. It wasn't much to look at, but it had rolled-up windows and gave me an idea.

I only hoped the passenger door was unlocked. It was. I jumped in and closed the door. The car smelled of egg salad.

Behind the wheel was an older man with old-fashioned, owl-shaped glasses and a bow tie.

"What are you doing, young lady?" he said.

"Shh," I said. "Drive."

"I am not going to drive. What do you want? I'm not interested in buying sexual favors."

"Do I look like a hooker to you?"

"I don't know what a hooker is supposed to look like, and I—"

At that moment a giant, growling wolf face slammed into the man's front windshield. It snarled and drooled and clawed at the window.

The man screamed. It was a low, rather tepid scream, but it did the job under the circumstances. It got his heart thumping, I'm sure.

"Hit the gas!" I said.

The bow de man did as he was told, and the Hyundai lurched forward. The werewolf rolled off the hood.

"God help me!" the man said.

"Sorry, Jack, I'm the closest you've got. Just don't crash." I looked behind and saw the wolf running after us. "He's coming."

"Ahhh!"

"Look out for the truck!"

The bow tie man swerved and almost nicked a truck going across Broadway. We were now getting into some light traffic. I wondered if the wolf had enough cheek to keep pursuing us. That was a silly question. Werewolves don't do much thinking when they're in this state, smelling blood, hunting prey. But when I looked back again I didn't see him.

"If you keep driving," I said, "you'll be fine. Just don't hit any red lights."

"What was that?"

"Oh, you know people in L.A. Probably on drugs."

"No, he had a hairy face. He looked like a monster."

"I don't believe in monsters," I said.

The lights stayed green and we went about four blocks before coming to a stop. The bow de man was breathing hard.

"Easy," I said. "We're out of harm's way now, I think."

"Who, may I ask, are you?"

"Thanks for the ride. Drop me off."

"Let me at least buy you a drink."

"You're a sweet guy, but I'm not interested."

"Suppose I make you interested." He said it in such a way as to pretend menace.

"Suppose I eat your eyes?"

He slammed on the brakes. "Get out!"

"You don't know how lucky you are," I said. And got out.

BACK HOME, BACK TO MY LOFT, BACK TO MY SAFE HAVEN. I WENT into the bathroom and checked out my arm. The werewolf had taken a bite out of my triceps area. The underside of my arm looked like the Apple logo.

I dressed it as best I could.

I was just about to settle in for a look at what was on TCM. They were having a Marx Brothers marathon. *Duck Soup, Horse Feathers, Monkey Business, A Night at the Opera.* Nice. I could settle in with Groucho and Chico and Harpo. I wouldn't even mind a little Zeppo. I just wanted to laugh and they were the perfect vehicle for it.

But then the air became eerily still. I have a calm-before-the-storm sense, and was definitely feeling it now.

Through my open window came the werewolf.

All I could grab was a softball bat. When I was with the PD's office I'd played on the office softball team, but hadn't picked up a bat since my re-upping. It was always in the corner, though, as a hopeful sign I might be able to play again someday.

Now it was for my survival as a normal-looking zombie. I did not want to be one of those helpless heads, like Mickey Cohen.

How had he managed to climb the building and burst in like this?

"Zombie!" he growled.

"We've established that," I said. "And unless you want me to hit your head for a triple, you'll get out."

"Zombie!"

"Yes! Good one! Who sent you?"

"Dead," he said. He started to circle around my sofa, looking for an opening.

"I hit .627 at the PD's office," I said. "This is going to sound great on your melon."

He kept coming, slowly, as I moved at the same pace, keeping the sofa between us. I knew he could spring over it at any moment. I held the bat in hitting position. I just kept thinking of his head as a slow-pitch softball.

He made his move, and I hit a solid double with his head. Then whacked him in the ribs. He doubled over. I dropped the bat and pushed his shoulders and he fell backward out of my window.

It was fifteen floors to the street.

Thinking clearly, I closed my window and pulled the blind.

I went through the garage and emerged on Main Street, then walked around the block as if I were returning home. A small crowd was gathered there now. Police had cordoned off the scene.

"What happened?" I asked a patrolman keeping watch on the crowd.

"Please move along," he said.

"But I live here. This is my building."

"Oh, then please wait. The detective would like to speak to the residents."

"Which detective is it?"

"His name is Mark Strobert."

CHAPTER TWENTY-ONE

I FOUND him over by the splat scene. He looked up and saw me, but didn't seem all that surprised. I was always fouling up his work, it seemed.

He came over and nodded. "You want to tell me what's going on?"

"How about *you* tell *me* what's going on?"

"Take it easy. I'm the police officer here."

"And I'm a defense lawyer. I guess that means we're natural enemies."

For a moment the cop look dropped from his face. It melted off him like frost from a windshield when the sun hits it. There was a starting to speak, a stopping, then he said, "It doesn't have to be that way." Oh, how I wished that were true. In some miraculous way, right now on these mean streets, a transformation, a saving, a newness of life, and a cop and a lawyer able to drop everything else but just *being*.

"I think it has to be that way," I said. "You're doing your job, you have to, even if it includes accusing me of knowing what happened here."

"I haven't accused you of anything."

"Yet," I said.

"Now look—"

"No, you look. I want to know why there's a dead thing outside my building."

"That's interesting."

"What is?"

"You used the word *thing,*" Strobert said.

Whoops.

"You're not being upfront with me, Mallory. I mean, Ms. Caine, criminal defense lawyer. We detectives don't like it when people are not upfront with us."

"All right, Detective Strobert. You look like you can use a break. I'm going to give it to you. Be ready."

He waited, probing me with his eyes. Or killing me softly. "I've had werewolves sniffing around my place," I said. "I even had one chase me tonight. I have a feeling whatever corpse this is, it's very furry."

"Keep going," Strobert said.

"There's nothing else to say. Is that a wolf lying in the street?"

A voice shouted, "Detective, get over here. Quick."

Strobert hesitated, gave me a look that said *stay,* then followed the voice. I followed Strobert. A uniformed police officer tried to stop me at the perimeter. I told him I was a lawyer working with Strobert, which was technically true if you stretch the meaning of *working with.* And as a graduate of a prestigious law school, I can do that. My confident tone seemed to confuse the officer, and in the hesitation I pushed past as if I owned the street. Maybe someday I would.

I edged close enough to be able to hear Strobert talking to the uniform who had called him over. He was a wide-eyed young man, and certainly looked scared.

"He had hair all over his face," the young cop said.

"And then it started disappearing. It's gone. I swear he had hair all over him."

"Take it easy," Strobert said.

"It's gone now, how did it get gone? It just disappeared right off his face."

"Have you got an ID on him?"

"Here." The cop handed Strobert a wallet.

I took another step so I could look over Strobert's shoulder. I recognized the driver's license photo. I said, "Dwayne Dewey."

Strobert spun around. "Mallory... Ms. Caine, please step behind the tape."

"It may interest you to know I spoke with Dwayne Dewey recently. What do you suppose he was doing appearing as a werewolf?"

Strobert straightened and faced me. "What do you know about him?"

"What do *you* know?" I said.

"I'm getting tired of you answering my questions with other questions. Maybe I should take you down to the station and question you. You're a material witness, if not a suspect."

"Don't use the word *suspect* in my presence unless you are prepared to back it up."

He backed it up. He called over an officer and told him to take me in.

Twenty minutes later my zombie rear end was in the lockup at Central Division.

CHAPTER TWENTY-TWO

AROUND MIDNIGHT I HAD A VISITOR. "Well, if it isn't the son of Satan himself, Aaron of Hell."

"I wouldn't mock me, Mallory," Aaron said. "It stores up wrath."

"Really? Where? You have a wrath warehouse somewhere? Do you offer sofas and sectionals, too?"

He was standing right outside my cell, just like a lawyer would visit with a client. The place smelled of disinfectant. Aaron smelled of sulfur. Or maybe it was just me imagining he did. He looked crisp and cool, as if he was just about to appear in court.

"What brings you down to the jail at this hour?" I said. "And how did you happen to know I'd be here?"

He smiled in that confident way he had. When I was alive those pearlies could wrap me up and melt me like cheese in a burrito. Now it just ticked me off.

"I want you to use your head," Aaron said.

"I have no idea what you're talking about, which isn't surprising."

"I'm talking about you leaving Los Angeles. There's no reason for you to stay."

I curled my lip, trying to look like Bette Davis in *All About Eve*. "What's your connection to Dwayne Dewey?"

Aaron didn't reflect anything in his face. "Who?"

"Come on, Aaron. I was attacked by Dwayne Dewey tonight. He was in wolf form, too. A real sweetheart."

"I understand you had something to do with a death, yes."

"Oh come off it," I said. "Dewey worked for Garza, and you're tight with the mayor. You and your so-called father are trying to take over this town. It's not a secret."

Aaron didn't answer right away. Instead he looked like he was considering a flat out denial again. But then he said, "Why shouldn't we?"

"There's a little matter of God opposing you, isn't there? I mean, if there's a devil there's a God."

"You're so naive, Mallory," Aaron said. "So much you don't know."

"Why don't you enlighten me, Aaron? I'm just so fascinated."

Aaron brushed the sleeve of his coat and straightened his bright red tie. "You want to be sarcastic, go ahead. Won't change anything. You've always thought you could do that"

"Do what?"

"Make a difference in the world. Isn't that what you thought? Pitiful." He let his eyeballs scan my cell, then brought them back to me. "You're one little zombie in a sea of gods and ghosts. You don't matter at all."

"Then why are you here, bothering with me?"

"For the last time, are you going to leave Los Angeles?"

I said, "I can't. I have tickets to the Hollywood Bowl."

He clenched his teeth, bared them at me. "Then you can rot for all I care."

"Oh, you care, Aaron?"

He put his hands on the cell bars. "Damn you, I do! But it's gone too far now for either of us. We could have had so much. You could have had it all."

I shook my head. "All isn't worth it if the price is too high."

"You'll see," he said. "It's coming."

"What is?"

He didn't answer.

He left.

Detective Mark Strobert came in about a half hour after Aaron left.

"You doing okay?" he said.

"You're asking me if I'm okay being locked up here?"

"Yeah," he said, not giving an inch in voice or look.

"At least give me a harmonica," I said, "so I can play 'Swing Low, Sweet Chariot.' "

"Is that the way it's going to be? You know I can hold you twenty-four hours."

"Why do you want to do that, Detective?"

"I want you to talk about what you know about the killing of Dwayne Dewey tonight. You let me know when you're ready."

He started to leave.

"Wait," I said. I grabbed the bars. My head was going light on me. "You got some coffee?"

IN AN INTERVIEW ROOM, STROBERT GAVE ME A COFFEE. EVEN zombies can drink coffee, and the coffee bean produces its effects in our undead tissue. But I needed some real nourishment, and soon. If I didn't get some cow brain in me I knew I wouldn't be able to be responsible for my actions. I was a ticking reanimated flesh bomb.

"You don't look good," Strobert said.

"That's what makes you such a great detective," I said. "The power of observation."

"I mean it. I can take you to an emergency room."

I almost snorted coffee out my nose. Maybe that would have been the best thing. Distract him, maybe get him to cut me loose. But something came over me. If I hadn't been a zombie I might have called it the milk of human kindness. But I have no idea what sort of liquid, kind or unkind, dwells in my brittle skin.

"All right," I said. "I'm going to give it to you between the eyes. I shouldn't do this. I don't like talking to cops, and I don't like my clients to, either. In my experience you don't cut many breaks. So here it is. Off the record, okay?"

He paused, then nodded.

"I am what you've heard. I'm a zombie. I'm not going to go into how I got this way, but I will tell you that I am not an eater of human flesh. I am in recovery. I am a law abiding citizen. And I am also the subject of a lot of attention from City Hall, Aaron Argula and now Dwayne Dewey. Dewey was a werewolf and he came after me tonight. That's what you should be looking at, Detective. He chased me down the street and I got to my loft. But he actually scaled the building and came in through my window. I hit him with a softball bat then pushed him out. It was a clear case of self-defense. And that's the honest truth."

Mark Strobert rubbed his hands together like he was making snakes out of clay. He took a few deep breaths.

"Look," I said, "I'll be happy to talk to you about tonight, give you a statement, anytime you want. But I have to go get something to eat."

He lowered his hands. "Like what?"

"Don't worry," I said. "I'm off the hard stuff."

"Can you assure me of that?" he said.

"That's what I'm telling you."

"Because if I ever find out you have, you know, killed ... I'll have to come after you. I'll have to . .."

I said, "I know. And I understand. And I wish it could have been different between us." And I so did wish it at that point. I wanted him to take me in his arms and tell me it was wrong, all wrong, for a cop to love a lawyer, but he was going to do it anyway, and we were going to run away together, far away from here, from this town, and everything that's going on.

But it could never, ever be that way.

He let me go. I walked out of Central and back to my loft. Funny thing was, weak as I was feeling, I didn't even want to eat anybody. For those few minutes, I just felt sick.

When I got home I took out some calf brain from my freezer. It was about as appetizing as chair cushion.

CHAPTER TWENTY-THREE

THE NEXT MORNING I showed up in the family law court of Judge Martita Tarot-Danelaw. Not having much to do with family law I did not know her well. Her profile on one of the websites rated her as tough, smart, and fair. I can deal with almost any judge as long as *fair* is one of the criteria.

Steve sat nervously beside me at the counsel table. For all his wolfishness, he was today just a man who wanted to see his children. And when his ex-wife walked in, I could feel him tense beside me.

I tensed a little at the sight of her lawyer, Charles Beaumont Manyon.

He was looking as he always did, sort of a portly country lawyer type. Walrus moustache and down-home way of talking. But I knew he was a vampire and plugged in with the powers of Los Angeles. I figured that was why he was representing Pat Ravener. It had something to do with Dwayne Dewey. The dead Dwayne Dewey.

Two lawyers who square off can fake congeniality. Manyon was good at it as we met between the two counsel tables.

"You're looking well," he said.

"I'm feeling good," I said. "Ready to make my case."

"You haven't got a case. You've got a werewolf."

"Who wants to see his kids."

Manyon shrugged.

"What about your werewolf?" I said.

"I don't think I know what you mean?"

"Dwayne Dewey."

Manyon shook his head.

"You're pretending you don't know?" I said.

"All I'm interested in is Mrs. Ravener and keeping her kids away from a dangerous man."

"Did you unleash Dewey on me?" I said. "I figure he was taking orders from somebody like you."

With an innocent smile, Charles Beaumont Manyon said, "Let's not get carried away today, shall we? It's always messy when you do."

THE JUDGE CAME IN AND CALLED THE CASE. MARTITA TAROT-Danelaw was tall and thin, a perfect Olive Oyl for an off-Broadway production of *Popeye*. Come to think of it, Manyon would have made a good Bluto. That left me to be the hero. But without spinach.

"I have spent the last several days reading up on lycanthropy," the judge said. "I know we are in a new era around here, and there are some people who say just kill all the wolves. Or the lawyers." She chuckled, but no one else in the courtroom did. She cleared her throat. "In any event, I find nothing in California's non-discrimination statutes that says we should treat a werewolf any differently than any other minority. With that in mind, I will hear from Mr. Manyon first."

Charles Beaumont Manyon stood up at his counsel table and said, "Your honor, this is a very simple case. My client and the petitioner, Mr. Ravener, have two children. It was unknown to Mrs. Ravener that the petitioner is a werewolf. He kept that information from her. And as your honor knows, having studied the subject, this condition may come upon him at odd times, as with the full moon, with the ingestion of potions, or randomly. I don't pretend to know how these things work—"

Oh, brother. Could he lard it on. He knew exactly what it was all about. I tried to keep a poker face.

"—but one thing is clear, your honor. The children are subject to danger when they are around the petitioner."

Judge Tarot-Danelaw said, "Is there a visitation order in place?"

"Yes, Mrs. Ravener has primary physical custody. But when she became aware of the petitioner's condition, she kept the children from seeing him out of concern for their safety."

"How long has it been since Mr. Ravener has seen his kids?"

"I believe it is six weeks now," Manyon said.

"All right," the judge said. "Ms. Caine?"

I stood. "Good morning, your honor. We are here because the respondent, Mrs. Ravener, is in violation of a court order regarding visitation. The proper procedure would be for her to seek a modification of the order, not violate it. The only issue before this court is whether she has contravened a previous court's order, and Mr. Manyon has just conceded as much. We ask this court to issue an order compelling the respondent to make the children available for visitation under the terms of the previous order."

"Is your client a werewolf?" the judge asked.

"Yes, but there is no law or case precedent which states that a werewolf is a danger to his own children. In fact, wolves are very loyal to their children, as can be observed in the wild."

"But we are not in the wild," Manyon said. "We are governed by the law which says that the best interest of the child is always the standard. And when there is an unknown danger, it is within the right of the custodial parent to do what is in their judgment the safe and expedient thing."

"Ms. Caine?"

"Well, your honor, it is somewhat surprising to hear my learned opponent make that claim. In fact, it is well settled that an appeal must first be made in a court of law, because only then are we to be saved from false expressions of danger."

"They are not false!" Pat Ravener said.

"Please do not speak," the judge said. "Mr. Manyon, instruct your client to remain quiet."

Manyon leaned over and whispered something to Pat Ravener.

I took the opportunity to continue, pulling out a sheet of paper from my briefcase. "In fact, if I may quote a scholar on this subject, *The law is the great civilizing machinery. It liberates the desire to build and subdues the desire to destroy.*"

"Who are you quoting?" the judge asked.

This is a copy of an article from the Harvard Law Review, January of 1987. The author is one Charles Beaumont Manyon."

Judge Tarot-Danelaw smiled. I laughed, inside of course. Research is a beautiful thing.

Manyon said, "I hardly think that counts as precedent, your honor."

"Maybe not, but it impresses *me*. I am going to order your client, Mr. Manyon, to make the children available to Mr. Ravener under the terms of the previous order. Should you wish to change that, you may petition a court. But until such time, the children will be made available. Any questions?"

Manyon looked stunned. I *felt* stunned. As nice a move as I had made, I did not expect the court to go that way. Lately all the judges seem to be in the pocket of the mayor.

"There will be an emergency appeal," Manyon said.

"Better make sure you're not quoted there," the judge said.

Nice.

Beaumont and his client packed up with a huff and walked out without saying another word to me.

Steve shook my hand and said, "That was something. I didn't think it could happen. I say we celebrate. And I know just how to do it."

CHAPTER TWENTY-FOUR

STEVE'S WAY was for me to show up at The Freudian Sip, a coffee house and jazz club in NoHo. The crowd was all twenty-somethings, with a few older artist types with that this-is-the-place-to-be look.

And I felt like a high school girl meeting up with the football captain, trying to look good but not give too much away.

What was going on? This was not the Mallory who was in total control. I chalked it up to stress.

I got a stool at the bar and ordered a Libido Latte. A nice young man in a UCLA hoodie served me. I wondered what his major was, and what his brain might taste like. I immediately mumbled my mantra, *"No human, no human, no human."*

"Excuse me?" UCLA said.

"Oh, sorry, I was just saying *No Bruin.* I'm a USC girl."

"I'm sorry to hear that," he said with a smile. He served me the coffee as I waited for Steve, who'd said he would meet me here.

Before my first sip a voice whispered in my ear, "Thanks for coming."

Steve was dressed in blue jeans and a black T-shirt that accentuated his well-builtness. I kept cool. "This is an interesting place for a celebration," I said.

"I'm here to serenade you."

"Maybe you'd better switch to decaf."

"I'm on next."

"You sing here?"

"I'm glad you came."

His blue eyes were starting to look like a liquid embrace. "Steve, I'm glad to be here to listen to you sing. But let's just leave it at that. You need to get your life squared away with your kids and your condition."

"Suppose I can't wait that long."

"Wait for what?" I said.

"You," he said.

I closed my eyes as if to regroup and come out with just the right words. But I didn't have them. I didn't know what to say. There were about seventy-five different responses swirling around in my mind, duking it out. When I opened my eyes, he was gone.

A jazz quartet was just finishing their set. A smattering of applause from the crowd and then an emcee, a guy of about sixty, came out and said, "Ladies and gents, hope you're enjoying yourselves here at The Freudian Sip. My name's Tom, I own the joint. Our motto is, *What you let slip here, stays here.* And now it's my pleasure to introduce to you a singer of balance. Reminds me of the old days, of the Kingston Trio and Liam Clancy. Did you know that Liam Clancy was a great influence on Bob Dylan? And so tonight we have a guy who sings like no other that I've heard in contemporary times. Please put your hands together for Mr. Steve Ravener."

Applause, and I sat back and held a warm cup of coffee in my hands. Steve came to the little stage and sat on the stool, holding an acoustic guitar.

Bathed in soft light, I would have been hard-pressed to think of him as a wolf. He looked like a poet or a saint. And when he started to play, the sweetest music I'd ever heard came from that guitar.

And then he sang.

Oh where have you gone, Larry boy, Larry boy,
Oh where have you gone, Larry Talbot?
They took away your soul, they made your head roll
And they danced on your grave, gentle Larry.

Larry Talbot? He was singing about *The Wolf Man*. And in a voice so pure it filled my heart to overflowing.

It was ages gone by, when the children did cry,
And Larry came walking and singing his song.
But the people in fear, felt the stranger draw near
And with silver they killed gentle Larry.
Now the moon comes up white in the still of the night
And the howling is heard from the mountain
But the soul has gone home, not longer to roam,
For they took it away from dear Larry.
With a yow deedle dow, and a yay deedle day
Sleep sweetly, my dear brother Larry.

I wouldn't have believed a song about lycanthropy could sound like a holy hymn. The place erupted in applause. Steve stood up and shyly nodded his head. Then left the stage, with the crowd shouting for more.

"Why didn't you do another song?" I asked after he'd joined me at the bar.

He said, "That song takes a lot out of me. And I sang it tonight like I've never sung before."

I cleared my throat and said, "What made tonight different?"

"You have to ask?"

Oh, man. No way. Too much. Stop now.

Don't stop.

Stop.

"Steve, I just can't."

He looked like he might try to kiss me, and if he had I don't know what I'd have done. Maybe offered to run away with him and his kids and become fugitives or something.

Irrational, totally.

But then he backed away. "You're right," he said. "I'm sorry."

"Don't be," I said.

"I mean, I'm sorry we don't seem to have a chance." I said nothing.

"But on the good side," he said, "I feel like writing a ballad about lost love."

I took a sip of coffee and almost bit off some of the cup.

CHAPTER TWENTY-FIVE

IT WAS ABOUT ten o'clock at night when I got back to my office. It was darkness all around, but I didn't feel like sleeping. I was too hyped up on caffeine and thoughts of a werewolf. I wanted to lose myself in some legal research.

Which is what I did, burning the midnight oil as it were.

I heard footsteps out in the hallway. I thought at first it might be the janitor, who comes in about once a month.

The steps were too heavy to belong to Nick. Which meant I had an unwelcome caller.

My mind immediately thought, *Take-out meal.* The caffeine had made me hungry, and there was some sort of human being right outside my door.

So I waited.

There was a knock on the door.

I said, "Come in."

If I'd had to choose one man I did not expect, or want, to see, it would have been the man who walked in.

"Working late?" Sheriff Geronimo Novakovich said as he gently closed the door.

I got to my feet, keeping the desk between us. "What are you doing here?"

"The city never sleeps," he said. "And neither do I. I saw a light in the window. I've been waiting for you."

"Not tonight, Sheriff. I'm kind of working here, you know?"

"I don't care about that" He took a couple of steps toward my desk. "I care that you don't listen to me."

"I'm sorry, I missed that."

He didn't laugh.

"I'm going to have to ask you to leave," I said.

"I am not inclined to go anywhere, Ms. Caine. I am inclined to run you in."

"Run me in?"

"Arrest."

"Oh please, on what charge?"

He smiled. "I'll trump something up." He removed his gun.

"Now, Sheriff," I said, trying to keep my voice from trembling. "You're going to shoot me?"

"If I have to."

"That'll look real good. You walk into a lawyer's office and shoot her?"

"You said *lawyer*. That'll have public sympathy on my side."

I don't like getting shot. It puts holes in my clothes. But I wasn't going to go anywhere with the sheriff.

"Now come along," he said.

"I guess you're just going to have to shoot," I said.

"I will, you know."

"I won't die. I may have a few holes, and I'll be really upset about that."

"My clip holds ten rounds," he said.

Ack. Ten holes.

"You want something from me," I said.

"All you have to do is come along. I won't arrest you. But I will drive you over the county line and drop you off."

"This is getting really melodramatic. Where is Randolph Scott?"

"I'm not acting, Ms. Caine."

I paused. "Put away the gun and I'll go with you," I said.

"I'm not inclined to do that."

"Oh, come on, Sheriff. Treat this moment with a little dignity, will you? Let me get my purse."

"Ah-ah," he said.

"What, you don't trust me?"

"You're a lawyer," he said. "So the answer is no."

I shook my head. "You're not going to shoot me." I reached for my purse.

He shot me.

Right in the middle of my chest.

The bullet passed through me and into the wall. "You creep! This was my last good blouse!"

"Don't touch anything, Ms. Caine. Come along."

I looked into those Native American-Russian eyes. There was something dead in them, like me. Something that said he had sold his soul at a certain point in his life, to bring him to this. My soul had been taken from me. That's one thing. But to give yours away, whether to the devil or some other supernatural entity, that was quite another.

And from within me came a hunger of such massive proportions I can only ascribe it to my revulsion. Like when an ancient Aztec warrior would eat the heart of his enemy. I wanted so much to eat this aberration of humanity I almost salivated on the floor.

But he was the one with the gun, and that gun could ruin suits and skin.

"All right," I said. "You've won this round. But there will be more."

"I don't think so, Ms. Caine. I think you'll see things my way." He wagged the gun toward the door.

My undead heart was thumping my chest like a Cuban tap dancer. I felt my breath starting to tighten. As I took a step toward the door I bent my right knee a little extra, then thrust upward with all the strength I could muster. With my left hand I hit his gun arm, outwardly, and I drove the palm of my hand under his chin. This is a much more effective move than a fist, innumerable movie and TV fights notwithstanding. You break your hand using fist on face, but the palm well placed is highly charged.

Geronimo Novakovich's head snapped backward. I grabbed the gun and twisted it against his thumb and out of his hand. A Mossad agent couldn't have done it any better.

Now I had a gun and a stunned sheriff in my office. And only seconds to get the job done.

A nine-millimeter handgun really hurts when it hits you in the head. So I hit Novakovich in the head with it.

Down he went.

To my purse I went.

I withdrew Emily. I went down to one knee and drove my weapon of choice through his nasal cavity and into his brain.

Sheriff Geronimo Novakovich stopped moving. Forever.

I went absolutely crazy.

I tore into the flesh of the sheriff with an abandon that both frightened me and compelled me. The more repulsion I felt the more excited I became. Never before had I felt this way when eating human flesh. I'd always managed to keep my mind about me, analyze what I was doing, control the situation.

But now this man who had pushed me to the edge and plied me with another bullet hole fed both my appetite and my hatred. I was going to take out on him all the rage I had stored within me for all the sharpies and demons and hucksters and crooked politicians and fake lawyers and mothers who give themselves to fads because their brains are addled from too much pot and whatever hallucinogens have been ingested over the course of many years. I took it out on whoever set this crappy system up, that allowed zombies to walk around without souls through no fault of their own.

And I was hungry, just plain hungry for real food. And so I carved up Sheriff Geronimo Novakovich right there in my office.

Oh, there was blood everywhere. That was going to be a big

problem. But not as big as having to explain how the sheriff of Los Angeles County ended up a butchered remnant in my law office.

But I was unconcerned with that right now. All I wanted to do was eat his brain, eat raw flesh, eat his arm like corn on the cob. Eat his eyes like bonbons.

I was so out of it I scared myself. I thought I was in a place I would never return from.

I thought then that this must be what it's like to be a wolf, just living on raw instinct. That and the flesh of any prey you claw to death.

It took me half an hour to eat my way through a good portion of the sheriff. And when I finished I felt not satisfied or sated, but sickened. Was this the real me? Was this my inner Mallory Caine finally asserting herself? Should I just chuck this whole jive about being a lawyer and start wandering the streets eating whatever I could? Forget Father Clemente, forget trying to cure myself, just go with the flow?

I was panting and bloody and intoxicated with flesh.

I stood up and looked at the carcass. The room began to spin.

The lights dimmed and I wondered if LoGo had paid the electric bill. Then I realized it wasn't the lights going out, but me.

And that's all I remember.

CHAPTER TWENTY-SIX

I WOKE up in a vat of pea soup. My head was scrambled and my sight fuzzy.

What the heck? It was like coming out of a dream where you don't quite wake up, when you don't know for a second if you're in or out of reality.

Maybe it was death. That was one thought. Yeah, death. Where was the white light? Maybe I missed it. Maybe I was going to the other place. The place where there is no light

But there was light, here. I heard myself breathing. I wasn't dead yet, really dead, permanent dead.

I managed to open my mouth and say, "Where am I?" A form of some sort swam through the pea soup, looming at me. I tried to reach up and grab it, but my arms just lay there like sea lions on a hot rock.

The form swam away, but I heard voices muttering in some other part of the soup. Blinking my eyes like castanets I was able to clear my vision a bit. I was flat on my back in some kind of dimly lit space. It wasn't a bed I was on, that's for sure. It felt more like a slab.

Slab?

I tried to get up, but my body parts weren't connecting

through my central nervous system yet. Blacking out, I sort of remembered that. And the sheriff. In my office. Yes. Stuffing my face.

How had I gotten from my office to wherever I was now?

More muffled voices.

With the strength of a wounded jaybird I rolled left to look in the direction of the voices. I thought I saw a plain white door in the middle of a plain white wall. Could have been a mental ward in an old Roger Corman movie.

Okay, Mallory, think.

It's not law enforcement who put you here. You would be in jail right now if it was a cop who'd found you in your office with a sheriff carcass.

Maybe it was Nick. Could Nick have found me and called a couple of moving men to take me away?

But who could he call to do that without drawing attention? Nick did have some nefarious connections, though.

What if it was someone who wanted me dead? Well, why wasn't I then?

"Wake up, sweetheart."

Okay, now I recognized him. It was one of Mickey Cohen's boys. "What the—"

"Mickey wants to talk to you."

It must have been Mickey's digs I was in.

Why?

I heard the sound of creaky wheels. Another of Mickey's guys was pushing in a rolling stand of some kind, on top of which was Mickey Cohen's head.

"You been in quite a scrape," he said.

"How'd I get here?" My brain was banging around in my skull, like a soccer ball being kicked around a padded room by an insane man who thought his name was Beckham.

"Shorty here went by to check your office." The thug who had addressed me first nodded. "I ordered him to do that."

"But why?"

"I heard they got it in for you. I been kind of keeping an eye out. This Dewey guy, he was the one. He told a guy who told a guy who I know."

"Who told who what now?"

"Dewey worked for Garza. He was kind of a hatchet man, taking care of business."

"I know that," I said.

"Did you know that one of the items he was supposed to take care of was you? He was supposed to set you up to be arrested for murder."

"Yeah, but he croaked," I said.

"Somebody else made it happen," Mickey said.

"Made what happen?"

"Double murder."

My head squeezed. "What do you mean, double?"

"The two bodies in your office. A real mess."

As hard as it was, I sat up. "Two? Now wait a second. There was only one. The sheriff, Geronimo Novakovich. He came in and was going to arrest me. I guess I kind of ate him."

"Kind of! I wouldn't want to be on the other end of your appetite."

"But there wasn't anybody else there."

Shorty said, "There was when I came in. Two uniforms were on the floor. And you lyin' right between 'em."

I tried to picture in my mind what might've happened. No, there was no way there'd been another person in my office. The door had been closed.

"I passed out," I said.

"Any idea who this other one was?" Mickey said.

"I said passed out!"

"Okay, okay. No need to take it out on me. I'm the guy who got you out of there. We got to figure out how to keep you under wraps. The heat's gonna be on."

"This is absurd."

"No, murder."

"It wasn't murder!"

"You don't got to convince me," Mickey said. "Even if it was, gettin' rid of a couple of laws is no skin off my nose."

"I've got to think. The bodies. Can we get them out of there?"

Shorty gave a sad look toward Mickey, then back at me. "The cops are already there," he said.

I swung my legs over the side of the slab and stood. Woozily.

"Easy there, sister," Shorty said, catching my arm.

"We got a place you can hide out for a while," Mickey said.

"No," I said. "I'm not going to run. That's what they want me to do."

"I wish I could shake my head," Mickey said. "Because I'd be shakin' it now."

I looked down at myself. I was in some plain-looking dress, the thrift store variety. "Hey!"

'We got rid of your bloody clothes," Mickey said.

"You undressed me?"

"Nothin' we ain't seen before," Shorty said.

I tried to wish myself into a cornfield, but it didn't happen.

CHAPTER TWENTY-SEVEN

I DON'T KNOW how many miles I walked. It just seemed I was drifting farther into the night, and farther away from downtown. I knew I was roughly in South Los Angeles. The signs, the liquor stores, the gas stations, the buildings on Normandy, the boarded-up facades.

The moon was up and the air had a cold snap to it. I wasn't even thinking about flesh then, about eating. It was more like I was stunned, trying to take in all of what had happened and figure it out from there.

At some point I heard singing. It was upbeat and enthusiastic, some group engaged in collective and joyful noise making. As I walked on I began to realize it was gospel music.

Then I knew what it was. A flat-out, gospel-singing, raising-the-roof, honest-to-goodness church. It sounded so good, the music and singing. I had to go in and have a look.

What I saw from the back of the church was a choir clothed in red robes and rocking the house. This was not your primly-hold-the-hymnal-in-front-of-your-face kind of choir. This was singing-from-the-heels-to-the-head-and-springing-it-out-your-arms type of singing.

The congregation was into it. No one was sitting down in the pews. Everybody was up and clapping hands and shouting and raising arms to the sky. I tell you, there is nothing as powerful as a community in sync, coming together with a happy purpose.

I found myself wishing I had the kind of faith that they did, that would allow me to forget everything and just sing in praise and be happy.

Instead, I was like someone on the outside of an observation room, looking in and admiring but not experiencing. For a long time I just stood there, listening.

A man touched my arm and said, "Welcome, sister." He had a nice smile and wore a suit and tie. He looked very dignified. "Would you like to come in and join us?"

"I was just walking down the street and heard the music here."

"This is our midnight revival service. We've been prayin' and singin' for a couple of hours. You're welcome here. This is the Lord's house, not our house. Would you like to have a seat?"

"May I just stand here?"

"Of course you can. We'll be here all night. We're callin' for revival to rain down. And you just let me know if there's anything I can do for you."

"Thank you."

He nodded and walked into the sanctuary, leaving me alone in the foyer.

I looked in at the church through the glass in the doors. It was mesmerizing. I liked being able to just listen, letting the music wash over me.

Just above the doors was a framed photograph of a large man with a warm smile and wearing a pulpit robe. Underneath the photo it said, *Reverend D. Ray Hightower.*

Looking back inside I could see him, the Rev, up on the stage next to the choir, singing right along with them.

The singing went on for another few minutes, and then the preacher went to the center of the stage. He had a Bible in his hands.

"My children, we are facing a darkness like no other time on earth..."

Several voices murmured back at him, with *Well* and *Amen* and *Yes, sir* and the like. This continued throughout.

". . . yes, since the time of the Canaanites and the forty years of wandering in the desert. The devil is loose among us, children, and our battle is not against flesh and blood."

Reverend Hightower moved his significant frame around the stage like a dancer.

"And it came to pass after that the children of Moab, and the children of Ammon came against Jehoshaphat to battle. Then there came some to King Jehoshaphat, saying, 'A great multitude is coming against thee from beyond the sea!' And Jehoshaphat feared, and set himself to seek the Lord. Oh my children, do you fear the coming of these evil days? Then seek the Lord!"

Amens and *Hallelujahs* filled the church, hands waved, and voices added *Oh yes* and *Well said* and *Mm-hm*.

"And Jehoshaphat stood in the congregation and said, 'O Lord, art not thou God in heaven? And rulest over all the kingdoms of the heathen? And in thine *hand is there not* power and might, so that none is able to withstand thee?'"

The crowd gave back their affirmations again. "'Art not thou our God, who did drive out the inhabitants of this land?'"

Someone shouted, "Oh yes he did!"

"And then came the spirit of the Lord to say, 'Be not afraid of this great multitude, for the batde is not yours, but God's!'"

Voices: Amen! Oh yes! Well!

"'Go out against them,' saith the Lord, 'and I will be with you!'"

Oh yes!

"And Jehoshaphat appointed singers unto the Lord, that should praise the beauty of His holiness! And they went out before the army, singing, 'Praise the Lord for his mercy endures forever!' Did you catch that, children? It was the choir that went before the army! It was the choir that praised the Lord and inspired the fighting men, and gave them the victory! It was the singing that gave them the day!"

Hallelujah!

Oh yes!

"So sing out, children, for the devil will not have his way in our house!"

People shot to their feet, raising their hands and shouting *Hallelujah* and every other kind of praise. And the choir began to sing again.

What singing it was.

I looked around at the people, jealous for what they had inside them.

And then I recognized someone.

Cal Dutton had been a client of mine when I was with the public defender's office. I'd later used him as a source to find out what was behind a motorcycle gang's trafficking in underage girls. That I happened to behead eight of them and attempt to eat their brains was merely a side note. I had uncovered a very smarmy ring. Cal had been reluctant to talk about it, probably fearing that he would be killed.

But the last time I saw him was in the Men's County Jail. Now here he was in church. I've known many a convict who has "found Jesus" while incarcerated, thinking it would help them gain release. Every now and then it was something that stuck. I wondered how it would be for Cal.

Cal looked my way and saw me through the glass. He came running out to the foyer to greet me.

"Ms. Caine!"

"Cal."

"What are you doing here?"

"I just sort of wandered in."

"It is so good to see you!"

"Cal, what happened to you?"

"I found the Lord."

"I guess so."

"It was after I got out of jail," he said. "No one there to meet me. I had no place to stay. No place to go. Didn't know where my next meal was even going to come from. You know what? That never happened to me before. I had to stand on a corner and beg for money. I got a couple bucks and came down to Clifton's and got me a piece of pie. That was all I could afford. And as I was eating it a brother came up to me and said, 'You look like you are down on your luck, son.' I didn't know how he could tell, I was just a guy eating some pie. But he looked like he could see right into me. It was Reverend Hightower. And he sat down with me and made sure I had a regular meal. He bought me meatloaf and peas and mashed potatoes with gravy. It was the best-tasting meal I'd had in a long time, a long time since I was at my granny's and had turkey dinner for Thanksgiving."

All of those words spilled out of Cal as if he were making a confession under time pressure. Just looking at his face I knew whatever happened to him was real.

"Cal—"

"I want you to meet him."

"Who?"

"Reverend Hightower."

"Oh, I don't need—"

"Come on!"

He led me back to a small office, where we waited for the service to end.

THE REVEREND CAME IN, MOPPING OFF A LITTLE SWEAT FROM HIS face with a towel. Cal introduced me to him. He shook my hand. "We're going to be doing some praying in just a little while," he said. "And then we will sing again. Won't you join us?"

"That was some singing," I said.

"The Lord inhabits the praises of his people," the preacher said. "And there is just something about gospel singing that the devil can't stand."

"Do you believe in the devil?" I said.

"Well of course I do, child! I see his handiwork every day, and I hate it. To fear the Lord, the Bible says, is to hate evil."

I said nothing.

"What is it, child?" Reverend Hightower said.

"There's a whole lot of it, evil."

"Oh yes," the preacher said. "And we're going to do some blasting. Can I tell you a little secret?"

I nodded.

"There is coming a day, real soon, when this church, and churches like ours all over L.A., we are going to come together and we are going to let out some singin' like this old town has never seen. I don't just mean two or three churches, I mean dozens. I've been a preacher here for twenty-five years, and I've got lots of preacher friends in lots of churches, and we do love our choirs. Like Jehoshaphat did. The good old spirituals, the good old music, they lift the soul. We're gonna lift this city up."

"When are you going to do this?" I asked.

"Don't know yet," he said. "The Lord will lead! But when it happens, I do believe the power of it will be felt as far as Rancho Cucamonga." He laughed then, as if the contemplating of it was joy enough.

"Have your folks pray for the city, then," I said. "Will you do that? And have them sing up a storm?"

"Stay with us," the reverend said.

"Not tonight," I said. "Maybe another time?"

"Oh sister, you just come on back when you're ready," Reverend Hightower said. "We'll be here."

CHAPTER TWENTY-EIGHT

I WALKED BACK TOWARD DOWNTOWN. Los Angeles tonight was really quiet. Even the cars seemed to have quieted down. True, it was early-morning hours, but there is usually a hum of activity somewhere. I thought about the events of the night, that great warm feeling in Reverend Hightower's church, and about all the people who were trying to set me up. Why hadn't I been killed? It was a matter of some kind of protection, I knew that. Max had told me as much. Now, once again, I was being asked to choose sides. That's what Reverend Hightower had made plain.

But somebody was out to ruin me in another way, not through death, but through conviction for a double murder. Who?

The second body found in my office. Didn't make any sense. Was this just another way to force me out of town? I wondered if Aaron was behind it. Wouldn't put that convoluted scheme past him. He'd engineered my own murder and re-animation by Ginny Finn. Then a cyclops killed Ginny to keep her quiet. I couldn't prove Aaron knew about that, but a hunch was playing loud and long inside me.

Or the sheriff could have been acting completely alone.

Had this other deputy been conspiring with him?

How had he gotten in?

All questions, no answers.

And what about me being on the run? I wasn't cut out for the fugitive life. Running away would only make me look guilty. Maybe that's what they wanted, too.

So another plan started to form in my mind. If they wanted to try to take me out this way, what if I charged right at them? Because this was going to end up in a court of law, in front of a jury. That's where I always want to be. It had always been the thing that saved me and my clients.

Give me a jury, I used to say, and a place to stand, and I can move the world.

Now was the ultimate test. By the time I got back to the heart of downtown I knew I was going to go for it.

It was nearly 3:30 in the morning when I walked into the front desk at Central Division. There were two blue suiters there, looking at computer terminals. One of them, a young Hispanic, asked what he could do for me.

"I'm here to turn myself in," I said.

Skeptically, the officer said, "What is it you are supposed to have done?"

"Let's put it this way," I said. "The sheriff of the County of Los Angeles was found dead in my office earlier tonight. I would appreciate it if you would call Detective Mark Strobert and tell him that Mallory Caine is waiting for him in the lockup."

CHAPTER TWENTY-NINE

Key:
MS: Mark Strobert
MC: Mallory Caine
Time: 04:06

MS: Please spell your last name.

MC: D-U-P-E.

MS: Are you going to make this difficult?

MC: Sorry.

MS: That won't look good, you know.

MC: This isn't about looking good, Detective. The reason I asked for you is I think I can trust you. So go ahead.

MS: Before I ask you any questions I want to advise you of your rights under the law. Do you understand that I am a detective with the Los Angeles Police Department?

MC: You don't have to do this. I waive my rights.

MS: Let's just do it my way, so it's all nice and legal, huh?

MC: Fire away.

MS: You have the right to remain silent, and you do not have to answer any of my questions if you don't want to.

MC: I choose to talk.

MS: You have the right to talk to an attorney and have him here with you before I ask any questions. Do you understand?

MC: I waive that right.

MS: If you decide to answer the questions now, without an attorney present you still have the right to stop answering questions at any time until you talk to an attorney. Do you understand?

MC: Let me see. Yes.

MS: Knowing and understanding your rights as I have explained them, are you willing to answer questions without an attorney present?

MC: Let's do this thing.

MS: Please sign here. All right. Now, you want to make a statement?

MC: Just that I am innocent of any crime.

MS: To what are you referring?

MC: An incident that occurred in my office earlier this evening.

MS: Your office on Broadway, correct?

MC: That's correct. I was attacked.

MS: *You* were attacked?

MC: That's right.

MS: Tell me how this attack happened.

MC: I was in my office, working, when Sheriff Geronimo Novakovich, N-O-V-A-K—

MS: You don't have to spell it.

MC: He came calling.

MS: What time was this?

MC: Around ten p.m.

MS: Why were you in your office at that time?

MC: I work there. I'm diligent.

MS: What happened next?

MC: The sheriff pulled a gun on me. Said he was going to arrest me.

MS: Did he say on what charge?

MC: He said he would trump something up. That was his word. *Trump.*

MS: What happened next?

MC: I refused to go with him. And he shot me.

MS: He shot you? Just like that?

MC: Just like that.

MC: Where?

MC: Right through the chest. Have a look. ms: I'm turning off the recording at 04:10

I UNBUTTONED my blouse and revealed just enough to show him the hole. "You can stick a long pencil through me," I said.

Strobert said, "Why didn't you die?"

"I'm already dead, remember?"

MS: Back on the record at 04:13, Detective Mark Strobert questioning Mallory Caine, who has shown me a purported bullet entry and exit wound.

MC: Not just purported, buddy. And if you go to my office your boys will find a bullet in the wall, if they haven't already.

MS: What they have found are two bloodied, mutilated corpses.

MC: How did they get there?

MS: You tell me.

MC: You're assuming I had something to do with those bodies.

MS: They were found in your office. Explain that to me.

MC: I can't.

MS: You claim no knowledge?

MC: Of the presence of two bodies, I claim absolutely no knowledge.

MS: Let's keep it simple. Where were you all day yesterday, up until the time the sheriff came to your office?

MC: I am now going to refuse to answer any more questions until I consult with my lawyer.

MS: Do you have a lawyer?

MC: Yes.

MS: I will notify him. Or her.

MC: You just did.

MS: Excuse me?

MC: I'm going to represent myself.

Yes, yes, we've all heard the bromide: A lawyer who represents herself has a fool for a client. But I had a feeling I was going to have to pull something later on in court that I could only carry off if I repped myself. It had to do with my closing argument, something I'd been thinking about for my own father.

And when I think, I get very dangerous.

Strobert clicked off the machine. "I'll have to lock you up again," he said.

"I'm used to it by now."

"Since I took this report, I may be the one investigating."

I smiled. "You think I didn't know that? Why else would a perfectly innocent zombie lawyer like me stroll right in and ask for you?"

CHAPTER THIRTY

THE NEXT MORNING I made my initial appearance in court.

The judge, Roman Hegel, was someone who'd been friendly to me in the past, when I was defending someone. But now that I was an accused the tune would be quite different.

But he seemed at least a tad sympathetic when he called my name. The felony arraignment deputy for the DA's office was a woman I knew, Alodia Flecker. She was all phony-baloney toughness, the kind I usually chewed on for lunch.

"Ms. Caine, are you represented by counsel?" Judge Hegel asked.

"I am representing myself," I said.

"Are you sure you want to do that?"

"Absolutely sure."

"You know that I must strongly advise you against such a course."

"I know that, your honor, and I appreciate it. But there are reasons, and I have them, and I am fully aware of what I'm doing. So I will waive a reading of the charges and advisement of rights, and enter a plea of not guilty. I will also not agree to any continuances. I am putting the district attorney's office on notice that I am ready to go to trial within the statutory limit. Does Ms. Flecker understand that?"

"I will do the asking, Ms. Caine," the judge said. "Ms. Flecker, do you have anything to add?"

Alodia Flecker looked at me with a touch of nervousness. She wasn't used to attorneys pulling this, especially in capital cases. Which was what this was going to be. Death penalty time for your humble correspondent. That would be something to see. Get a lethal injection and then walk out of the chamber feeling like a rose.

I almost wanted to get convicted just so I could perform that little stunt.

"We understand Ms. Caine's position," Alodia Flecker said.

"All right," said Judge Hegel. "The defendant is remanded."

"With all due respect," I said, "I would like to be heard on the bail question."

There will be no bail, Ms. Caine."

"Your honor, you recall that I am defending myself? I need to be able to interview witnesses, to investigate. If I am denied that, how can I be expected to defend myself?"

"Ms. Flecker, do you have anything to say on this matter?"

"Indeed I do," the DDA said. But just as she was about to open her mouth she got a signal from another deputy in the arraignment court. She asked the judge for a moment and went to consult.

Alodia Flecker returned to the center of the courtroom. "Your honor, at this time the district attorney's office will not oppose Ms. Caine being released on her own recognizance."

What? They were actually telling the judge I could be let go OR?

"It's still up to the court," Judge Hegel said.

Knowing it was time to act compliant, I said, "Whatever your honor decides."

Roman Hegel pursed his lips and then said, "All right. I am going to allow Ms. Caine to be released. But I am going to impose a requirement that she report to this court in person every week until the matter is concluded. Is that understood, Ms. Caine?"

"Looking forward to it," I said.

OUTSIDE THE COURTHOUSE I WAS GREETED WITH AN ONSLAUGHT of media. Every news organization and website that had any traffic at all was represented out there on Temple Street. Somehow it had leaked out what was happening, and now here I was facing media attention, not like a celebrity lawyer but as a hybrid of celebrity lawyer and defendant.

Everybody was shouting questions at me. People jostled forward and I got bumped a couple of times. "Back off," I said. "You want me to make a statement, everybody be quiet and give me some microphones."

In about thirty seconds all the microphones within sight had been pushed toward me in some kind of makeshift knot. I raised my hands to quiet the crowd down.

"Ladies and gentlemen, thank you for your kind attention. I have been accused of murdering the sheriff of the County of Los Angeles, and one other deputy sheriff. I've been released on bail, because I'm going to prove my complete innocence of this charge. I did not murder anyone. I'm not a murderer, I am a criminal defense lawyer. I'm telling you the truth. And I will prove this in court."

"You're a zombie, isn't that true?" someone shouted.

"No secret about that now," I said.

"Did you eat the victims?"

"All the facts will come out in court."

"How many people have you killed in your life, Ms. Caine?"

"I am on an all-bovine diet," I said.

"You claim you've never killed anyone?"

"You'll all have to wait for the trial now." I started to walk past, but the scrum of reporters moved with me. They shouted more questions, stuck microphones and cameras in my face.

Managing to get to the sidewalk, I headed to Spring Street.

The reporters followed me, the younger ones running to get in front with their devices.

So I ran faster.

This was going to look good on the evening news.

HE WAS WAITING FOR ME ON SPRING STREET. IT WAS A convertible Ferrari, hot orange in color.

Steve Ravener said, "Hop in, Counselor!"

I looked behind me and saw the crowd rattling toward me like angry buffalo. I didn't bother opening the door. I jumped in. "Let's ride," I said.

He smiled, put on some shades, and burned rubber.

We crossed the freeway and cut over to Wilshire, which he took all the way to the beach. We got down to Pacific Coast Highway and pointed north.

"Quite a shock that my lawyer gets arrested for murder," he said.

"This is L.A. Anything can happen. Should I have expected a werewolf to show up in my office?"

"What I'm saying is, this makes things feel a little more personal."

"What do you mean, personal?" My heart started to drum a little faster, threatening to go all Neil Peart on me.

"What I mean is, you and I share something. We are not normal. We're part of the kinship, the kinship of the strange. I mean to say, I want to help you. You offered to help me once, now I want to help you."

"Steve, I'm facing a murder charge. I'm going to be defending myself. I don't think it's a good idea for you to get involved in it. You're a werewolf. What do you expect to be able to do?"

"I can intimidate witnesses," he said, but with enough of a lilt that I figured he was joking.

"Don't even think that in jest," I said.

He continued to drive. We were zipping up the coast, the ocean to our left. We passed Gladstones and the Chart House and Topanga Canyon Boulevard. Further north to Malibu and then Point Dume, Zuma Beach and just north of that Steve pulled the car over. From where we were, we could look out at the water. It was a clear day, the Channel Islands looking close enough to touch. The breeze was intoxicating. The ocean, the smell of it. I love the ocean. But because of the salt I can't get near the water. Another impediment of my curse.

"You know," Steve said, "I never thought I'd love water so much. Texas is not generally known for its waters. When I first saw the Pacific Ocean, I was a kid. My mom and dad brought me out here to visit my dad's brother. He lived in Oceanside. I think I was six or seven. I remember taking a plane out here, landing at the big airport at night. I think I fell asleep in the car, and I woke up the next day at my uncle's house. I heard the sound, like a whooshing. I got out of the bed in the little guest room and went to the window. It had an ocean view. I almost screamed, not out of fear but out of pure joy. I don't know." He looked sheepishly at his hands. "I'm just going on and on."

"No," I said. "I like it. I feel the same way. I didn't have a real normal childhood, and being at the beach was one of the nice things." I couldn't believe I was opening up to him like this. Where was my professional objectivity?

He turned and looked at me and put his arm on the head rest behind my seat. "This world eats people up," he said. "But the only chance we have is getting with people we are close to. I didn't tell you that before, because I was afraid."

"Afraid of what?"

"Afraid I'd lose you."

In my chest, my heart palpitations were clog dances.

"I wanted you to be my lawyer. But I also wanted you to be one of those people that you get close to, who understand and help. I thought it was just because you were a lawyer. But now that I know you're like me, one of the different ones, I find that I especially don't want to lose you now."

And I knew then I didn't want to lose him, either. His hand came off the head rest and went behind my neck. He gently pulled me toward him. I was exploding inside, wanting him to kiss me more than I wanted anything in my life, but also knowing that I might try to bite his lips because a food source was so close. But the kiss, the kiss! I screamed a silent prayer to an unknown god and let him kiss me. When his lips touched mine and his mouth opened and our tongues met, I fell headlong into the Grand Canyon, my arms out, picking up speed. I didn't hit bottom. I kept going, and my arms became wings and I rose up on the wind like an eagle or a hawk, and found to my astonishment that I didn't want to eat Steve Ravener. All desire for mastication was gone, or simply wasn't there. And as the kiss continued to pull me farther up into the clouds I thought, either I am free or I can kiss a wolf without fear. I wanted it to go on and on and on. I wanted to forget everything and everybody and just stay here, because I was flying.

And then, like Icarus, my wings melted and I pushed him away. "I can't. I can't get involved like this. I've got murder hanging over my head and I've got a father awaiting trial and a messed-up mother and I don't know what else to say I just want—"

I shot my lips back on his and kissed him again, hard, as the waves of the ocean broke onto the beach in all their metaphorical glory.

We sat in the sun silently for several minutes. Neither one of us knew what to do. At least I didn't.

I said, "I have to think rationally. What kind of future would we have? You're a werewolf, and that means, for some reason, I don't have the desire to chew your head. You know what that means to me? You know how I've longed to be able to feel this way about someone?"

He said nothing.

"But I'm a lawyer, and a zombie, I have an undead body. I

shudder to think what a wolf and a zombie coming together might mean."

"Suppose you let me shoulder that risk if I want to?"

"I don't know, I don't know! I can't. Not now. Oh man, what I wouldn't give for a big old martini."

"Done," he said.

CHAPTER THIRTY-ONE

WHEN I GOT BACK to the office, Nick was stomping his foot outside his office door. There was still police tape across my own door and a police override lock on the door handle.

Which meant that I would be squeezing into Nick's office for the time being. Nick, being gnomelike, had everything in his office at about half size. Whenever I was in here I felt like I'd stepped into some grade school kid's diorama.

"You took some sweet time, you did," Nick said.

"I needed to do some thinking," I said.

"And with who did you do this thinking?"

"What do you mean by that?"

"I saw you drive away with him."

"You were at the courthouse?"

"Of course! You are supposed to pay me, you are, and how can you do that when you are in jail?"

"As you can see, I'm not."

"So what were you doing with that wolf?"

"He's our client."

"Yeah? Any more than that?"

I didn't answer him. I wasn't sure I couldn't insult him.

"Answer me," he said.

"Listen, short stack, what gives you the right to be nosy about my personal affairs?"

"I'm an investigator, remember? That's what I do. Also, I'm a barometer—"

"Oh, brother—"

"—and I can sense when something is going on, and there is, and I do not like this thing that is going on, no."

"Suppose you let me handle my own personal life, and I'll let you handle yours."

"A personal life I don't got!"

"You need one then. When was the last time you went out with a woman?"

He narrowed his eyebrows at me. "You are making fun."

"No."

"Look at me! I'm an ugly little creature, cursed by the Saturnalia. I was not like this once! I was handsome once, I was. And could lift a table with my teeth! But now I am like this forever!"

"Nick—"

"You got two murders hanging on your head!" His voice cracked a little. He cared about me, he really did. I felt like a jerk.

"All right," I said. "Let's get to work."

He looked at the floor.

"Nick," I said. "I didn't mean that short-stack crack."

He waved his arm.

"I'm a little stressed out, you know?" I said.

"You are not the only one!" He waved his other arm.

"I can't do this without you, Nick. You're invaluable to me."

He rubbed the back of his hand under his nose.

"What do you say we beat the crap out of the DA?" I said.

Nick took in a couple of deep breaths, then took out some colored markers from his desk. He had an easel with a large pad of blank pages by his window.

"You talk, I draw," he said.

"Okay," I said. "The sheriff comes to my office. He wants to try some intimidation. He wants me out of town. Why? I must've represented something of a threat to him. Why would I be a threat?"

"You have to ask?" Nick said.

"I'll do the jokes, thank you. He kept talking about the bikers out in Sunland. Remember?"

"How could I forget?"

"So somebody tipped him off to me. Somebody who wants me out of Los Angeles. There are a lot of people who want me out of Los Angeles, I mean people who aren't really people. Let's start a list."

"Going to be a long list," Nick said, but he got his marker ready.

I ignored him. "We have Aaron, Manyon, Mayor Garza, and a host of demons. We have Lilith, Marduk, Dagon, and Ishtar."

Nick's marker squeaked across the page as he wrote the names.

"Second question," I said. "Why would the body, the dead body, of the deputy sheriff also show up in my office? You have any thoughts on that, Sherlock?"

"Somebody wanted to make it look like you killed this other guy, too."

"If so, we need to find out more about this deputy. Who was he? What was he into? Who did he hang with? You getting all this?"

"I will find the answers. I am a bar—I am pretty good at this stuff."

"We need to do a little triangulation. We need to make a connection from one of these people who wants me out of town, to Sheriff Geronimo Novakovich, and to the dead deputy. Somewhere in there is the answer." Nick folded the first piece of paper over the easel, and on the new blank page he drew a triangle. At the top of the triangle he wrote *Mastermind*. At the bottom left he wrote *Sheriff*. At the bottom right he wrote *Deputy*.

"So what does this look like to you?" he said.

"A triangle," I said.

"Oh, you are good. How did I get so lucky, finding a good lawyer like you?"

"Can the sarcasm, buddy. Get ready to write. Okay, *Mastermind.* Who is calling the shots? Let's assume there is something to this idea that Lucifer, that a real devil, is actually setting up something here in Los Angeles. You would have to assume he is the one at the top. But as far as we know he hasn't shown his face yet. He's got surrogates out there doing all the dirty work. So my take would be that he's put some people in charge of carrying out the actual tactics. What do you think?"

Nick contemplated this for a moment. "I think you are right. The devil is always leaving his dirty work to his slaves."

"Slaves?"

"The Book says the devil makes you a slave to evil. Even if you don't know it."

"So who are our chief suspects in the mastermind? Write down these names. Ronaldo Garza, Aaron Argula, various gods."

Nick wrote.

"Now which one of those names would have a direct contact with the sheriff?" I asked.

"The mayor."

"Probably. But we have to also assume that it's possible any one of these gods that have been showing up is getting in contact. My mom is a perfect example. She was in with Lilith at one time. So I don't put it outside the realm of possibility that our sheriff was making time with some god or other."

"What about the deputy sheriff?" Nick asked.

"We don't even have a name yet. They're withholding the police report until the preliminary hearing."

With a twinkle in his eye, Nick raised his finger in the air. He went to his miniature filing cabinet, pulled out a drawer, pulled out a file, pulled out a paper. "His name is Wesley Oates."

"Well done."

Nick shrugged. "I know people."

"So have you found anything out about this guy?"

"Only that he joined the Sheriffs Department six years ago. He was kind of young."

"Any idea of his background?"

"Not yet. But give me time to work."

"Take all the time you need, my friend. We are going to war."

"You mean trial?"

"Same thing," I said.

PART TWO

I care not how hard the case is—it may bristle with
difficulties—if I feel I am on the right side, that cause
I win.
　　—Rufus Choate, legendary lawyer

CHAPTER THIRTY-TWO

BEING on trial for murder is a definite inconvenience.

Especially if you have to keep alive on less than human brain.

For the two months until the trial started, I was good. I was going straight. I was attending Zombies Anonymous meetings. But it wasn't making me any stronger. It was not an appetizing or pleasant experience, but I did it. I had obligations.

For one, I still needed to defend my father. I put myself on a speedy trial schedule to get mine out of the way. Dad didn't mind being in jail. He kept telling me that. So we got a continuance until my own situation was resolved.

Now all I had to do was be acquitted so I could defend my father. Easy peasy melted cheesy.

My theory was going to be self-defense. But I would have to find some way to explain that other little something, that second body in my office.

What Nick had been able to find about Deputy Oates was exactly nothing. The Sheriffs Department gave out only his record, which was impeccable. He was thirty-two years old and had been with the department for six years. No stain on his performance. No disciplinary marks.

Oates was a complete and utter mystery to us. Yet somebody had killed him.

We had a copy of the autopsy report on Oates from the coroner's office. According to which the cause of death was the same as that of the sheriff. The bodies had been conveniently cremated shortly after the report so I had no chance to have my own expert examine them.

Gee, what do you know about that?

The judge gave a big yawn when I moved for exclusion of the coroner's evidence. The trial would go on, and the evidence would be admissible.

The fix, in other words, was definitely in.

Which was why I wanted to get in front of a jury, and quick.

There was media from every part of the globe stuffed into Los Angeles now. My trial was drawing attention even from China and North Korea. Reporters of various colors and languages were haggling with security at the courthouse to try and get in. It was like the worldwide meeting of the Abyssinian Rug Merchants Society. Everybody shouting, wheeling, dealing, and waving their arms.

And why not? Another celebrity trial in Los Angeles! The country, indeed the world, cannot resist this. It all started with O.J., because we were actually inside the courtroom for that one. Before that, trials weren't widely televised. There was a mystery, an aura of secretiveness about trials. I kind of wish it was that way again, because I wasn't going to like being center stage when my own life was on the line.

But by this time everybody knew about me. Everybody knew I was a zombie, there was no hiding that fact anymore. My story had been told many times in many places. Geraldo did an hour about me, how I was subsisting on cow brains, trying to go straight in a crooked world. And while I put on a seemingly normal front, for an undead person at least, there were serious vibes going down in L.A. of the supernatural and demonic sort.

But people didn't seem to care. The city was running pretty much like a well-oiled machine now. Traffic was better, the mayor was popular, and when people are getting the services they want they don't ask many questions.

OUR JUDGE FOR THE MURDER TRIAL WAS THE HON. GREGORY Thaw, white haired and regal. I'd been in front of him before. He acted like a federal judge, which is one step below God. But on the federal bench you serve for life. In California you can get voted out. Judge Thaw didn't think you could get rejected if you acted like Moses and spoke like James Mason. Thaw had perfected the cadences of Mason, complete with the nasal voice. It was irritating, but you have to play the cards you're dealt.

As Nick and I took our places at the defense counsel table, I took note of the space that would be my home for the next couple of weeks. I've always loved courtrooms. Love the great seal of California above the judge's bench. The two flags—one of the United States, the other the bear flag of California—flanking where the judge sits. And the jury box, empty now but soon to be filled with people who would hold my fate in their hands.

I have felt comfortable in courtrooms ever since my training days with the PD's office. A little strange, perhaps. But maybe not so much when I think about it. I never felt quite at home in the world. The courtroom always seemed to be the place where I could truly live and move and have my being.

I checked out the cameras for the courtroom feed, and decided just to never think about them. If I wondered how I looked I'd lose all mojo. It's like anything, from golf to painting to writing to acting—if you're thinking about it too much you're not really in the moment. And you won't be as effective.

The gallery was packed with pool reporters and a few lucky spectators who got entry tickets after standing in line most of the night. The natural heat arising from the bodies gave the place a stuffy feel. I had no doubt it would get hot very soon.

Then I saw Steve. He'd made it in. He'd told me there was no way he would miss the trial.

Five weeks ago he'd finally gotten to see his kids. I'd been able to get enforcement on visitation, though it had been supervised by an LAPD officer that Steve had to pay for. He didn't care. He was able to see his children again, and that was a start.

He smiled at me. I gave him a nod, so as not to cause too much attention. The last thing I needed was somebody poking into a love story during my murder trial.

Yeah, I said love. It was happening in spite of myself.

But those thoughts snapped closed when Aaron and his lead investigator, Detective Mark Strobert, came into the courtroom from the back. That was a privilege of the district attorneys. Aaron was dressed impeccably. Not a wrinkle in his suit, shirt or tie. His hair was neatly combed back and he walked as if he owned the place.

But he didn't own me.

Strobert looked at me and I was unable to read his face. We hadn't spoken since he officially arrested me, and that was to be expected. I was in the system now, a defendant. His job was to gather evidence against me. And, I should note, to alert Aaron to evidence that tended to show my innocence.

Of which there was none, but I just thought I'd note it anyway. The only evidence on my side was my story. The jury would have to believe me when I told them it was self-defense.

But I wanted Mark Strobert to believe me, too. Deep inside, I really wanted him to.

Aaron motioned for me to join him in the middle of the court-room, where we could talk without being heard. I wanted to muss up his hair. But I acted professionally and just gave him a cold stare.

"Well, Counselor," Aaron said, "are you ready to become a superstar criminal?"

"Sure. We're forming a union."

He nodded impassively. "So you ready to talk deal?"

"Which would make this a deal with the devil, am I right?"

His beautiful face—and it *was* beautiful, deadly beautiful—

broke into a grin. "I always loved that about you. Your guts, even if it means you're being stupid. We're talking about a real deal here. Try to remove yourself from your ego for once, Mallory."

"It's all a setup and you know it."

"The jury is not going to buy that"

"We'll see. Give me a jury, even with Jack the Ripper as my client, and I'll take my chances."

Aaron said nothing for a long moment. He just looked at me, the way he used to back in law school. I would have done anything for that look at one time.

"I still love you, Mal," he finally said. "That's why you should reconsider and marry me. We would make such a great team."

"Yeah, with me wondering when you were going to try to kill me again."

"I thought by now you'd understand why I did that. It wasn't to keep you dead, but to bring you back to a new life."

"You call this a life?"

"It can be. You've tried to fight us, and you can't. You're about to be convicted of murder. But I can arrange to have the charges completely dismissed, and then we can be together."

I couldn't believe he was still trying. But then he dropped his bomb.

"One thing more," he said. "I can give you your real life back."

My body quavered. Real life? No more flesh eating?

"No more eating flesh," Aaron said.

The possibility of it, just that much, weakened my knees. Oh, if I could only believe that it was true.

But then again, this was Aaron Argula, son of the devil. "But at what cost, Aaron?"

"There is no cost. We'd be married."

"There's always a cost. I'm afraid I wouldn't like my in-laws."

He shook his head. "Don't get taken in by the wrong side. Everything you think you know about it is wrong. My side is the good one. The other side is about being slaves to laws and regulations and priests." I glanced over at Nick then. He was looking right at us, as if he could read our lips. His eyes met mine. And his elfin head shook slightly.

If I had to pick someone to trust, it would be Nick. "Do your best, Aaron," I said. "And get ready to watch me walk out of here a free woman."

"Zombie you mean."

"Maybe. But never Mrs. Aaron Argula."

That got under his skin. He didn't bother with any more words. He went to his table and started arranging his papers for the battle to come.

CHAPTER THIRTY-THREE

WE BEGAN PICKING A JURY. I knew Aaron liked to use consultants to help him. I never use them. First of all, they cost too much. Second of all, they usually want to rely on data over gut instinct forged in actual courtroom battle.

My way of picking a jury was the old-fashioned way, the way Darrow and Rogers and Edward Bennett Williams had done it. By knowing what questions to ask and reading faces.

Aaron had insisted on jury questionnaires, so we had a lot of information up front. What I was looking for, my ideal juror, was a woman who knew what domestic violence was all about. And all women either have experienced it or know someone who has.

That was going to be easy for Aaron to counter. I was sure he'd use his peremptory challenges to get that profile off the jury.

Which left me to sandbag him. I also wanted men who had good family ties. Pillars of the community. You might wonder why, me being less than the pillar type. But I was going to argue justice in this case, and that appeals to fathers.

The clerk called twelve potential jurors to the box and we began the *voir dire* process. This is where the lawyers get a shot at questioning the *venire,* the good citizens called to be jurors.

Right off the bat I found a roly-poly man, a friendly-looking sort, who fit exactly my profile. In my mind I dubbed him Santa Claus. Not because he had a beard, but because he seemed the sort to play that role on Christmas. He had a wife and a couple of young kids, attended church, and was a Little League coach.

Just the sort of juror this zombie was counting on.

I tried not to let Aaron know it by asking too many questions.

But this was the first juror Aaron used a peremptory challenge on.

Same thing happened with the next juror I really wanted to keep, a mother from Boyle Heights. Aaron used a peremptory on her, too, and she was gone.

I got rid of a couple of jurors I didn't like, too. But then Aaron booted the third juror I was really hoping for, and I started to get suspicious. It was like he was reading my mind.

Which got me thinking ... I took a quick look out to the gallery, scanned the faces. And sure enough, in the back corner, there was someone staring hard at me. A mind reader. Aaron would know how to get a real one. He had connections, so to speak.

To test the theory, I glared back at this person, a woman about my age, but very dark of feature, from her black hair to her midnight eyes. In my mind I said, *I know who you are and what you are doing. You have mustard on your blouse.*

When she looked down at her blouse then, I knew I'd pegged her. She looked back up at me furiously.

I thought, *Nice try.*

When I went back to questioning jurors, I kept putting in my mind a vivid memory, one of my mom's old exercise videos. Richard Simmons, *Sweatin' to the Oldies.* I recalled his screechy voice shouting out commands. If there is anyone who can read thoughts through that cacophony, I don't know who it is.

Jury selection went a lot more smoothly for me after that. By the end of the day we had managed to seat twelve, plus two alternates. There were at least four jurors I thought I could count on. If nothing else, I would get a hung jury, I was sure. But I was going for all-out victory.

THAT NIGHT NICK AND I GOT TOGETHER TO GO OVER THE DAY and strategize. We still did not have many facts about the deputy sheriff, Wesley Oates. For all anyone knew he was a good, loyal member of the sheriff's team. He had a spotless record. He was just starting to gather some commendations.

He was single, living in Silver Lake in a condo.

And he was a complete dead end as far as my defense went.

"I see no other way than to go right into the teeth of the tiger," I told Nick.

He knew what that meant. We'd gone over it and over it.

It was going to begin right in the opening statements.

I wasn't going to hide any balls with the jury.

Everyone would know what this case was all about from the get-go.

CHAPTER THIRTY-FOUR

"LADIES AND GENTLEMEN OF THE JURY," Aaron said, "what you are about to hear is a story so bizarre, so foul, so deadly and disgusting, that it will require your full attention just to prevent your becoming ill."

It was 9:15 AM, and the start of the trial. The jurors were seated, the courtroom again packed. The cameras were rolling.

The trial of Mallory Caine was on.

For this opening day in court I wore a pleated gray skirt and matching gray jacket, with a burgundy blouse, and black pumps. Aaron was going to portray me as a flesh-eating horror. Well, I guess that's what I was. But I was certainly not going to look that part.

Didn't matter to Aaron. He took off right after me. "This case involves the vicious murder of two law enforcement officials, the sheriff of Los Angeles County himself, Geronimo Novakovich, and one of his deputies, a man with a bright future ahead of him, Deputy Wesley Oates. They were in the process of carrying out their sworn duty to keep us safe from crime, when they happened into the office of a ravenous monster, a zombie to be exact, an eater of human flesh. Yes! A masticator of membranes, a consumer of craniums."

Oh, brother.

"And that monster is the defendant, Mallory Caine, sitting at that table right there, preparing to defend the indefensible. Don't let her looks fool you. She appears to be a competent and well-appointed attorney-at-law. But make no mistake. She would eat each and every one of you if she had the chance!"

I shot to my feet. "Is this an opening statement or an audition for the Royal Shakespeare Company?"

Judge Thaw said, "All right, Ms. Caine, you may be seated. Mr. Argula, if you will please confine yourself to the evidence you wish to present. You know the rules."

Aaron made a half bow to the judge. "And the evidence is all I'll need, your honor."

Oh, brother, again.

But then he went at it. He laid the groundwork expertly. I wouldn't have expected any less of him. Despite being a devil, he was still as good a trial lawyer as I've seen. Maybe those two things aren't entirely at odds with each other.

Using graphic photographs of the crime scene—my office—and other exhibits, Aaron presented a full-on show of bloody magnificence. It was like a dinner theater performance of *Sweeney Todd*. All Aaron had to do was sing and we'd be going to Broadway.

It took him two hours to complete. By the time it was over the jury looked like it had a collective case of post traumatic stress disorder.

Then it was my turn.

THERE ARE DIFFERENT WAYS TO DELIVER AN OPENING statement. You can tell a story, which is usually the best thing. The jury wants to know how the evidence is going to fit into a pattern that makes sense. Or you can start with the client's background and try to build up some sympathy.

Or you can do something totally outrageous, because that's the only way to get the jury's attention back from the prosecutor.

That was my option. I had not given Aaron one hint of what my defense was going to be. I'd waltzed through the preliminary hearing for just that reason. My list of potential witnesses didn't tell him a thing. In fact, they weren't supposed to. I'd put that list together as a ruse. I wanted him and his investigative team out there scrambling around after witnesses I might not call.

Prosecutors do that all the time to us defense lawyers, so I was just returning the favor.

But now I had a jury to talk to, to get to listen to me. Outrageous. That was the only way.

"Ladies and gentlemen of the jury," I said. "I ate the sheriff. But I did not eat the deputy."

Dramatic pause.

"I ate the sheriff, but I swear it was in self-defense."

One more pause. Yes, I had their attention indeed.

"Ladies and gentlemen, you will hear the evidence. You will hear the facts. You will hear about a sheriff who was corrupt, who tried to drive me out of town because he didn't like the threat I posed to him. And what was that threat? It was the threat of exposing his ties to a corrupt and crooked administration. Yes, Mayor Ronaldo Garza's administration is going to be on trial here, not just one lawyer falsely accused of murder."

Aaron objected. The judge had us march up to the bench.

"I am asking your honor to rule out all evidence concerning the mayor. It's irrelevant and immaterial to this case."

Judge Thaw nodded. "Unless you give me an offer of proof, Ms. Caine, that shows a direct tie, I will not allow any more mention of the mayor or the administration, is that clear?"

"I'll make the offer when the time comes," I said.

"She's bluffing," Aaron said.

"No more talk of it," Judge Thaw ordered, then sent us back to our places. He then told the jury in his drawn-out, James Mason way: "Ladies and gentlemen, the statement by Ms. Caine about Mayor Garza and his administration has been ruled inadmissible by me. You are not to give it any thought or allow it to influence your decision. Remember that what the lawyers say here is not evidence, only what they assert the evidence will prove. You twelve are the sole judges of the facts of this case. Continue, Ms. Caine."

Thanks for nothing.

"You will hear, ladies and gentlemen, how the sheriff threatened to arrest me on trumped-up charges, and then shot me with his gun. Because I am a zombie, the bullet did not kill me. But it did set off a fear of imminent bodily harm that led to my defending myself. I defended myself the only way a zombie knows how.

"The sheriff had given up his place as a respected law-enforcement official and was a common criminal himself. That is why I ate the sheriff, and that is why it was in self-defense.

"Then you'll hear that I knew nothing about the deputy, Wesley Oates. I will be presenting evidence to you that may explain how he got into my office after I had blacked out. Yes, I defended myself against deadly force and then everything went dark for me, which I will tell you about in due course. For now, it's important to note that only the sheriff was in my office at that time."

In reality, I still had no idea how Oates got in there. But I wanted them to be thinking I did, and I hung on to the hope that Nick and I could figure something out.

Sometimes trial work is just about faith.

"But as you await the evidence, ladies and gentlemen, I ask you not to form your opinions too soon. These are strange times in our city, and the things that are happening are beyond most of your experiences. Keep an open mind. Let justice be done. I'm confident you will bring it to pass."

CHAPTER THIRTY-FIVE

AARON SAID, "I call as my first witness Dr. Dezyderiusz Mintz."

A wide man with a bald head waddled in from the gallery. This was the coroner for the County of Los Angeles. I'd cross-examined him before. He was the big gun on all the major homicide cases. A cannon. He came across as a trusted uncle type, the hardest kind to deflate in front of a jury. Plus, he'd testified hundreds of times. He knew all the tricks.

After the coroner was sworn, Aaron began his direct testimony.

"Doctor Mintz, please tell us what your current position is."

"I am the coroner of the County of Los Angeles."

"And how long have you been so employed?"

"Thirteen years next January."

"And in that time you have conducted a number of autopsies?"

"Oh my, yes. Or overseen. I've lost count. Several hundred."

"I see. And did you conduct an autopsy on the body of Sheriff Geronimo Novakovich?"

"I did."

"Do you have your report with you?"

"Yes."

"Can you tell the jury, please, what the cause of death was?"

"Exsanguination due to massive tissue trauma, caused by aggressive laceration."

"In layman's terms, what does that mean?"

"He was literally torn to shreds," Dr. Mintz said. Aaron paused. He wanted it to sink in. He'd already shown the graphic photos to everyone. Now he had the official medical cause of death.

"Did you also perform the autopsy of Deputy Wesley Oates?"

"I did."

"And what was your conclusion?"

"Same cause of death."

"Just one more question, Doctor. In all your time as a medical examiner, and coroner, have you ever seen bodies in such a condition before?"

"Only once," Dr. Mintz said. "It was when a drunken man jumped into the tiger exhibit at the L.A. Zoo. He apparently thought he was Tarzan. What he was, was meat."

The courtroom laughed.

Some joke.

"Your witness," Aaron said.

I got up and smoothed my skirt and smiled. "Good morning, Doctor."

He regarded me warily. "Good morning."

"Does your description of the deceased tell you anything about what was in my mind?"

"Your mind?"

"Remember, Doctor, I have already admitted that I ate the sheriff."

He looked repulsed.

"Can you answer the question, Doctor?"

"I cannot fathom any reason anyone would eat anyone."

"Then this is an area beyond your expertise, is it not?"

"I don't know what you mean."

"You can hazard a guess as to the cause of death, but not the *reasons* for it. Isn't that true?"

"I can surmise that the death was violent."

"A car crash is violent too, isn't it?"

"Yes, certainly."

"But a person who dies in a car crash is not the victim of first-degree murder, correct?"

"Well, no."

"That's all, Doctor. Thank you."

When you get a good admission from a hostile witness, save it for the summation. Get what you're after and stop. Too many lawyers keep going, to their ultimate disappointment.

AARON CALLED A DETECTIVE NAMED BRUNO HUNSUCKER, WHO had been the first detective at the scene. He was angular, with sharp points for his chin and elbow. His thin eyebrows pointed down to his nose, like streams joining at a nasal delta.

"Detective Hunsucker," Aaron began, "when were you called to the scene of the crime, Mallory Caine's office?"

"At 11:30 p.m. My partner and I arrived about one half hour later."

"And what did you do upon arrival?"

"I spoke to the patrolman who called it in. He told me he had been notified by his division that a janitor had called in a report of blood on the floor just outside the defendant's office door."

"What did you do next?"

"I secured the scene and called for SID."

"Did you enter the office?"

"Only after SID arrived. I directed the scene from there."

"SID is..."

"Scientific Investigation Division. They are primarily responsible for the collection and interpretation of evidence at the scene of a crime."

"And they took photographs and so forth?"

"Yes, they completed a forensic investigation of the scene, including gathering of blood samples."

"What did you personally observe at the defendant's office?"

"Two bodies, one later identified as Sheriff Geronimo Novakovich, and the other as Deputy Sheriff Wesley Oates."

"What was the condition of the bodies?"

"Both of them were mutilated. They had flesh torn off their arms and legs and torso and neck. Their faces were unrecognizable."

"What did that indicate to you?"

"It indicated that they were killed by a zombie."

I didn't object. I wasn't denying who or what I was. Aaron did a little more *addax yadda,* then turned the witness over to me for cross-examination.

"Detective Hunsucker," I said, "did you examine the bite marks on the two bodies?"

"Yes, I did."

"And what method did you use?"

"Eyesight."

A few titters from the gallery. I let them tit, then said, "I was under the impression this was a serious trial. I'm glad you find my fate so amusing." Hunsucker clamped his jaw shut.

"Ask your next question," Judge Thaw said.

"I'll try again. Using that dynamite eyesight of yours, what evidence did you examine?"

Hunsucker huffed through his nose. "I examined the medical examiner photos and the description of the wounds. I examined over a hundred and twenty-five photographs."

"Did you examine the bite marks on each of the faces?"

"Yes, of course."

I was going to go into a short riff to establish that he was not an expert in bite wounds when I heard *Pssst.*

I turned to the gallery and there in the front row, sitting on top of a reporter from Channel 7, without the reporter even knowing it, was the ghost of Elizabeth Short.

"I need to talk to you," she said.

"Now?" I said.

"What was that?" Judge Thaw said. "Ms. Caine?"

I faced the judge. "Your honor, may I request a short break so I can consult with my . . . investigator on a certain matter?"

Judge Thaw looked at the clock, sighed, and said, "Fifteen minutes."

When the jury was all filed out I looked at Beth Short and motioned for her to come to the counsel table. The reporter from Channel 7 shrugged. I waved him off. He waved back.

Beth Short floated through the railing and I saw, once again, only her top half. She wore the same black halter dress she had on the night I met her, but no legs went with it. She settled her ectoplasm between me and Nick, who saw her, too.

"He's a liar!" Beth said. "I was at the morgue just the other night, talking to some of the new spirits, and one of them started talking about the trial, and you, and he saw this detective with the bodies when they first came in, heard him talking to the coroner. The coroner told him the bite marks were different. Said it right out loud."

"Are you sure about this?" I asked.

"It's what the ghost told me, and we don't lie to each other. No reason to. And the detective said not to put that in the report."

Stunning. But... "How can I prove that? I can't put you on the stand. It's hearsay on hearsay, from a couple of phantoms."

Nick said, "We got pictures." He took my iPad out of its case. We had the prosecution's photo evidence in there. They were, of course, hand selected to give us the least possible information. We'd had them analyzed by an expert, who couldn't offer anything that differed from the official conclusion.

Beth looked at me pleadingly. I remembered her telling me that if she could help solve a murder, that would bring her peace in the afterlife and make her whole.

When in doubt, a good trial lawyer knows how to blow smoke. As long as there is some basis in fact for said smoke, you blow away. Especially if you know that witness is lying. You blow smoke in his face and maybe you can get him to cough.

I looked at the clock. "We have ten minutes to put something together."

"Will you try?" Beth Short said.

"For you, sweetie, anything."

WHEN WE WERE BACK ON THE RECORD I HAD NICK FIRE UP A slide show from the iPad. The first slide was of the bite-marked face of Sheriff Geronimo Novakovich in all its gory glory. It was a mass of red gouges, with the two eyes missing and black sockets staring out in blind terror.

"I show you now what has been identified as ME photo number forty-two. You are familiar with that photo?"

"May I refer to my report?"

"Of course."

Hunsucker took his sweet time turning to a page in his notebook. "Yes, this is one view of victim number one, Sheriff Novakovich, specifically the left side of the face."

"I direct your attention to the lower right quadrant of the photo. Bite marks, so identified by the coroner. Do you see that, sir?"

"Yes, I do."

"I'm now going to put up, next to it, ME photo number eighty-seven, which is, I believe, the same left-side view, only of Deputy Oates. Can you confirm that?"

He looked. "Yes."

"Now look at those side by side. Do you see similar bite marks to the face of Deputy Oates?"

Hunsucker stared. "I see marks that appear to be bites."

"Let me ask you a question, sir. If an expert witness were to testify that the bite marks on Sheriff Novakovich and the bite marks on Deputy Oates were made by two different sets of teeth, would that alter your opinion about this case?"

What I was asking was a hypothetical, which is allowed under the rules of evidence.

"I wouldn't draw any conclusions one way or the other," Hunsucker said. "I'd have to assess the evidence and the expert myself."

"Are you an expert in teeth marks, sir?"

"No. But the coroner is."

"I see. And did you consult with the coroner about these marks?"

He hesitated. "Not consult. I was given an autopsy report."

I gave him a knowing look, right between the eyes. "Isn't it true that you met with the coroner in the morgue first, to discuss what would go in the report?" His right cheek quivered like a cold mouse, but he kept his voice even. "No, that is not true."

"Isn't it true, sir, that you were told the bite marks were different, and that the coroner should not note that in his report? Isn't that true?"

Before he could answer Aaron was on his feet, shouting an objection. The judge summoned us to the bench.

"Outrageous," Aaron said to the judge. "There is no basis at all for this conjecture. Ms. Caine is simply trying to taint the jury."

"There better be a foundation for that question, Ms. Caine," Judge Thaw said.

"I can call a ghost to the stand to testify to my basis," I said.

"A *ghost?*" Judge Thaw said.

"Competent to testify," I said. "Just like any other witness."

"This is too much," Aaron said.

"I quite agree," Judge Thaw said. "Ms. Caine, I will not sanction you this time. But I warn you, any other question like that which is not supported by someone who is actually alive I will consider contempt. Is that clear?"

As I was holding five unmatched cards in my hand, I said, "Clear." And back we went. I might have planted a small seed of doubt in one or two jurors' minds, but without further ability to hammer this witness and maybe see him crack, those seeds would dry up and produce nothing.

To the witness I said, "All right, Detective, I will ask you the same question I asked the coroner. You have no idea what was in the mind of whoever was responsible for these deaths, do you?"

"Murder was on your mind."

I turned to the judge. "Your honor, I ask that his answer be stricken, and the jury admonished to disregard it."

Judge Thaw shook his head. "The jury can make up its own mind on that. Move along."

"Then let's go with it," I said. "You're a mind reader, is that it?"

"No, but the evidence—"

"You solve murders with tea leaves, yes?"

"Objection," Aaron said.

"Sustained," the judge said.

"I have nothing further for Carnac the Magnificent," I said, and sat down.

AARON CALLED MARK STROBERT NEXT.

It was déjà vu all over again. I'd tangled with Strobert in court before, in the Traci Ann Johnson murder case. And then again at my father's first trial. Aaron ran Strobert through the statement I'd made to him when I turned myself in. It didn't add anything to the evidence as far as I was concerned. Then it was my turn. Cross-examination time.

I love cross-examination. Hostile witnesses are my meat. So many lawyers, and people who watch too much TV, don't understand the purpose of cross. It's very simple: to argue your case to the jury. It's not to argue *with* the witness, but *through* the witness.

Rarely do you catch a witness in a lie. Especially a cop who has been through cross-examination many times before. With most witnesses, then, you create a box. Or, rather, you let them construct their own box by leading questions. Leading questions are allowed on cross-examination, and the skilled lawyer will lead the witness into limiting his own effectiveness.

Which was the strategy I would now employ on Detective Mark Strobert of the Los Angeles Police Department.

"Detective," I said, "do you believe in the supernatural?"

Strobert paused, sizing me up, trying to discern my purpose. "In what way?"

"Is the question ambiguous to you?"

"I'd like to know what you mean by *supernatural.*"

"I mean things that cannot be explained by science or are beyond our experience." I watched his eyes to see if I could catch a memory there, a memory of rolling eyeball guacamole. He didn't know I knew about that. I'd been disguised as Amanda at the time.

If he was remembering, he didn't show it. "Can you be more specific?"

I said, "Things like angels and demons. Do you believe in them?"

"I haven't given it much thought," Strobert said.

"What about creatures like zombies and vampires?"

"Well, I've come to see that they exist. You are a prime example."

There were a few appreciative laughs in the courtroom. Which I didn't like one bit. "Your honor, I would move to strike that last answer as non-responsive and argumentative."

The judge nodded. "So ordered. The witness is admonished to answer only the question asked."

I smiled.

"In fact, Detective Strobert, I have helped the LAPD before, advising you and one of your partners about the reality of zombies, isn't that correct?"

"You did on one occasion, yes. The Carl Gilquist matter."

"And tell the jury what that was."

Strobert looked at the jury and said, "There was a man, a plumber named Carl Gilquist, who we found beheaded. His mouth had been stitched closed and there was salt inside it Ms. Caine was called in because we knew she had some experience with these matters. We didn't know she herself was a zombie at the time. Now we know."

"And tell us what you know about zombies," I said.

"That they eat human flesh, especially brains. That they can't be killed by normal means."

I took a dramatic pause by walking to the counsel table and picking up a piece of paper on which I'd typed some notes. I then set the paper down as if it actually had something relevant to my next question.

"In your experience as a detective, have you come across people who have killed in self-defense?"

"Sure."

"And when those people describe what happened, are they usually in a state of mind that is calm and reflective? Or are they likely to have adrenaline pumping through their body and acting primarily on instinct?"

"Mostly, they're going to be pretty excited."

"Are they likely to use whatever force is available to them at the time?"

"I don't follow."

"For example, an intruder comes into my house and threatens me. If a baseball bat or a lamp is nearby I might grab it without giving that much thought, correct?"

"That's possible."

"And what is the weapon of choice for zombie?"

"I'm not sure I know."

"You said it yourself, they eat flesh. Would it not then be reasonable to assume that a zombie, in fear of being killed or maimed, would use teeth for a weapon?"

Aaron stood up to object. 'Your honor, the detective is not here as an expert on zombies. This cross-examination is going beyond the scope of the direct."

"I quite agree," Judge Thaw said. "Move on to something else, Ms. Caine."

"Detective Strobert, I turned myself in after killing Sheriff Novakovich in self-defense, didn't I?"

"Objection," Aaron said. "States a conclusion that is the subject of this trial."

"Sustained," the judge said.

"Let me put it this way," I said. "After the death of Sheriff Novakovich, however it came about, I voluntarily turned myself in to the police, did I not?"

"Yes."

"And I asked that you be the one to take my statement, correct?"

"That's right."

"Was I cooperative?"

"Yes."

"Did I show you the bullet hole in my chest?"

Strobert cleared his throat. "You showed me something you said was a bullet wound."

"No further questions."

AND THEN FOR SOME REASON, AARON CALLED THE WOMAN WHO is the bane of my rental existence.

LoGo was sworn and asked to place her ample bulk into the witness chair. The clerk asked her to state her name.

"Lolita Maria Sofia Consuelo Hidalgo."

Aaron began his questioning. "You are the manager of the building where Mallory Caine rents a law office, correct?"

"That is right."

"And how long has the defendant rented an office in that building?"

"Oh, I think it is maybe two years."

"I see. And in that time, has the defendant been perpetually behind in her rent?"

"Objection!" I said. Aaron, the jerk, knew that question wasn't relevant.

But the judge said, "Overruled."

"What?" I said.

"You heard the court's ruling, Ms. Caine."

I heard it, but I couldn't believe it.

"You may answer the question," Aaron said.

"Yes, she is the deadbeat," LoGo said, surely not intending the play on words for a zombie. LoGo wasn't the firmest bean in the chili.

"And on the night of the horrendous murders in the defendant's office, did you have occasion to be in your shop?"

"Yes."

Liar!

"What were you doing there at that late hour?"

"The inventory. I am doing that sometimes in the late times."

I had *never* seen LoGo there at night. Not once. She got out of the Smoke 'n Joke as fast as she could after it closed.

"Now Ms. Hidalgo, are you able to see who comes and goes to the second floor of your building?"

"Yes."

"Did you happen to see Sheriff Geronimo Novakovich come to the building on the night of the killings?"

"Objection," I said. "Leading the witness."

"Sustained."

"All right," Aaron said. "That day, who did you see coming into the building?"

"I saw the sheriff."

"Did you recognize him?"

"Yes. He's on TV all the time."

"So you knew he was the sheriff of Los Angeles County?"

"Yes, I did."

"Was there anyone with him?"

"Yes," LoGo said. "Another sheriff."

"A deputy?"

"Yes, a deputy."

Aaron put a slide up on the screen, a shot of Deputy Oates as he appeared before losing his face. "Is this the deputy?"

"Yes, it is."

"So Ms. Hidalgo, you are absolutely certain that these two men went upstairs to Ms. Caine's office together?"

"I am very sure, yes."

"Thank you. That's all."

I got up. "Ms. Hidalgo, am I currently paid up in the rent?"

"This time."

"So your answer is yes?"

"I guess so."

"You're guessing now? How much guessing have you been doing with the prosecutor?"

Aaron objected. Sustained. The judge warned me. *Yadda yadda.*

"Ms. Hidalgo, in point of fact, you are never at your store past six o'clock, isn't that true?"

"No, that is not true."

"In fact, someone has coached you to give the answers you've given here today."

"No! No one has done the coaching."

I didn't stop, hitting her with questions as fast as I could say them.

"You claim you were doing inventory?"

"Yes."

"How many Chinese finger traps did you count?"

She frowned. "I don't remember."

"Maybe that's because you were counting in the dark."

"No! I have a little light."

"Oh, a little one?"

"Yes."

"So you can see what's in front of you, right?"

"Yes."

"But that doesn't light up the whole store now, does it?"

"It does not need to. I see what I need to see."

"And make up what you need to make up?"

Aaron objected. "Argumentative."

"Sustained."

"But the light," I said, "was small, correct?"

"That is all I need."

"But it is not enough light to see the faces of two deputies coming into the office, is it?"

That got her. She squinted and didn't answer. "Why don't you just tell us who coached you, Ms. Hidalgo," I said.

"No!"

"You won't tell us?"

"No!"

"Because you don't want to let out the secret identity of this person?"

"No! I mean, no. I mean, no, there is no person!" When a witness is dog paddling in the water, best to leave it right there. I sat down.

And with that we were done for the day. The court adjourned after the judge told the jury not to discuss this case among themselves. Fat chance, I thought. How could you not talk about this case?

A TON OF REPORTERS WERE WAITING OUTSIDE THE COURTHOUSE, naturally. Judge Thaw had neglected to issue a gag order, so I was free to speak. I would make this count, because he could slap a no-talk on us tomorrow.

"It was a good day in court," I said. "The incompetence of the prosecutor and the weakness of his case were on display. I used to play a game as a little girl picking up plastic fish with a magnetized fishing line. I got to be so good at it there really wasn't a challenge to it anymore. I only wish Mr. Argula was offering more of a challenge. But he's a fish. Any questions?"

A reporter shouted, "So you have admitted you're a zombie?"

"Some of your best friends could be zombies," I said.

"Aren't you afraid the jury will hold that against you?"

"I have full confidence in the jury system, because it is a vehicle for truth and justice. So long as I tell the truth in court, justice will be done."

"You don't deny that you killed Sheriff Novakovich?"

"Ate is the operative word here."

"Then it's homicide."

"Sir, you do not know whereof you speak. Stay tuned."

"How much human flesh do you eat each day?"

"I am a recovering zombie," I said. "I do not eat human flesh."

Except when I do.

I WENT INTO EVENING GOING OVER THE COURT DAY WITH NICK. He told me he was trying to turn over every stone, contact every person or creature he could in the city who might know about Deputy Oates. But no luck so far. No public records existed.

I needed to clear my head. Sometimes the best preparation for the next day of the trial is to just let everything sit in your subconscious. Let the girls in the basement work on it while you do something else.

That something else, for me, was Steve. I asked him to come get me and drive me into the Hollywood Hills. I wanted to look down on the city and feel human for an hour or so. I wanted to feel his reassurance. I wanted to think there was something waiting for me after the trial. A werewolf and a zombie. Why not? This was L.A., after all.

From where we parked in his Ferrari, we could look down at the Chinese Theater, the Magic Castle, and out toward the west. Except for a police helicopter or two, the night was quiet. I leaned my head back against the seat.

"You were great in court today," Steve said. "You command that space. I've seen great actors and singers who can do the same thing."

"Now if I could only act and sing my way out of this," I said.

"You're going to beat this thing. I have faith in you."

"Why?"

"I never thought I'd be able to see my kids again. You made that happen." He paused. Then: "I never thought I'd be able to love anybody again. You made that happen, too."

I waited for what I knew would happen next. Steve leaned over and kissed me. It was warm and long and wonderful, and I knew if he asked me to marry him right then I would say yes.

"I want you to marry me," Steve said.

"Yes," I said. "I mean, no."

"What?"

I put my hand over my eyes. "Nothing is changed. I don't see how anything has changed."

"No," he said, "things are the same. That's the point You are who you are and I am who I am. We are the ultimate outsiders. We need to be together. We don't need anyone else."

"But I may end up in prison," I said.

"That's not going to happen."

"What are you talking about?"

He looked down at the lights below. "We have ways of getting people out of prison."

"Who is *we?*"

"The people I run with."

I turned toward him. "Now Steve, it wouldn't do to have you get taken out because you have some wild prison escape scheme."

"I don't care! I want you in my life and I will never let you go."

He grabbed me and pulled me to him. This time the kiss was more intense, and I was full of Southern California wildfire. The most amazing thing happened to my body. It felt more alive at that moment than any other time I can remember even when I was really alive. I moaned and Steve kissed me harder. His hands dug into my back.

Or should I say, claws. Because my face got full of fur. I recoiled and saw that Steve had gone wolf.

He looked at his hands in horror. His eyes widened in the realization that the lycanthropic tides of his cells had taken him out of his humanity.

A terrible thought hit me. Maybe it was sexual passion that triggered the change. If that was true, then the frightfulness of his condition would be that he could never truly love anyone because it would only make him become what he hated.

"Steve, don't—"

He looked up at the sky and howled. It was the most mournful, pitiable sound I'd ever heard come out of any creature on earth. He jumped out of his car and tore his shirt off. His chest was all dark, matted hair. And then he leaped over the car, over me, and landed on the other side where the hill descended into darkness. And down he ran.

"Steve!"

Only another howl came in return, fading like a train in the distance.

Now what?

I waited about half an hour for Steve to come back. At least he could have done me that courtesy. Or was his wolfness carrying him away on animal instinct? Where would he go in these hills packed with homes? I hoped the pet dogs were all inside.

So here I was with a Ferrari and no way of knowing where the driver was. The only solution: drive the Ferrari out of there. Let Steve find me when he returned to normal.

Before I could start it up my phone played Prokofiev. It was my ring tone for Nick.

"Where are you?" he said, sounding breathless.

"I'm up by the reservoir," I said. "What's wrong?"

"Hang onto your mat."

"Hat."

"Just hang on! I got something for you. On the deputy, on Oates. Something you want to know."

I slid further into the driver's seat as if that would help me hear better. "Spill it."

"Spill what?"

"Talk to me!"

"I am trying! I found a dame and gave her a sawbuck."

I rubbed my eyes. "Okay, Mr. Spade, what did this woman tell you?"

"She works for the heat. In the records department of the sheriff's office. And she used to be the girlfriend of Carl Gilquist."

"What?"

"Am I a good shamus or what?"

"Yes, you're aces, you're the bee's knees! All of that. What did she tell you?"

"She told me she knew all about you and Carl, always liked you, and what could she do to help? I told her I wanted the records of where Oates was when he was working. And she had that."

"What did it tell you?"

"There was one thing. Two days before what happened in your office, he went to a place you might know. A little bead store in Glendale."

CHAPTER THIRTY-SIX

STEVE'S RIDE got me to my mom's trailer home faster than Geraldine ever could. I pounded on the door until she opened.

The place reeked of Mr. Ganja. This time I went in and overturned the table with all the weed on it.

"Tell me what you told that deputy sheriff," I said.

"Honey," she said in a dull, senseless way. "How about some orange juice?"

I grabbed her shoulders and shook her. "There was a deputy sheriff who came to your bead store, remember? He ended up dead in my office. Tell me what you told him."

Her eyes were glassy and sad. She shook her head. "You need the light," she said. "Won't you join me?"

"Mom, I need your help."

There was a long silence. She shook in my grip. And then she started to cry. She fell to her knees and put her head in her hands. Out of some drug-induced fog she was somewhere, somehow, sorry for something. She was so far gone. I wanted to slap her.

I got on my knees and cradled her in my arms.

She wept into my chest.

I stroked her hair. Once, when I was seven, I came back to our dingy little trailer in tears. A big girl had pushed me down and stolen my bike. Just like that. Deliberate cruelty like I'd never experienced before. It hurt me in ways I couldn't understand, but felt like a sickness in my chest.

Mom was inside watching *All My Children,* which was for her like going to church. I was not to interrupt her viewing, ever. But my sobs rang out and she did not hesitate. It wasn't even a commercial, but she shut off the TV and took me in her arms and stroked my hair. I loved her hand on my head, and I cried for the hurt and I cried for the longing of my mother's touch. And she did that until I stopped and fell asleep on her.

And now here I was, holding her.

The roles had been reversed. I wondered if she wanted my love now, finally.

When she finally stopped crying I grabbed a dish towel and wiped her face. I sat her at the kitchenette table. I made coffee—instant was all she had, so I made it strong—and gave her a cup.

Mom took it gingerly. Her hands shook slightly, rippling the coffee. The spirits and demons and gurus and drugs had really done a number on her.

"Mom, come back to me," I said. "I want you so much to come back."

She closed her eyes. "He asked about you."

"Who? The deputy?"

Mom nodded.

"What was he asking?"

"I didn't tell him anything," Mom said. "I didn't turn you in."

"For *what?* What did he want to know?"

"He kept asking about a friend of yours. At least I think it was a friend. "

"What friend?"

A flash of fear swiped across her eyes. She shook her head.

"What's wrong?" I said.

"He said not to."

"The deputy?"

"Uh-huh. Not to talk."

"He's dead, Mom. He can't do anything to you."

"Dead?"

"Haven't you been following my case?"

"What case?"

Oh Mom. Oh blissfully unaware Mom.

"Just tell me the name of the friend," I said. "No one's going to hurt you. And I need to know. Just believe that I need to know."

Mom sat back and took my hand. "I'm so sorry, baby. I have not been a good mother."

I put my other hand on top of hers. "I haven't been the perfect daughter. But perfect doesn't come around in this world. What counts is family. Let's make it count."

My mother sighed, then said, "I can't remember the first name of the friend he kept mentioning, but I remember the last name. Because of Huckleberry."

"Huckleberry?" I said.

"Finn, of course," Mom said. "Even I remember Huckleberry Finn."

"Ginny? Was the first name Ginny?"

"That's it," Mom said. "A funny name."

"Did he say why he was asking you this?"

Mom shook her head. "I didn't tell him anything. I know about the fuzz."

I kissed her cheek. And told her I had to go. She walked me outside. When she saw the Ferrari she said, "I'm glad you're doing so well, dear."

I let it go at that.

I SHOT DOWN TO WEST HOLLYWOOD, TO MED ZEPPELIN, THE retro coffee bar and medical marijuana place where Ginny Finn used to hang out. It was late, but the poets and laptop writers were all basking in the effluvium of hemp and creativity. Maybe some high IQs in here. Good nutrition. I fought that back.

And behind the coffee bar one of Ginny's closest friends, Imac-

ulada Kino. She was about thirty, a pretty Asian with a wide mouth
and short attention span. Always a dozen different things going on
in her head, but I only wanted one.

When she saw me she looked like she wanted to run out of the
place. But there was nowhere to go.

"Hi, Imaculada," I said. "How is the bean and seed
business?"

She came up close and looked down, whispering, "What are
you doing here?"

"Need to talk."

"Don't you know you're on trial for murder?"

"Let me have an espresso shot," I said.

"You better just get out of here. If they see ..."

"Who sees, Imaculada?"

I felt a tap on my shoulder. I turned around and looked at a
leather jacketed James Dean look-alike. "Can I have your autograph?" he said.

"I'm having a conversation," I said.

"I'm a big fan."

"Do you have any idea who I am?"

With a loopy smile, he said, "No, but you kind of look like
somebody."

"You look like somebody, too. Why don't you give yourself your
own autograph and leave me alone?" He put his arms up in surrender. "Whoa, now I don't want your autograph."

"Another tragedy in the city," I said.

I turned to Imaculada once more but saw nothing but the
coffee machine. I looked up and saw her backside scurrying up the
stairs.

I followed, almost tripping over a guy reading Bukowski on the
floor.

At the top of the stairs I heard a door slam. I went to the door.
It was marked *Private*.

"I'm not going away," I said, pounding on the door. "You hear
me? I'll start singing show tunes out here and interrupt the vibe.

You ever had your vibe interrupted by Ethel Merman? It's not pretty, Imaculada. You better talk—"

The door opened a crack. "Please be quiet."

"Let me in," I said.

Imaculada opened the door a little more. I squeezed through.

The interior was stuffed with papers and books and files and a desk where a computer was, somewhere.

Imaculada said, "They might shut us down. We are not supposed to talk."

"I want to know about the deputy sheriff, his name is Oates. He had a special interest in Ginny and me."

"Mostly you," Imaculada said. Then added, "Oops."

"What about me?"

She said nothing.

"I mean it."

Imaculada shook her head.

I started to sing. Loud. "There's no business like show business like no business I know! Everything about it is appealing—"

"Please—"

I threw open the door. "Everything the traffic will allow! "

Imaculada bounced over and slammed the door closed. "Okay. Just this time, but then you have to leave."

"Happy to," I said.

"Okay, how can I put this? The deputy, he was trying to gather evidence about Ginny, about who might have killed her."

"And?"

"And he thought you might have done it."

"Me? I was talking to her when she got the knife in the back."

"That's the official story, I guess."

"It was a cyclops."

"Nobody saw one."

At least no one we could find. "But that case is cold."

"Not for him, for the deputy," Imaculada said.

"Why not?"

"Because he was Ginny's brother."

I took a moment for processing. "I didn't know she had a brother."

"Yeah. Her real name was Virginia Oates."

"And that doesn't exactly say hip. But she never talked about him."

"He was sort of on the other side, you know? Law? And Ginny was Miss Events that push the limits. They had to be careful with each other."

I ran my fingers through my hair, which felt brittle. "All right, then who would have a reason to kill this guy?" Imaculada looked at me sheepishly.

"You don't think it's me, do you?" I said.

She shrugged. But I couldn't blame her. That's what all the evidence suggested.

"Mallory?"

"Yes?"

"Would you please not sing anymore?"

"Probably not for a long time." I patted her cheek.

CHAPTER THIRTY-SEVEN

"But your honor, this is absolutely crucial to my case!"

I was arguing my butt off the next morning. But Thaw was not warming.

"You have made the assertion," the judge said, "but I'm not going to halt a major felony trial so you can go rooting around for irrelevant material."

"She's bluffing," Aaron said. We were in the judge's chambers before the day's festivities. Thaw's chambers looked like something out of a Dickens novel. He liked old, leather-bound books to give him the appearance of a wise old sage. But he wasn't fooling me. "This is newly discovered evidence," I said.

"Ms. Caine, first of all, you are offering a potential statement from a potential witness about something Deputy Oates might have said. I am not convinced that even what he said would be relevant."

"It would show at least he had some sort of motive to come after me," I said.

"But your position is that you didn't eat the deputy," Aaron said. "And I also think you owe an apology to Eric Clapton."

Judge Thaw said, "I quite agree."

"Fine, I'll call Eric Clapton," I said.

"Not that! I'm talking about your theory of the case. You can't be arguing you had no knowledge of the deceased and then, at the same time, argue that his knowledge of *you* somehow mitigates his death. I don't see it."

"But Mr. Argula's theory is that I killed them both," I said. "I have an absolute right to refute that."

The judge pursed his thin lips, which made them disappear entirely. "Mr. Argula, your response?"

Aaron paused a moment, then a nausea-inducing smile smeared his face. "I will leave the issue to you, your honor. Further, we have proved our case. The People will rest."

Boom.

Nice move, Aaron. Hit me with a surprise.

Okay, I'll return the favor.

"CALL YOUR FIRST WITNESS, MS. CAINE," JUDGE THAW SAID when we were back on the record.

"I call myself," I said, and walked to the witness box. It was good theater. I could feel the vibration in the air, the sense of anticipation in the crowd. Which did not include Steve Ravener.

I was sworn in and sat in the chair. It would be me, facing the jury, and that was all.

"Ladies and gentlemen, there are only two people who know what happened in my office that night. One of them is me. The other one is the person who planted the body of Deputy Oates into my office."

"Objection," Aaron said. "Assumes facts not in evidence."

"Sustained," Judge Thaw said.

I continued. "Right now, sitting here in court, I am the only one who knows and can talk about it. I'm going to ask you to look at me as I do so, because you are going to be the ones to judge whether I'm telling the truth or not. I'm going to tell you the absolute truth. It will be your decision after that."

I paused to scan the jurors' faces. It was hard to tell, it always is, what a jury is thinking. They have collective thoughts and they have individual thoughts. All I needed was one. All I needed was one to hang up this jury. But I was going for all twelve.

"I am a zombie, as you know. This was not something I chose. In fact, I was murdered, and then brought back to life. Or what is a form of life. And the man who murdered me is sitting—"

"Objection!"

Aaron insisted we go to the bench. He told the judge what I was going to tell the jury, and he was right I was going to name names, starting with Aaron's. But the judge looked at me and told me there was no evidence to back that up and I was not to speak of it again. I knew I could go ahead and say it anyway, but that would risk alienating the jury. And the judge was right. Without some evidence to present, it would just be something I said.

So I got back on the stand and behaved myself.

"For some time now, I have been on the wagon. In zombie terms, that means I have given up eating human flesh. I go to a recovery group, Zombies Anonymous, and I'm trying to make my way in this world without hurting anyone. But that does not mean I cannot defend myself. And that is exactly what happened in my office.

"Sheriff Geronimo Novakovich told me he wanted me to get out of Los Angeles. Wanted to run me out of town, just like some sheriff in the old West. When I refused, he took it up a notch. He came to my office to arrest me, and said he was going to drive me out of the county. I suspect he was going to kill me."

"Objection."

"Sustained."

"The sheriff drew his gun. When I did not follow his orders and tried to get that gun away, he shot me. I would've produced a bullet for you, but that bullet conveniently disappeared from the evidence locker at LAPD."

"Objection."

"Sustained."

"But I will show you a picture of a bullet wound." I nodded to

Nick and he put up a slide on the screen. It was a photo of the bullet hole just above my left breast "That is the perforation caused by the sheriff's bullet. I fully expect the prosecutor to claim that it wasn't so made. But once again, I am the one who was there. Look at my face as I tell you this. I'm telling you the truth."

Aaron again objected. "Statements about who is telling the truth are opinion only, and irrelevant on direct."

"Sustained," the judge said. "The jury is admonished not to consider any opinion this witness has about who or who is not telling the truth. Ms. Caine, you will confine yourself to evidence that is admissible only."

"Of course, your honor. What is admissible is this. I was shot. To protect myself from being riddled with bullets I stopped the sheriff the only way I could. It's a brutal thing zombies do under those conditions. But brutality is not the measure of self-defense. It is when someone acts under the threat of severe bodily harm. And I'm telling you now that that's what I was under. That's what happened."

I paused, let that sink in for a moment, then said, "It is a fact of zombie life, if I may use that expression, that too much intake of flesh too fast results in something like a state of drunkenness. That can cause a blackout, just as if someone were to take shooter after shooter of tequila. That's what happened to me. I blacked out, and when I woke up I was not in my office. I had been removed by a friend. It was he who informed me that there was another body in my office."

Another objection, and another sustained.

"Ladies and gentlemen of the jury," I said. "If I had truly wanted to eat the sheriff with malice aforethought, would I do it in such a way as to insure my conviction for murder in the first degree?"

I left it there. I'd made my plea. It was all I had. But now I had to face Aaron's cross-examination. "Good morning, Ms. Caine."

"Good morning." You unctuous slime.

"You are a lawyer, is that right?"

"Yes."

"A good one, according to reputation?"

"I'm not allowed to offer my opinion," I said. "But if I were, I'd say you bet."

Laughter in the courtroom.

"As a good lawyer, you know the law concerning self-defense, do you not?"

"Of course I do. That's why I'm here."

"Let's walk through it, shall we?"

"Is that a rhetorical question? I'd rather stroll." More laughs.

Aaron wasn't fazed a bit. "We'll go at your own pace, Ms. Caine. I want the jury to fully understand."

"Objection," I said. "Mr. Argula is arguing."

"Proceed, Mr. Argula."

"Ms. Caine, surely you know that under the law you may only use deadly force for self-defense when the force against you is also deadly, correct?"

"Deadly or severe bodily harm," I said.

"Let's take those one at a time," Aaron said. "A zombie cannot be killed by a bullet, isn't that so?" Okay, he knew what he was doing.

"Did you understand my question?" Aaron said.

"Yes, of course. No, a zombie generally cannot be killed by a bullet."

"Generally and specifically, correct?"

"There might be exceptions."

"Can you name one?"

"Not right now."

"All right." Aaron did a little pace in front of the jury box. "Since you were not in danger of being killed by Sheriff Novakovich, if we even believe he shot you, that leaves us with only one other justification, that of severe bodily harm. Correct?"

"That's what it was. Severe bodily harm."

"Severe is defined as something more than mere bodily harm, correct?"

"There is no one definition of it, as I am sure you know, Mr. Argula. It depends upon the circumstances, and what a reasonable person might infer."

"Or a reasonable zombie lawyer."

"Is there a question lurking in there?" I said.

"Indeed there is. You have told us that bullets do not kill a zombie. And they do no severe bodily damage, either."

"Holes in my body, that's damage."

"Did the alleged hole in your body keep you from gorging yourself on Sheriff Novakovich?"

"Now look—"

"Answer the question, please."

He had me backed into a corner.

"I was running on pure adrenaline," I said.

"That's curious," Aaron said. "I didn't think zombies had adrenaline. Do you have medical testimony to offer this court?"

I glared at him.

"I didn't hear an answer," he said.

"I am telling you what was in my mind," I said.

"So the answer is no, you have no medical testimony."

"Not now."

Aaron smiled. "I think this would be a good time for a recess. And a meeting of the lawyers in chambers."

CHAPTER THIRTY-EIGHT

"It appears the district attorney has you over a barrel," Judge Thaw said.

"What is that supposed to mean?" I said.

"It means that I'm not going to allow you to argue self-defense to the jury. You have not met your burden of proof."

"What!"

"I will instruct the jury that not guilty by reason of self-defense is not an option. It will not be within their power to acquit you on that basis. I am willing to allow them to consider what was in your mind, but if they believe you it will be voluntary manslaughter."

"You can't do that."

"I can and will."

Suddenly it was hard to breathe. The air was full of the stench of corruption.

Aaron said, "I am perfectly willing to make a deal with you, Ms. Caine. I will consider involuntary manslaughter, but you will have to agree to do the maximum sentence under the law."

"You two make a really great pair," I said. "How long have you been planning this?"

"I will let that comment pass for the moment," the judge said. "I know you must be a little shocked. Under the circumstances, I would strongly advise you to accept the offer of Mr. Argula. It sounds pretty generous to me."

"We're not finished with this trial yet," I said.

"In my opinion, the trial is not going your way. The prosecutor is giving you a chance, frankly more of a chance than I would give you under the circumstances. But there you go. It's your choice."

Choice. There was that word again. My whole life I've been choosing to fight. Why stop now?

"I'm ready to go back in there," I said. "No deal."

"I tried," the judge said to Aaron. "Let's get this thing over with."

I ONLY HAD ONE ARROW LEFT IN MY QUIVER, AND IT WAS A LONG shot. But I was going to take it.

I rested my case and the judge called for a lunch break. I really wanted to eat a judge. It would've made me nice and strong if I found a smart one, but those are increasingly rare. Nick wanted to talk about the case, but I just wanted to be alone.

But where? I was a media sensation, a notorious zombie, a celebrity defendant. But I had a good hour and a half. So I got in Geraldine and drove to Hollywood, to the little church that had been my sanctuary so many times before.

Inside I met with Father Clemente and Jaime and his mother. They said they had all been praying for me. I asked them how to pray. Jaime was the one who gave me the answer. "You just talk to God like he is your friend."

I needed such a friend. I asked for a quiet spot.

Father Clemente gave me the small prayer chapel, which seats about five people.

It was nice to be alone.

I did what Jaime told me. I just talked. I hoped there was a God and that he could hear me. I told him that I needed something like a miracle. I told him I was ready to be shown what to do.

I asked for a sign. I wanted lightning. I wanted an angel to appear. I wanted specific directions on a piece of paper.

Nothing came. But I will say there was a quietness in my zombie heart for a moment, and I thought maybe something touched it. A reassuring hand like my mother used to give my cheek when I was sick as a little girl.

She had done that. She'd come through, and even though she was way off the beam now, I couldn't forget those times.

Maybe it was just me hoping, or maybe it was really reassurance from above. I didn't have time to quibble. By the time I was finished praying it was time to get back to court.

CHAPTER THIRTY-NINE

CLOSING arguments are usually the dramatic high point of the trial, as long as the lawyers don't blow it. Most read notes and bore the jury.

You try to pick the other side's story apart. Pick, pick, pick and hope at least one juror will come alongside you. That's the standard option.

But I was representing myself, and had been cooking up something else. Something that would slam both Aaron and Judge Thaw against the wall of their complacency. There's no way I could have gotten away with it if I was representing someone else. But being my own lawyer gave me this small opening. It was about the size of a water glass, and I was on a fifty-foot high diving board.

Aaron, as the prosecutor with the burden of proof, argued first. He would also get another shot after I was done, on rebuttal. Two bites at the apple.

I was going to blow that apple up.

As the judge had indicated, my perfect self-defense argument was not going to be allowed. Aaron made sure the jury understood this. Under the law, he told them, they would not be able to find me not guilty by way of self-defense. It was going to be whether they believed it was murder or manslaughter. And it involved two victims, not one. What he was telling the jury was the least they could do was find me guilty of manslaughter of at least one of the victims.

A nice little net pulled tight. Or so he and the judge thought.

It was a little after three in the afternoon when I stood up to make my final plea to the jury.

"Ladies and gentlemen," I said, "I thank you for your kind attention throughout this trial. I need that attention now. Because I'm going to tell you something you perhaps have never heard before, but it is as much a part of the law as anything you'll find in a book of statutes. It is this: you are the law in this courtroom. When you go back to deliberate you can reach any conclusion you desire, anything you think is right, despite what you are told by the judge."

At which point Aaron Argula pitched a conniption fit that was worse than a prom queen with a wardrobe malfunction.

Why?

A little item called jury nullification.

It is one of the great legal principles in our American jurisprudence, and they don't want you to know about it. *They* being the judges, the grand pooh-bahs, the authority figures, the big bosses. What they don't want you to know is that a jury can find a defendant not guilty *in spite* of the law and the evidence, if they think she should be let go.

Yeah.

It goes all the way back to the colonial days. A guy named John Peter Zenger was a printer and publisher in New York City, back in the 1730s. He printed a paper that contained a highly critical opinion of what was then called the royal governor of New York. The law was on the books that even if you printed the truth, if you went too far you could be arrested on a charge of seditious libel.

Which Zenger was, after his royal governorship got extremely cheesed off.

So here was the thing. Under the law at that time, Zenger was guilty. But his lawyers argued to the jury that the law itself was unjust. And after hearing all the facts, the jury came in and acquitted Zenger, even though the presiding judge wanted to toss him in the clink and throw away the key.

In other words, the jury nullified the law. And there wasn't a thing the judge could do about that, because juries *don't have to explain the basis of their verdicts.*

You see, the real power is not in the government, or in the judiciary. It's in the people! And we should never forget it.

But you can't say that in front of a jury. You see, the black-robed ones are scared stiffless because every defense lawyer in the universe would argue for jury nullification if they could. They would be telling jury after jury to let their guys go because some law is unjust. And in some cases it is. Sending a guy away for life on a three strikes rap because he stole a wedge of pizza? Please.

There would be a lot more hung juries and mistrials and even outright acquittals if lawyers could tell juries they didn't have to convict just because a silly thing like the law says they do.

So if a lawyer tries to argue this, they are immediately stopped by the judge and threatened with contempt. They can be fined and even tossed in jail if they persist. They can even be removed as counsel for the accused.

But here, oh reader, is the twist your humble narrator has inserted into the rib cages of prosecutor Aaron Argula and Judge Gregory Thaw—this time the lawyer herself is the client! They can't keep throwing me in the can and then having to dismiss the jury and then starting the whole thing all over again!

This is why Aaron's head was exploding in open court. And why, deep inside, I was all *BWAHAHAHA HAHA!*

Aaron's objection was sustained by Judge Thaw, but that didn't matter one bit to me.

"Ladies and gentlemen, they're going to go crazy," I said.

"Ms. Caine!" the judge said.

"Because you have the power—"

"Enough!"

"And because they are both in league with an unnamed defendant in this court—"

"The bailiff will take Ms. Caine from the stand—"

"The devil himself," I said. "Lucifer, Satan, the Prince of Darkness—"

The bailiff was at the witness chair, reaching for me. I stood on the chair, then jumped up to the judge's bench. "The devil will not have his way, ladies and gentlemen, the devil—"

And which point the entire courtroom began to sway.

CHAPTER FORTY

EARTHQUAKE.

If you've lived in L.A. for any length of time, you know what I'm talking about You know the signs. You know when the San Andreas Fault is getting restless. You just never know how big it's going to be.

The next few seconds usually tell.

There was a low rumble, like giants bowling in the mountains. The ball was rolling down the lane. It would either subside, or crash like a ten strike.

This was more like a hundred strike.

The room started shaking.

Everyone in the room screamed.

And everything went black.

The next few seconds: glass breaking, wood cracking, feet scrambling, voices shouting. The bailiff told everyone to "Stay where you are!" Yeah. Like that was going to happen. I could sense, rather than see, a river of humanity rushing toward the door.

I knew it was a losing battle to get out. We were on the fifteenth floor and the elevators were going to be on auto lockdown.

We were all prisoners in a building that continued to shake.

"It's here!" a voice shouted, high pitched and hysterical. I knew it was Aaron. I could not see him. But I could smell him. The stench of sulfur hit me and then the hard-boiled-egg smell of his mouth as he said, close to my face, "See you in hell!"

I wanted to scream at him for his dreadful dialogue—or maybe the devil specializes in clichés—but I was too busy trying to keep from getting hit by debris.

The shaking and screaming and chaos went on. Not subsiding, but growing in intensity. Gad, this would have to be a big one. Maybe *the* big one that everybody in California talks about.

Whatever it was, it wasn't stopping.

And I was the defendant in a murder trial who was, at the moment, free.

And intended to stay that way until I could figure out how bad things were.

Shafts of faint light crisscrossed the courtroom. Smartphones. Reminded me I had my iPad in my briefcase. Now the trick was to find the briefcase.

The shaking went on. Wails of fear burst like gunfire at a shooting range. I heard one woman crying and screaming for God to save her.

But the quake continued.

I fell once, held on to the ground. It was like being on top of a giant washing machine overloaded on the spin cycle.

Plop. Thud. Bang. Stuff hit the floor.

If it was this bad up here, what must it be like on the street?

I decided to just hold still until the shaking stopped. When it finally did I had no idea how long it had been. I only knew it had to be one of the worst earthquakes in the history of California.

I pushed myself up to my knees, waiting, listening. Aftershocks would surely come and be plentiful. Now the question was how to get out of here before the whole thing collapsed.

Someone hit me from behind, a body blow. I went face first into the floor. The body stayed on top of me. It was not an insubstantial body, either.

"Get off me!" I managed to say, but the body stayed.

I wondered if it was dead. And then I wondered what it would taste like. Here in the dark, with all the commotion, I was feeling hungry. I hadn't had a decent brain in weeks.

But first I had to get out from under the fat person who had fallen dead, or fainted, on top of me.

Scraping along the floor, I pulled my arms into my body. Pushing with my elbows I managed to raise the hulk and, using my left leg, I pushed it off my back. It thudded to the floor like a wounded tree sloth.

My eyes were adjusting to the dark now, so I at least could see the face. It was Juror number eight. An overweight plumber from Downey.

He wasn't breathing.

Heart attack maybe?

My head told me to get out of there. Now was my chance. In the confusion I could get out and regroup. Find people who could help me. But here was a giant Roto-Rooter jockey, a man with a family. Why should I care about him? I couldn't figure it out, but something kicked in and made me want to do CPR on him. I originally thought about doing New York CPR. That's where you get in the guy's face and scream, "Get up or you're gonna die!"

Instead, I started pushing down on the guy's chest. I pulled his neck up so his head tilted back and gave him mouth-to-mouth.

You don't know what mouth-to-mouth resuscitation is until you've had it from a zombie. Best that you are never conscious. Because I so wanted to eat his lips. I wanted to eat his nose.

Try to imagine a famous boozer, maybe Hunter S. Thompson, giving mouth-to-mouth to a bottle of Johnny Walker Red. Do you think he wouldn't take a nip or two?

Just don't do it, I told myself. I pulled my face back and gave him more pumps on the chest. Then heard him gasp. Doggone if the CPR didn't work. He started to come to. He gasped for air like a man who'd had the wind knocked out of him. I waited there a moment on my knees and said, "Can you hear me?"

"What happened?" he said.

"Earthquake. Court has been adjourned."

"What!"

"Your best bet is to just stay here. It's a mess in the building."

"You're the defendant!"

"Not right now, friend."

I got up. Immediately a strong hand was on my arm. It was the bailiff. "You're coming with me," he said.

I yanked my arm away. "Go help the people out in the hallway."

"You are my prisoner."

"Don't you understand? There's a lot more important things going on."

"I can't let you go, Mallory."

"Chuck"—his name was Chuck and I'd known him for some time—"I'm not going to leave Los Angeles, if that's what you're worried about. There's going to be no room in the jails. It's going to be bedlam here in the courtrooms. You can trust me. I'll be back."

"It might mean my job. I can't let you go."

"I'll take full responsibility," I said.

He grabbed my arm again. "I have to put cuffs on you, Mallory."

I pushed him. He was a strong guy, but I had the leverage. And with that I ran toward the hallway behind the courtroom. It was like running through the forest in darkest night. Only the trees were moving and they were people. Back here in the hallway was where the judges and other court personnel moved. But they would not be able to use their private elevators, either. They'd be making for the stairs.

I fell in with some people moving that direction. It was going to be one big massive exodus. But I had to get out and into the street. For some reason I knew that's where I had to be.

But the sweating mass of humanity awaited us in the stairwell. I got pushed from behind and entered the traffic jam. It was like the 405 at rush hour when there's roadwork, too. Dark except for the lights of the phones and some miniature flashlights dangling from key chains. It was enough to illuminate faces around me, behind and in front. Everybody looking around to see who was who. Voices murmuring to colleagues all at the same time. And me stuck in the middle, slowly descending.

But there was something else going on. Imagine someone who had been lost at sea for thirty days, without food or water, drinking in the raindrops when they fell. Almost dead from lack of nutrition when rescued. And then he's dropped in the middle of a 7-Eleven warehouse. Every conceivable kind of snack food is suddenly around him. He would just start ripping open bags and throwing whatever he could into his mouth. He would feast until he burst and then he'd probably die anyway.

That is the picture of the recovering zombie suddenly thrust into a sea of humanity and stuck there.

I wanted to eat everyone. My body was telling me to chomp. My mouth was salivating. I was beginning to resemble those fake movie zombies that shuffle around grunting and acting like slobbering feeding machines.

I tried to fight it. I knew I needed help. I needed my recovery group. Anybody. Maybe I could call my sponsor, Sal. I fished around in my pocket and took out my phone. But there was no service. Everything was going to be overloaded.

Imagine a whole city unable to communicate. Now we would find out what we were made of.

I sure knew what everybody around me was made of. Flesh. I put my own fingers in my mouth and tried to stop the visions of brains dancing in my gullet.

I heard snippets of conversation as the human mass slowly headed down. People talking about earthquakes and emergency measures and getting home to family. There was even some laughter as a couple of jokers tried to keep things light by talking about a giant conspiracy to kill all the lawyers.

Ha ha.

And then someone, way down in the stairwell, shouted, "Fire!"

CHAPTER FORTY-ONE

LIKE A HORROR MOVIE AUDIENCE, the entrapped crowd screamed. And a stampede started the other way, back up toward the door I'd just come through.

People fell, got trampled. I got pushed. I yelled at everybody to slow down, but of course I was paid no more heed than a middle school hall monitor.

It was steaming, screaming, bad breathy, flailing pandemonium.

In front of me a woman fell. I stumbled over her and kneed her in the back.

That made me mad. I spun around and kicked out at the guy behind me. Got him right in the chest. It was a momentary respite from the push of humanity. I jumped up and grabbed the downed lady by the collar and dragged her upward. Luckily we were right at the open door, and I managed to get both of us out into the hallway.

It wasn't much of a relief as the frenzied masses ran back and forth crying out at their desperate plight.

The smell of acrid smoke wafted in.

The woman I'd grabbed was fighting for breath. She was middle-aged, puffy of face. Not dressed like a professional. I wondered if she was one of the court watchers who wander from courtroom to courtroom, looking for a juicy trial.

"Thank you," she said.

"You okay now?" I said.

She burst into tears. "I don't want to die. Please don't let me die here."

I gently patted her shoulder. "All right, hang on. I got no guarantees. We've just been through a major earthquake."

"Can you get me out of here?"

"Everybody in the world is trying to get out of this building," I said. "Best thing is to wait for rescue workers."

"Fire," she said.

"Don't panic. Panic doesn't get us out of here. Can you stand?"

"I think so."

I helped her up. She was hefty. She was ample. She was a week's worth of nutrition. She was also hurt. "My leg," she said. "I can't walk."

Great!

"Don't let me go," she said.

I propped her up against the wall. And tried to think.

We were trapped, no doubt about it. If there was a fire on a lower floor, it was going to be heading up. There were only three choices. Stay put, try to get down, or go all the way to the top of the building.

The middle option was out. We'd just tried it.

The first option meant the hope that some sort of rescue would be forthcoming, before we were completely engulfed in flames or choked by smoke.

I didn't like any of the options, frankly. But if I could get onto the roof, at least I'd be in the air and able to see what was going on.

Getting up on the roof would probably be just as hard as going the other way. But I sure was not in a sitting mood.

"I'm going to try to get up top," I said to the woman.

"Don't leave me."

"Look, there's not anything I can do for you," I said.

"Please!"

"Fine! Hold my arm and try to keep up with me."

She grabbed me and I pulled her into the hallway flow. She limped along, slow but at least steady.

THERE WAS A MAINTENANCE STAIRWELL AT THE END OF THE hall. That much I knew. I'd used it a couple of times when I was with the PD's office. You're friendly with enough of the staff around the courthouse, you get some inside information.

I took my limping companion down the hall. It was thinning out a little bit as people were going out to the courtrooms and interior hallways to try and figure out what to do. There were some people frozen in the corridor, a few on their knees in what looked like an attitude of prayer.

When I got to the end of the corridor I came to a locked door with a keypad. No one was attempting to get in. I wondered if the code was still the same. I have a memory for numbers, and this one came back to me as if I were just coming into the office for work a few years ago.

Bip bip bip bip.

The door clicked open. I hesitated. I didn't want a whole crowd shoving through immediately. That would get somebody trampled again. Then I opened the door and helped my large charge through.

"We have a ways to go upstairs," I said. "Can you make it?"

"I think so, if you'll help me."

"Well, I've got nothing else to do this afternoon. Come on."

Upward we went. A moment later I heard the door slam open and other people coming in. They started downward. I kept going up. Two flights. And then there was a shorter stairway up to another door. The roof access. I had never been out on the roof of the criminal courts building. No time like the present.

The rooftops of Los Angeles buildings are not romantic like the ones in New York. You're not going to find *West Side Story* up here. Instead of water towers, the CC building had some klieg lights, a couple of satellite dishes, and the typical outer workings of cooling and heating systems.

And it was darkness at noon. Heavy black clouds obscured the sun, and there was a palpable odor of smoke in the air.

The woman and I were not alone. Some others had made it up here, including a couple of the court security staff. They were motionless, looking outward. There were cracks on the surface of the roof. Some major.

"You better wait here," I said. "I don't want you falling."

"All right," she said. "May I know your name?"

"Mallory."

"Mine's Dina."

"Sit tight, Dina."

I carefully negotiated my way toward the south edge of the building.

And stopped in shock when I could see over it.

The world was in flames.

At least, my world was.

The majestic towers on Bunker Hill were sprouting fire from various levels. It was like 9/11 all over again, only this time it was six skyscrapers at once.

Closer, I could see the Times Building's classic facade, now a crumbled ruin along First Street.

The new police headquarters, engulfed in fire.

The streets were a mass of cracked asphalt hills.

Cars overturned. Bodies strewn.

Farther out, toward the ocean, fires bloomed like desert roses.

My own classic corridor, Broadway, looked like Beirut, circa 1985.

Eerie screams rose up from the streets all around us.

I took a quick scan of other views of the city. The same scene. From Chinatown to Union Station, from South Central to the San Gabriel Mountains, the place was barely recognizable amidst the fire and smoke and rubble.

But the biggest fire was just to the west of us. It took up an entire city block, because that was the footprint of the Cathedral of Our Lady of the Angels.

It was not just suffering from a few hot spots, no. It was completely, utterly covered in flames. The heat of it hit my face like the noon sun in summer.

Yet there was one building that did not, at least at first glance, seem to have any discernible damage. It stood pristine and content, and if a building could be said to have its chest thrust out, this would have been it. It was like it was announcing to the city that it was the one place to look to, the one place to trust.

I'm talking about City Hall.

More people joined us on the roof. Sirens were sounding all around the city. And then came the helicopters, a fleet of them. They appeared out of the south like a flock of geese, and spread. It was clearly a concerted effort. They were black, too, which would raise all sorts of conspiracy theories.

One of them flew close by and I could see the lettering on it. CITY angels, it said. It made a loop around the civic center, then hovered at our level. A voice boomed out of a speaker.

"Do not be alarmed," the voice said. "We will take you to safety in an orderly fashion."

"We're going to burn up!" a man shouted. He was in a suit, about sixty years old or so. He looked like one of the old-time lawyers who did daily business in court. He ran toward the ledge closest to the chopper.

"I repeat," said the voice. "Stay calm. You will be rescued."

"Get us out of here now!"

And then he slipped and fell, screaming, over the side of the building.

For a second it felt like there was a collective, shared stream of horror running through everyone on the roof.

The voice from the helicopter: "Stay where you are! We can all make it if the city sticks together! "

And I wondered, how had they managed to mobilize so fast? If there was someone who'd done the planning for contingencies surrounding the "big one," there ought to be a big bonus coming.

Bonus.

I thought, what if there was a bonus on the other side? What if this earthquake was not a natural disaster, but a man-made—no, demon-made—shaker?

Would that explain the fire that was consuming the cathedral? Were churches being torched?

Father Clemente!

I had to get to the Father.

Father...

My own father! He was in jail a stone's throw from here, at Central on Bauchet Street! Was that on fire? And if it was, were the inmates being cooked to death?

I went back to find Dina, but she had disappeared. Had she gone back down the stairs? Panicked? Fallen over the side?

The air filled with shrieks.

The building actually started to sway. Or rather, list. We were all at an angle now. Somebody once said that if you turned the world on its side, everything loose would land in Los Angeles. Now the building was tilting, and everybody was leaning toward one corner, the southwest.

I had to get out of here, but there was no way. I went to the stairwell and tried to open the door. No go. The stress to the building had caused the doorway to collapse on itself and the door would not open.

So it looked like we were stuck here waiting either for a helicopter to lift us off or for the building to completely collapse. I'm a zombie. I could survive, but what condition would my body be in?

But I wasn't going to wait to find out. I started scoping the top of the building, looking for some kind of escape route. Maybe there was something in the heating or cooling system. Like in those movies where a guy gets out crawling through the ducts.

Sure, like that was going to happen. But what other choice did I have?

232

I ATE THE SHERIFF

Smoke was choking me. It was like the whole city was sitting under a pile of volcanic ash. How far had this earthquake gone? If it was indeed something Satanic, maybe all of California was like this. Maybe the whole country.

Maybe this was the beginning of the big battle, Armageddon.

Or maybe it was just a freaking earthquake.

I scoured the roof looking for an escape. One of the cooling contraptions was loose. I pulled at it and it wouldn't budge. It had to be a fool's errand anyway. I wasn't going to go anywhere through any of these things.

Still I looked.

I worked my way up to the northeast corner. It was like being on the prow of a ship. But there was no access to anything remotely usable.

I cast a glance over toward Chinatown. There was smoke rising from the area where the Men's Central Jail is.

Dad.

"Get me out of here," I said aloud. Maybe it was a prayer.

A voice behind me said, "You got to look in the right places."

I turned around. Tucked into a fissure of an electrical access box was a large bat. Its wings were folded over it, but its beady little eyes looked at me and the rat face seemed to be smiling.

Could have been a vampire. Now I have defended vampires in court, and I am not a natural enemy. But I also know that demons like to appear in that form when they can. So I didn't know whether to trust this one or not.

"I'm waiting," the bat said.

"Say something else."

"You want I should tell you a joke?"

"Max!"

"You are expecting maybe Perry Como?"

I wanted to grab him and hug him. But then again, he was a bat and he had always been an owl before. I don't know about you, but I would rather hug an owl.

"You're wondering maybe about why I'm here?" he said.

"I thought you were dead."

"I am dead. I'm a spirit. But when they got me, they locked me up. You can lock a spirit up."

"Who locked you up?"

"Them. The bad guys. The demon forces. You know, they got a jail just for spirits like me?"

"How did you get out?"

"I escaped. Just like Steve McQueen."

I didn't have the heart to tell him that Steve McQueen didn't make it in *The Great Escape*.

"But why the bat?" I said.

His beady eyes went back and forth a couple of times. "I'm in disguise. I figure they're not going to take much notice of a bat. They got lots of bats on their side. Now do you want to stand here yakking or do you want to get off this sinking ship?"

"You know a way?"

"You think I'm just another pretty face? Why do you think I showed up?"

"All right, I'm ready."

Max slid out of the crack and spread his webby wings. He was one huge bat. His body was the size of a small boy. His wingspan must've been six feet. "Ah," he said. "That feels good."

An aftershock hit. The building listed even more. "You better work fast," I said. "Which way down?"

"Right over the side, baby."

At first I thought I didn't hear him right. But then he gestured with his bat head over the ledge.

I glanced over. There was nothing between me and the street but open air. I turned back to Max. "What are you talking about?"

"Grab my feet," he said. He extended one of his bat feet toward me. It was gnarly.

"You have got to be kidding," I said. "You think you're going to fly me to safety? How much do you weigh?"

"No fat jokes, thank you. We aren't going to fly anywhere. We're going to float. Down."

"Oh no."

"Just like Mary Pippins and her umbrella."

"Poppins."

"Whatever! You want to stay here? Is that what you're telling me, Tchotchke?"

This is what they call in the law the horns of a dilemma. Or you're damned if you do, and damned if you don't. Only I was damned already, so what did it matter?

"All right, my batty guardian," I said. "But remember, this body is the only one I have and I'd like to be able to keep walking around in it."

"Don't worry your pretty little head," Max said. "I'm getting good with these things." He flapped his wings.

"Getting good!"

"Let's go!" He winged up into the air and hovered.

I swallowed hard and grabbed his—do you call them ankles?—with each hand.

"You'll love the view," Max said, and with that we flew out into the open air.

And dropped like a stone.

It was about four floors of sheer downward direction before the momentum slowed. Max was straining to keep his wings expanded and filled. His little bat face was wincing with the effort.

"Oy!" Max shouted. "You put on weight or something?"

My arms felt like they might pull out of my sockets at any moment. My joints weren't the best anyway. But they held. And so did I.

We hit Temple Street like a hang glider and rider. It wasn't smooth. I let go of Max and flopped forward on the hard, broken asphalt. A big clump of broken street stuck me in the ribs.

But I was free of the criminal courts building.

Max came down next to me. "That landing reminds me of the time I bombed on *The Tonight Show*."

"I've got to get over to the jail," I said, getting to my feet.

But how?

Here at street level it was like the middle of giant junkyard after a hurricane. Cars upended and scattered like toys. People running around like rats. The flames and smoke of the Cathedral fire in the middle of it all.

Whatever direction I went it wasn't going to be easy walking. No smooth streets or sidewalks.

The sound of the chopper. It was almost directly above me. Then the voice: "Stay where you are! Do not attempt to move."

Was that a general directive? For some reason it sounded like it was being leveled at me.

I looked up and saw a guy in shades and a white helmet leaning out of the chopper. He pointed at me.

What? Focusing on little old me?

"The noise, yet!" Max said, reminding me I wasn't alone.

"Max, will you take a flyover and find me the best way to get to Bauchet Street?"

"You think I got a map with me or something?"

"It's over there." I pointed in the general direction. "Just over the freeway. I need to find out the best way. The jail may be on fire."

"But what for?"

"My father. He's in there!"

Max paused, then saluted with one of his wings. "I'm on the job."

Up he flew, heading toward the remnants of the freeway.

As a screaming fireball came right at me.

And then I realized it was a man.

THERE ARE CERTAIN SITUATIONS IT'S IMPOSSIBLE TO PREPARE for. A flaming person is one of them, and I mean that in the literal sense. This poor man, whoever he was, was shrieking for help.

My brain told me there was nothing that could be done. I had no way of putting out the fire. Unless I tried to smother it myself, with my own body, in which case I would become a Joan of Arc impersonator.

But with little time to think and feeling just so doggone sorry for this guy, who would probably die anyway, I let him run to me and got him down on the ground. I threw my body on top of him, covering my face with my hands. I rolled around and yes, it hurt. But I thought maybe I could make it, like somebody walking across hot coals. If I moved fast enough and steady enough back-and-forth, maybe I wouldn't get scorched in any one place.

It took me thirty seconds to put the flames out. At least that's what I estimated, I wasn't exactly keeping track. I had to pat out a few loose places on his legs and that's when I realized he was wearing a burned-out robe.

It was a priest.

I hoped that he had made his final confession. His face was a mass of burned flesh, hardly recognizable as a face. His eyeballs were gone. He was motionless on the ground except for spasmodic movements of his lips.

He was trying to say something. Just like in the movies. I felt like Jimmy Stewart in *The Man Who Knew Too Much*. I bent over so I could hear anything he might say.

All that came out was a deep, guttural groan.

"I'm listening," I said.

He groaned again, a little louder.

"Yes?" I said.

"Wit..."

"Wet?"

"Wit... nests..."

"Witness, yes. What do you need to say?"

I'll never know because he died at that moment.

WHERE WAS MAX?

How long did it take a bat to fly over a small area? All I had to know was how to get across the freeway.

I wasn't going to wait. I made my way down to Main Street.

I cut left and just decided to go for it. This was the straightest path to where I wanted to go. But as soon as I got to the 101 I ran into yellow police tape and a uniform telling me to stop.

He wore shades and his uniform was crisp. He was young, with short blond hair, emotionless features. "I'm heading over to the Plaza," I said.

"No one is allowed to go by," he said.

"Oh, really? Do you want to tell me why someone is stationed on the street at this location, with police tape yet?"

"Ma'am, if you'll just wait for the situation to settle down."

"Settle down? Look around you, man. I find it a little strange that you're concerned about one little access point to the other side of the freeway area. Who gave you these orders?"

"That's not your concern, ma'am. Please go back and find a secure place to wait for further instructions."

"Instructions from who?"

"The City Angels will help."

I looked past his shoulder and saw that the pavement of Main Street was certainly cracked but by no means inaccessible.

"You've done your job," I said. "I assume full responsibility." I started to walk past.

He grabbed my arm. "Go back the other way or I will place you under arrest."

I yanked my arm out of his grasp. "You're going to arrest me? With all this going on around you? For what? What are you hiding? You and the so-called City Angels?"

"Stay back or I will incapacitate you."

"You going to Tase me, bro?"

He said nothing.

I ran past him. I broke through the yellow tape.

A split second later he tackled me. Tackled me! We rolled around on the hard, cracked sidewalk for a few seconds until I managed to get to my feet. As he did. Now he put both hands on my shoulders and pushed me hard.

That's when Max made his return appearance. He started flapping his wings wildly in the cop's face. The cop waved his arms frantically, trying to beat him back.

Max looked at me and shouted, "Get going!"

I got going. As I crossed over the 101 I could see L.A.'s worst nightmare—the traffic jam—frozen now in permanent aspect. Cars like scattered Legos, smoke from fires rising. People wandering through the automotive graveyard like lost souls.

I made it over the freeway to Arcadia Street. The old Pico House, an L.A. landmark since the 1800s, was dust and remains now. The debris impeded my progress through the Plaza to Alameda and then over to the jail.

But just as I found a clear access, Max flew in front of me and kicked out with his feet. The sharp little talons impaled my head and sent me reeling.

"What are you doing?" I shouted, putting my hand on my forehead. A huge flap of skin came off in it. No. I was falling apart!

The crazy bat just flapped there, hovering.

"Say something!"

No reaction in his rodent eyes. Which is when I realized it wasn't Max. It was another bat of the same size.

"What is your name?" I demanded, positing that it was a demon. But instead of complying, the bat face just laughed. Out of its mouth came the sound of a madman, hysterical at something in his fevered brain.

"What is your name!"

The laughing face quieted down, and it said, "I have no name. It has not been given. Your demands are nothing. You are nothing. I am everything. I have won."

And then the bat laughed again.

For some reason, I recognized the voice. Or maybe not the voice so much as the cadence of the words. Where had I heard them before?

I looked around for a way to run. The Plaza was almost

deserted. There were two or three bodies lying motionless on the ground, and one on the bench.

That's when it hit me. I had encountered this bat before, but in human form. And right here in this spot.

"The sheriff," I muttered.

"You thought you would never see me again, didn't you?"

In astonished tones, I said, "You are now one of the wicked dead. The demon looking for a host."

"And on the winning side, too."

"This is it, isn't it? The big move. The devil's play date."

"All zombies will die and stay dead."

Now he was just making me mad. I remembered an incantation Father Clemente had taught me. "In the Name above all Names, be gone!"

Sheriff Geronimo Novakovich, bat demon, shrieked like a stuck pig (I have never heard a stuck pig squeal, and don't want to) and exploded. Black goo whapped me in the face.

The bat body was gone. Only the wings were left, lying on the ground like discarded kites.

The wicked dead spirit of the former sheriff of Los Angeles County was not apparently present. Probably off to look for a new host somewhere.

Which let me finally head over to the Men's Central Jail.

Inside the dark, stinking corridors I smelled the smoke and heard panicked screams. They echoed off the walls like sirens of death.

And one of them could have been my father.

I had no idea where he was in this steel hive. I knew he was a K-10, highest security, and that was on a top tier, near the roof.

How could I possibly get up there?

As I made my way down the first-floor corridor I saw flames shooting out of one of the locked doors at the end.

I confess now to you all, my first thought was not to save anyone. My first thought was barbecue. This would be a feast for a zombie, human flesh fried up nice and crisp. It was like an undead diner on the cooking channel.

Yes, that is what I thought and lusted after, and I'm no angel. I might have gone for it had I not heard someone scream, "Ms. Caine!"

It was coming from a lockup to the left, and a face pressed against the bars.

I recognized him. Andrew Panama. I'd defended him when I was with the PD's office.

I ran to him.

"Get me out!" he said. "They took off."

"Who took off?"

"The deputy sheriffs. Leaving us to die!" Andrew's thirty-year-old eyes were big as fists.

"I haven't got access," I said.

"Do something! It's all goin' down!"

"What is?"

"The devil, the city, he's gathering the troops!"

"Wait here," I said to Andrew, then realized what a completely idiotic statement that was. But I didn't know what I was going to do except that it had to be more than standing here waiting for the flames to engulf us.

I went back the way I'd come. The deputies had a small office just off the front desk. The door was open. Inside were a couple of monitors showing rotating camera feeds from all tiers.

It was a smoking, horrid scene.

Men, sometimes five to a cell, were pressed against the bars, flailing, mouths open and eyes wild.

But there were just as many cells, maybe even more, that were open and empty.

I looked at a console full of buttons and switches. I doubted I could do anything from here, as each tier had its own control bay.

But I didn't even get the chance to try.

"Hold it!"

I turned around to find a female deputy, her sidearm drawn and pointed at me.

"Help me," I said.

"On the floor," she said.

"Listen to me carefully—"

"On the floor!"

"I want you to forget everything you think you know about your job right now. There are things happening in the city that would melt your hair. You've got to listen to me."

"This is my last warning."

"Listen to me!"

"I'm going to shoot you!"

"Fine! Do it! And you're going to buy me a new suit after this! Fire at me already!"

She didn't do a thing. Her hands shook. The gun wobbled.

I stepped closer to her. "Will this help you? You want to fire now?"

Her eyes betrayed a fear she had never known before. I reached my hand out and gently pressed the gun down. She didn't fight me. "My name is Mallory Caine, I'm a lawyer. I'm also a zombie. I could eat you right now. In fact I want to eat you right now. But I'm not going to do it. Because my father is in here and he's going to be burned up. Every incarcerated individual here is in danger of being consumed by fire. You are the one who is responsible for this. So I'm telling you right now, open up every cell door."

She started breathing fast. "I don't have that authority."

"You are the only authority here now. Can you hear them screaming?"

A deaf person could have heard them screaming. She looked at me and said, "Oh, my God."

"Exactly. Do it now. Please."

It took her three tries to holster her weapon. She moved to the main console and her fingers hovered over the keyboard. She wiggled them like a piano player getting ready to play. And then she started pressing buttons. "Dear God, I'm letting out killers."

"You're saving lives."

"But they're going to be unleashed on the city."

"The city is in total chaos right now. It's better than letting these people die. Are you done yet?"

"Almost." She pressed and typed and watched the monitor. After an interminable two minutes she said, finally, "It's done."

That's when I heard the sound of feet and voices heading our way.

"Give me your gun," I said to the deputy.

"I can't do that."

"I know. And I'm sorry for what I have to do." I smacked her in the jaw with a right cross. It didn't knock her out entirely, but stunned her enough that I could push her down on the floor and take her weapon away. Poor thing. This was not the duty she'd signed up for.

I charged out into the lobby.

The first of the thundering herd came through the access door. They were a mix of black, Latino, Asian, and white. Major crime in Los Angeles knows no color barrier.

I put my hand up and said, "Stop! You have to hear this!"

I was met with a few choice epithets. So I fired one shot into the ceiling. That got their attention. "Line up behind the desk," I said.

A crazy woman with a gun is something gangbangers and most men in general do not have much experience with. And if she can put on a horrific look like I am capable of, it makes for a pretty persuasive moment.

One of the faces recognized me. And I recognized him. It was Carlos "El Cuello" Herrera. A very big and very bad dude I repped once. I had gotten him a deal that kept him out of state prison so he could be with his girlfriend and daughter. I knew it would only be a matter of time before he was back in here, and lo and behold here he was.

"Hey, Ms. Caine," he shouted. "What's going on here?"

"Carlos, come over here."

One thing I knew about Carlos was that he would be one of the guys who commanded respect in the joint. He had prison muscles and a huge head that sat on a neck as thick as a freeway pylon.

He separated himself from the rabble.

"I need you to help me keep these people under control. I just need a couple of minutes."

"This place is on fire."

"Not out here. Not yet. Go throw some muscle around and get them lined up and quiet."

Carlos knew exactly what to do. He got some of his own boys and passed along my instructions.

I kept looking for my father's face. If he didn't make it out in time I didn't know that I'd ever be able to forgive myself. I had done all I could, but I wondered if it was enough.

Carlos and his guys did a great job. It didn't take long for the whole area to be filled with what I can only euphemistically call a captive audience.

Still no sign of my father. I wanted to run to him myself, but I knew the flames would be such now that it would be useless. I had responsibility for an overwhelming number of criminals who were anxious to run out of the place.

"All right, listen to me," I said. "There has been a major earthquake in Los Angeles. Everything is out of control out there. And I know exactly what you're thinking. It's looting time. Well, I'm here to tell you there is a lot more going on than you know. This is biblical proportions stuff. This is heaven versus hell, and there are demons and bats and all manner of creature out there. You are getting a reprieve. I'm a lawyer and I've represented some of you. I'm telling you right now don't blow this. Go find your families and friends. But leave everybody else alone. I don't expect all of you to follow my advice. But if I ever do find out that you've been involved in massive criminal activity, I'm going to forget that I'm a defense lawyer. I'm going to remember that I'm a zombie and I'm going to hunt you down and I'm going to eat you. Do you hear that? I will eat you. If anyone does not believe me let him come forward now and I'll eat him right here. Have I made myself understood?"

There were no answers but more than a few confused looks.

I fired another shot into the ceiling. "I said, do I make myself clear?"

Now I got some nods. That was about all I could expect under the circumstances.

"Now that we understand each other, I will let you go through these doors. What I suggest is that you go find some way to help people. There are injured people, scared people, confused people. Go do some good for once in your life. You know what? That is going to make a difference to the man upstairs." I pointed a finger in the air. I could hardly believe I was doing that. "Now get out of here."

They didn't need to be told twice. They started running and jostling out the front doors of the Men's Central Jail.

I watched them go. Carlos came over and shook my hand and said, "I'll try to do better this time."

I nodded at him and he was gone.

They streamed by like obedient schoolboys. It was probably the first time they'd ever looked like that. Where was my dad?

When the last of them had gone I gave up hope. I could feel heat from the flames now. The fire was heading toward me.

Meanwhile the deputy sheriff had staggered out of the security office. Her face was completely white, drained of blood. She was going to have one hell of a case of PTSD. I took the magazine clip out of the gun so she wouldn't hurt herself. I placed the gun in her holster. She didn't fight me. I said, "Go outside and do what you can to help somebody."

I took her by the shoulders and pointed toward the doors and gave her a little push.

Then I heard a voice say, "Mallory."

"Dad!"

He was flat on his back behind the front desk. Being one of the older guys, maybe the oldest, he'd been left behind under the trampling feet of self-interest. I helped him sit up.

"Are you okay?" I asked.

"I've been better. I have a shoe print on my chest."

"Can you stand up?"

He grabbed my blouse the way a thug might grab somebody he was shaking down for money. "Listen to me. The words you said. I heard them."

"What are you talking about?"

"What you just told those people. Told them not to commit any crimes. Told them to be good. Told them about the man upstairs. I heard you say all that. I had a vision last night. There is a reason."

"We haven't got time to discuss your visions, Pop. We've got to get out of here."

"No. This is the important time. This is the moment. You have to do something."

"What do I have to do?"

"I don't know!"

"That's not helping me a lot here, Dad."

"The vision stopped. All I know is that out there is something for you to do and it will mean the survival of the human race or the death of it."

Oh, thank you. No pressure at all.

I helped him to his feet. "Dad, listen, let's get out of here and find a place to regroup."

"No time! He is coming!"

I led him outside into the dark smoky air of Los Angeles under siege.

CHAPTER FORTY-TWO

"HEAD FOR THE LIGHT!" my father shouted.

"What light?" I said.

"*The* light."

My poor father was still caught up in some religious enthusiasm. In truth he had never been quite right since he wandered out of Mexico many years ago after his sojourn there.

And yet he kept seeing things that made sense later on. He predicted the future. And he said he had heard my words before I said them. I don't think he was lying about that. One thing my father didn't do was concoct stories. He had enough of them in his head already.

I put my arm around his shoulder and said, "Let's just go on together and we'll make our way."

"We have got to get to the light."

"Sure, Pop."

Another voice said, "He's right."

It was Max, flapping around our heads.

My father screamed and started waving his arms. "Devil bat!"

"No, Dad, I know him."

"Evil!"

Max said, "He must have seen my act when I was alive."

"It talks!"

"Everybody calm down!" I said. "Max, what's happening in the city?"

"Boy, it's a madhouse like you wouldn't believe. But your old man is right. You're supposed to be somewhere where there is light."

"What does that even mean? And who is telling you all this?"

Just then a beam of brightness flashed in front of us. A ball of silver flame descended about twenty yards away. I had to close my eyes.

Then a voice said, "This is the way you must go." The voice sounded vaguely familiar. I peeked a little bit and saw that the brightness had died down, leaving the form of a woman in brilliant white robes standing there. I knew this woman. I had just met her. "Dina?"

"Follow me," she said.

"What the heck? What are you?"

"An angel, Tchotchke," Max said.

Dina said, "You have one more test."

"I don't want a test!"

"Tough," Dina said.

DINA LED US THROUGH CHINATOWN, WHICH HAD MANAGED TO find repose. We could hear sirens and choppers and screaming and yelling and the crunching of buildings as bits and pieces dropped from rooftops and windows.

The way was not smooth. We had to keep stepping over detritus and chunks of road and broken items of every sort. There were giant holes in the streets. A dirty little secret about our Los Angeles infrastructure is that it's a lot of infra and not much structure. The roads are in terrible condition, and the city doesn't have enough money to patch them up. Sinkholes are a real problem. I even saw a Mini Cooper halfway down a giant hole in the road, its little rear end stuck up in pitiful surrender.

"Where are we going?" I asked Dina finally. She was floating in front of us, which I guess is an angel's privilege. She didn't answer, but motioned with her arm.

We gradually made our way back along Broadway and across the freeway to Temple Street, then cut over to Grand. The Disney Hall, which looked like a bunch of bent aluminum siding anyway, didn't seem any different. But the sidewalk and street all around it was cracked.

To the left I saw City Hall, still looking pristine.

We were now at the top of Bunker Hill. All around we could see the damage the earthquake had wrought.

I even saw the poor cars of Angels Flight lying on their backs on Hill Street like dead turtles. That was the unkindest cut of all. The symbol of our community, one of the oldest and most enduring in all of Los Angeles, now upended and useless.

We started on the downgrade of Grand, heading toward Fifth Street, where the central branch of the Los Angeles Public Library was. Across the street from the library was the tallest building in Los Angeles, the US Bank Tower. I had to wonder how damaged it was. But it looked pretty solid, its majestic cylindrical form shooting upward and disappearing into the clouds.

Then Dina stopped us. "In there you must go," she said, pointing at the Bank Tower.

"What? In that building?"

She nodded.

"But what about all the damage?"

"You will find the way."

"I don't want to find anything. Maybe somebody can just show me."

Max said, "Show? Show more respect."

"Now listen, everybody," I said. "I've been trying to be a good soldier here, been trying to listen and follow all those things you're talking about. But I'm tired of not knowing exactly what role I am playing in this whole mess. What is it I am supposed to do? Just come out and tell me for crying out loud. Then maybe I can do it."

Nobody in our little group said anything. And I was just about to issue another rant when I heard a boy shout my name.

I looked behind me and saw Jaime at the top of Bunker Hill.

CHAPTER FORTY-THREE

WHAT WAS HE DOING HERE? How had he gotten downtown? I couldn't know, but Father Clemente was with him, and that was enough for me.

"I have to go to him," I said to Dina.

"No!" my father said. "Into the building! Into the light!"

Dina told him, "Let her go."

That was all the inducement I needed. I started back up Grand, which is not an easy way to go. It's steep. But I knew I had to be with Jaime and somehow felt like this was part of whatever plan was unfolding in front of my eyes.

But before I reached the top of Bunker Hill one of those City Angel choppers swooped out of the smoke like a predatory pterodactyl. It made a quick circle above the heads of Father Clemente and Jaime. They both looked up.

A rope dropped out of the chopper and immediately a black-clad and helmeted man jumped out and lowered himself to the sidewalk. It happened in a flash. He kicked Father Clemente in the chest. The old priest went down.

The City Angel intruder put a hood over Jaime's head and pulled a cord that tightened it. I heard Jaime's muffled scream and saw the hood expand. Then another scream. I can only surmise that Jaime had breathed fire, but that his captor was prepared for that. The hood was fire resistant. The rope started pulling the man, who had Jaime in his left arm, upward.

I opened my mouth to shout, but what came out was not words but flame.

Concentrated flame, and it hit the chopper rope at midpoint. The rope snapped and man and boy fell to the ground. The man on his back, Jaime on top of the man. The man was stunned. Jaime got to his feet and pulled the hood off his head.

"Mallory!" he screamed.

He ran toward me and I toward him. We met in the middle of the street and he threw himself into my arms.

"I've got you," I said.

It was the last thing he heard before his little body, and mine, were riddled with bullets from above.

CHAPTER FORTY-FOUR

IT WASN'T WHITE.

It was blue.

The color of sky but deeper than sky.

There were no clouds.

There was no noise. No sound of any kind.

Jaime.

I looked around but saw nothing, just more blue.

Had I been blinded? Deafened?

I tried to move but could not, yet felt as if I were running.

It was like a dream.

And just as in a dream you cannot always speak, I tried to cry out for Jaime, but no sound came out of my mouth.

Was I dead?

But I couldn't be dead. I was a zombie. I had not been killed the zombie way.

I tried to look at my body to see if there were bullet holes in it.

My body was a faint blur. What was I? An ink blot?

Jaime! He was real, and he could not have survived what had hit him.

I wanted revenge. I wanted to kill every one of them. Comfort hit me. I shoved it away. It hit me again, overwhelmed me. Not light, not a voice . . .just comfort. As if I had been given a drug.

Was this to be eternity for me? Maybe I was in some place that was between heaven and hell, a place where creatures like me go. Can't get into the good place, somehow saved from the bad.

Comfort once more. Like I had intravenous tranquility in my arm that pumped every minute.

That wasn't so bad. Could I be serene forever?

I'd like to have some books. It would be nice to read some books.

Jaime.

Dear God, let him go to heaven. Let there be a heaven. And let there be a hell for all the scum that kill little kids.

Comfort.

Words.

Words in my head, not from an audible voice but some deep sense of knowing.

Now when they have finished their testimony, the beast that comes up from the Abyss will attack them, and overpower and kill them. Their bodies will lie in the street of the great city . . .

A voiceless voice.

Who was it?

Where was it?

For three and a half days men from every people, tribe, language and nation will gaze on their bodies and refuse them burial. The inhabitants of the earth will gloat over them and will celebrate by sending each other gifts, because these two prophets had tormented those who live on the earth.

Yes. Father Clemente, he had read this to me once.

But after the three and a half days a breath of life from God entered them, and they stood on their feet, and terror struck those who saw them.

I wanted to say something. I wanted to see something. I wanted to go back.

CHAPTER FORTY-FIVE

"YOU'RE BACK."

I opened my eyes.

And saw Father Clemente.

"What?" I said.

He helped me to a sitting position.

The smell of the room was palpable, telling me I had indeed returned to my former reality. I was on the floor of what looked like had been, at one time, an expensive office.

"Where am I?" I said.

"The fifty-ninth floor." He took my hands, got me to my feet. My legs were paper. Father Clemente helped me to the window, the glass of which was shattered. "I want you to see," he said.

"See what?"

"What's coming."

The view was to the north. What had been a wasteland now looked at least like a boxer rising from the canvas. There was street activity, some vehicles moving, and something more, the most astounding thing of all. From every direction crowds of people were on the move, toward City Hall. A sea of them pooled around the base and outward, waves of humanity.

"What's happening?" I said.

"You've been gone," Father Clemente said. "Three days."

"Three?"

"The mayor has called for a noon press conference. He wants as many people as he can have downtown, to hear it live. He wants a show of popular support. For the city and the world. I suspect this is it."

Voice still thick, I said, "This is what?"

"The beginning. Of the end. The final battle." Final battle? I rubbed my head.

Three days? No wonder I was weak.

"Jaime," I said. I grabbed Father Clemente's robes. "Where is Jaime? What have they done—"

The old priest gently took my wrists and lowered my arms. His face shone kindness and calm. "It's all right, Mallory. He's in the other room."

"Dead?"

"Alive."

"But how?"

"The two witnesses shall rise."

A wind whipped through the broken window glass. It touched my cheek like a cold hand.

Father Clemente said, "You and Jaime both were dead on the street."

"But I couldn't. You can't kill me with bullets."

"I can only report what my eyes saw. And the whole world saw. There were cameras—"

"Then how did I get up here? And Jaime?"

He put a hand on my shoulder. "You have friends. Your friends got you here. We have been fighting off the City Angels. They've been trying to find you."

I put my hands in the air and waved them around. "Wait, wait. What friends are you talking about?"

"They have gathered downstairs. They have made camp. And they seem to be dressed in jail clothes. They're waiting for you."

"To do what?"

"Lead them."

The sound of a squeaky door opening hit my ears. Then I realized it was a sigh coming out of me. "Father, I don't want to lead anything or anybody. I'm getting out of here. I'm going to take Jaime and his mother and go someplace where we can be left alone. I've had it. I've had it with the cosmic battle and the people of this city just blindly following the mayor. They are the real zombies, did you ever think about that? They are the ones who are dead, from the neck up. Let them have this place, then. If they're going to go along with City Hall—"

"But why should they? They need someone to convince them otherwise. Someone who knows how to deliver a closing argument."

I said nothing.

"They will see you alive after they've seen you dead. That's the whole point! You have been given a witness unlike any other the world has ever known."

I started to say something, then heard a squeal. Jaime had pushed through the door and was running to me. Alive and running! He grabbed my waist and I wrapped my arms around him. We stayed that way for a long moment, then I stepped back to look at him. His body was not marred. He was in every way a healthy kid again.

"Will you at least see them?" Father Clemente said. "Your friends?"

We took the stairs. A lot of stairs.

THEY HAD TAKEN OVER THE SECOND FLOOR. AND KNOCKED down the walls to make the whole level one big room.

There were dozens of jail inmates there. My father and Carlos Herrera stood among them, and it was my father who told everyone to quiet down when I stepped in with Father Clemente. Jaime was on my left, holding my hand.

Nick was there. And somehow he had gotten hold of a fedora, one that was a bit too big for his head.

"You look like a million bucks, doll!" he said.

"Hubba hubba," I said.

On the other side of the room were a whole bunch of people I didn't recognize. Except for one face, the friendly-looking game show host kind. Pat Sajak smiled and came to me. "I just want you to know," he said, "that we're with you."

I said, "All these people are your, um, pack?"

"From Malibu to you by way of the zoo," he said. "We're here to fight. This is our town, too. Just because we howl at the moon on occasion and tear a few people up doesn't mean we don't have feelings. Consider us your security force. Which reminds me."

Pat Sajak turned and snapped his fingers. From the back of his pack a commotion erupted as two men brought forth a third, this one gagged with a rope around his upper body.

It took me a second to recognize their prisoner.

Steve Ravener.

He struggled and moaned in the grip of the two men. They brought him to me as if I were some queen with the power of life and death.

"What do you want us to do with him?" Pat Sajak said.

"I don't get it," I said.

"Why is this man bound?" Father Clemente said.

"He's the guy," Pat Sajak said. "The guy who left you all alone in court." He looked at Steve. "Do you want to tell her, or should I?"

Muffled protests issued from Steve's gagged mouth.

"Do you want to buy a vowel?" Pat Sajak said.

Steve stopped struggling. His eyes met mine and I saw in them fear and regret.

"Let him tell me," I said.

Pat Sajak nodded and one of his men unwrapped the gag.

Steve let out a huge breath. His chest heaved. He dropped his gaze to the floor.

"So go on," Pat Sajak said.

He didn't have to. "It was you," I said. "You killed the deputy."

For a moment Steve didn't move. Then he nodded, once.

"Why?" I said. "How?"

"Tell her," Sajak said.

"She won't believe me," Steve said.

"Try me," I said.

He took a breath, then said, "Okay, you're the lawyer. You're the one who can tell if a witness is lying. Look me in the face. This is how it was. I was watching out for you, following you. Wanting you. Okay, I was obsessed."

"Wolves get that way," Pat Sajak added. "It's a hazard."

"It wasn't like that!" Steve said. "I wanted just to be with you. It was night and I went to your place, but you didn't answer. I walked to your office. It was night. And it was open. I went up. I went in. And saw the blood. All the blood! And you on the floor, and the mangled flesh."

He stopped, looking like he had to gather strength.

"And all that blood did something to me. It wolfed me. I started turning. Just as that deputy came in. He went for his gun and I went for him. I got him first. I got all over him. I tore him up. And then I got out of there."

"And left her holding the bag," Pat Sajak said. "We ought to put you in a trap."

"No," I said to Sajak. "Let him loose."

"What? Why?"

I said, "There are more important things than revenge right now."

Father Clemente said, "Does that mean you'll do it? You'll lead us?"

"I didn't say that," I said. "Don't put words in my mouth. The only thing I want in my mouth is—" I stopped before I said *brains*.

Pat said, "We've been scouring the fast food joints around here. There may still be sandwich makings in the Subway around the corner."

I didn't have the heart to tell him what I needed was human flesh.

At least I thought I did.

I found myself looking at the people in the room, wondering which ones have the most advanced education. I thought maybe Pat Sajak himself should be the one. After all, he was witty. You have to be smart to be witty. I looked at his impish face and thought about extracting his brain. But when I did a strange thing happened. I got nauseous. The thought of a human brain was making me sick.

But my mouth was salivating.

What? How?

Quickly I said, "Yes. Get me a sandwich. Some kind of meat, and put everything else on it."

Pat Sajak smiled and shouted, "Make it so!"

"Let me get it," Steve said.

I nodded yes, as if I were in charge.

Sajak said, "Are you sure?"

"I'm sure," I said.

He looked at Steve. "The category is Food and Sandwiches. Understood?"

Steve nodded. Sajak signaled his guys to release Steve, who immediately ran for the stairs.

"You'll never see him again," Pat Sajak said.

"I think you're wrong," I said.

And then we heard fireworks.

CHAPTER FORTY-SIX

WE CROWDED at the window and saw pyrotechnics popping in the sky. Though we couldn't see City Hall from this vantage point, at the bottom of Bunker Hill, they certainly seemed to be coming from that direction.

Father Clemente said, "That's the beginning. The mayor is calling for attention. We haven't got much time."

"Time for what?" I said.

"For you. To speak at the top of Grand. You'll look right over the Metro plaza and have a full on shot at the crowd."

"Hold on," I said. "First of all, no one will hear somebody speaking up there."

"That's being taken care of. Look over here." Father Clemente pointed down toward Fifth Street. A blue van with skull, cross-bones and a caricature of Johnny Depp on it was parked at the corner. I knew that van. It was Sal's van, his band's wheels. He was sitting in the driver's side and looked up at me looking down at him. He gave me the thumbs up sign.

"He's got a speaker in the back of his van," Father Clemente said.

"But I haven't prepared anything. What am I supposed to say?"

The priest took both of my shoulders in his hands and said,

"You must tell them to choose. And you must tell them why they should choose the side of good over evil."

"But what's the offer?" I said.

"Speak the truth. The truth is its own offer. And then it is up to them. It will be their call."

"And if they refuse?"

"The devil wants to gather as many as he can. You must snatch as many as you can away from him."

I said, "Look, Father, the devil is your business, not mine. I've told you that before—"

"Look," someone said.

I glanced back down to the street and saw a dozen or so people dressed in strange white togs. No, not togs—togas. They were marching lockstep like ducklings down the middle of Fifth Street, heading east.

I only had a moment to see, but in that moment I fully understood. The head of the ducklings was Gig Shivley. I knew that because, right behind him was the unmistakable bulk of that security guard of his, the one they called Laertes.

And at the tail end of the line, moving like one of the walking dead herself, was my mother.

"Mom!" I shouted, but my voice seemed to fall to the ground with an ineffective thud. She was too far away. I wanted to grab something, a chair or a chunk of concrete, run down there and clock Shivley and take my mother away from him.

But I realized she would have to choose to get away from him. Because that's what this was about. The city was full of people like my mother—the walking dead, like zombies, only not the flesh eating kind but the kind that gave up their minds willingly to others, listened to hucksters and demons and lies.

There was a single shard of broken glass at the window, sticking up like a sword point I kick-punched it with the heel of my shoe.

When I turned back to face the group of second-floor mavericks, my face must have done the talking for me.

"We'll clear a path for you," Pat Sajak said.

With Jaime, Father Clemente and my own father beside me, I marched to the stairwell and down to the first floor, surrounded by the rag-taggiest looking group of rebels the city had ever seen. And that's saying something.

As soon as we came out onto Fifth Street, Steve appeared with a sandwich.

"What's going on?" he said.

"Just follow," I said. I grabbed the sandwich and took a huge bite. Oh, sweet taste! Salami and pepperoni, onions and mustard, lettuce and tomatoes. I could taste them in all their savory glory!

It was all I could do not to stop and wolf it down. Instead I cried up at the sky with something that must've sounded like *Thank God.* Because I'm sure that's what I said even with my mouth full.

We got to Grand and started up the hill.

Sal was already gunning his van toward the top. The street was relatively quiet, the center of activity being a quarter mile to the east. Up we went, toward Disney Hall and the Music Center. Up to where I would make the most important closing argument of my life.

It was a scene all right.

The corridor that runs from Grand to Spring Street was overflowing with people. It was like the Washington mall when Martin Luther King spoke. It was Central Park with Simon & Garfunkel, or Rod Stewart at Copacabana Beach.

It was a cross-section of Los Angeles, not spread out into various 'burbs, but together for once, centrally located. Along First Street was a line of news vans. Nothing like that even for my trial, or other celebrity roasts in the criminal courts building.

We were elevated, and while there were gawkers up there with us, we had room to spread out.

And Sal was there, ready for the moment. The back of his van was opened and a speaker that filled the entire opening was pointed outward toward the mall.

Sal had his guitar strapped on and he was smiling. "I always wanted to do this," he said, "just like Michael J. Fox at the beginning of *Back to the Future*."

"It's time, then," I said. "Give 'em a few licks of Purple Haze."

"Classic!" Sal plugged in his guitar and flipped a switch on the speaker, turned a knob. I heard a loud hum, like the buzzing of a million bees.

With a look of pure ecstasy Sal laid some Hendrix on the assembled multitudes.

I could almost feel the sound waves as they rumbled toward City Hall.

Thousands of heads turned toward us.

Roving news camera crews trained their video eyes our way.

They were covered with Purple Haze.

And then Sal stopped cold, reached for a handheld mike at his feet, and tossed it to me.

"Go," he said.

CHAPTER FORTY-SEVEN

"CITIZENS OF LOS ANGELES, thank you for your kind attention! This is Mallory Caine, someone you all thought was the only good kind of lawyer, a dead one. But as you can see and hear, I am not dead. And I haven't much time to speak. So listen carefully.

"You are about to be lied to by the mayor of Los Angeles. He is going to tell you that you must pledge your allegiance to City Hall and all will be well. In fact, you will be giving away your souls. Listen to me, because I almost gave away mine. I almost gave it away because I refused to take a side. I refused to choose between good and evil. And that is the only choice you have now. This is a battle no one can sit out. Your choice will determine the future of Los Angeles, and maybe even the whole world. Because it is the devil himself who demands your allegiance."

I paused to look down at the people. It sure seemed as if I had their attention. I tried to picture myself in front of a jury. I could do this.

But before I spoke again something caught my eye to the left, coming from Temple Street. It was an advancing army in full trot. Black clad, like an LAPD riot line, only not LAPD.

"City Angels," Father Clemente said.

Charging like Spartans.

So it would come down to force after all. No real chance for anyone to think for themselves, or choose without coercion.

But then, out of the sky came a strange and wonderful sight. A swarm of bats raining down on the heads of the City Angels.

Max! It had to be, along with all of his guardian friends.

Down they came, flapping and pecking like one of Alfred Hitchcock's nightmares.

The riot squad flailed at them with batons.

"Keep talking!" Father Clemente said.

I raised the microphone. "Do you see that, people? You cannot be crushed if you stand together and fight. Do you want this city to be your home again? We have been too long at the mercy of City Hall, which is in the hands of a man who has sold his soul. Stand up to them!"

From just below me came a shout, a man's voice that was louder than any human voice I'd ever heard unamplified.

"She's lying!" he said.

I knew that voice.

Aaron. Only when I looked it wasn't the Aaron I knew from law school or the courtroom or from within my embrace.

This Aaron was about fifteen feet tall, a monster Aaron from a 1950s sci-fi movie.

And he was growing.

Now we definitely had the attention of the people of Los Angeles.

Even more so for the ensuing onrush of dark clouds. No, not clouds. Forms. Wraiths wrought of black paint and smoke. And howling like a choir screaming discordant music.

Out of the sky they came and swirled around the increasing Aaron Argula. When I saw one form shaped like a woman with snakes wrapped around her, I knew what these were. The demon-gods I'd faced before. Lilith and Dagon and Marduk and who knew what other tin-pot deities.

Still Aaron grew.

Until he was face-to-face with me, only his face was the size of a house. I couldn't help myself. I thought of Mr. Stay Puft, the giant marshmallow man from the end of *Ghostbusters*.

And took courage from that.

Mr. Giant Head Aaron glared at me, the demonic forms swirling around his head like swallows returning to Capistrano.

Then his lips parted and his giant white teeth bared.

"You can't win, Mallory!" Aaron boomed.

"I could always beat you in court," I said. "I'll beat you now."

He threw back his gargantuan head and laughed to the sky. And then began to change. From Aaron Argula, lawyer, to a pillar of flame, a swirling tornado of fire.

The blast from the heat knocked me backward.

I went sprawling on the asphalt, splayed, looking up.

The Aaron-conflagration widened and thickened and formed a clamshell of fire, like the amphitheater at the Hollywood Bowl.

It would be enough to cover the entire street and burn up everything on it, including me and everyone else at the top of Bunker Hill.

And down it started to fall.

Which is when another river of flame shot upward. I looked right and saw it was Jaime, his face clenched in effort. He was literally fighting fire with fire to protect me.

His oral inferno was like a fire hose aimed at an ocean wave. I spat fire, too, trying to help.

Within the roar of the Aaron-blaze I heard another peal of laughter.

And then I heard something else.

IT WAS SINGING. IT WAS SINGING FULL-THROATED AND ROUSING. It was coming from Disney Hall, and out of the Music Center, and down Grand.

Rolling, I cast a glance and saw a blue-robed choir on the Disney steps. They were swaying and busting a gospel song, and there was Reverend Hightower right front and center.

I heard words, the words clear and clean and, best of all, loud.

Ole Satan is mad and I am glad,
   Ain't got tired yet!
   Missed a soul he thought he had,
   And ain't got tired yet!

The fire above me, a sky of orange and black, hovered like a zeppelin.

Oh, been in the war so long, so long
   Ain't got tired yet!

Dozens and dozens of singers, waves of them pouring over steps and curbs, in choir robes of blue or burgundy or gold, they were marching forward like a mighty army.

They kept coming. The dozens became hundreds. From every direction, some in robes, some in street clothes. Men and women and children, all lifting voices in song.

My knees acquainted with the hillside clay!
   Ain't got tired yet!

And then the voices were nearly drowned out by the loudest, craziest, most nightmarish scream I or anyone this side of hell has ever heard. It was issued from out of the fire, and as soon as its first pitched wail had thumped the street, the flames funneled backward, downward, like a pillow case being sucked into an industrial strength vacuum cleaner.

And just as a second before the sky had been hot and fiery, it was now clear and blue. And cool.

And still that choir sang.

Feet placed on the rock of eternity.
   Ain't got tired yet!

Jaime and Father Clemente and a host of my band were scattered on the street. We all clambered to our feet, like shipwreck victims dragging themselves onshore.

My Dad was one. Our eyes met and he smiled.

For some reason I ran my right hand along my left arm. Maybe just to feel if I was still there. The skin was smooth, smoother than it had been in two years.

No, more than that. Regenerated.

Human.

Real.

The singing reached a crescendo, like a melodious thunderclap.

I wanted to cry. I wanted to shout

My face. My cheeks. My hair.

Restored.

And then the singing stopped, and the crowd erupted in spontaneous applause. They cheered and whistled.

I heard a flapping. A large bat was at my side. I nearly belted it with my fist.

But Max, in his unmistakable voice, said, "You really got their attention now, Tchotchke. Talk to them."

"Max! I'm ... look at me!"

"You look marvelous. And now that we got that out of the way, talk to the people!"

"But how do I top what just happened?" I said.

He flapped himself higher, just above my head. "As my agent, Morty Scheinbaum, used to say, You don't got to top it, kid. You just gotta keep 'em from leaving the theater. Go!"

And so I did. For five, ten minutes I talked, something like that. I only stopped when the LAPD cruiser, sirens blaring, screeched from around the corner of Temple Street and headed for me.

CHAPTER FORTY-EIGHT

IT CAME to a stop with a skid mark.

From the driver side stepped a uniformed officer.

From the passenger side came Detective Mark Strobert.

"What's going on?" I said.

"You are," he said. "It's a full-on takeover of City Hall. They don't want the mayor. They want you."

"Who does?"

"The whole crowd," Strobert said. "They dragged the mayor off the steps, away from the microphones."

"You didn't stop it?"

He half smiled. "I guess I didn't. But they're shouting your name down there. I'm here to take you."

"Serious?"

He said, "I don't know what just happened up here, but I have a feeling you can tell me. I want you to tell me. After you talk to the people."

I looked over at Father Clemente.

"Go, Mallory," he said.

Without another word I got in the back of the police car. The officer and Strobert got in and we started to ride. Back to Temple, then down toward Spring, passing the old Hall of Justice, long abandoned, but still standing even after all the events of the past days. Still standing. Like the city itself.

I didn't know what the future held for Los Angeles. Who could? It was going to be up to the people. That's what I would tell them. And if enough of them believed me, maybe we could keep this place from becoming Satan's headquarters. We could get our city back and hold it.

As we neared Spring Street, I said to Strobert, "I have to tell you something. It's important."

"Well," he said, "anything you say seems pretty important right now."

"It's about you and me."

Strobert turned fully around in his seat.

I said, "I don't know exactly how to put this, or what it means exactly. But I need you to know this. I don't have any desire to eat you."

He said nothing. He looked at the driver who looked back at him.

"Well," I said, "what do you think?"

Mark Strobert cleared his throat. "I think it's a good start."

AFTERWORD

The persons and accounts in this tale are fictional, with the exception of Elizabeth Short, the famous "Black Dahlia." Her torture-murder has long been one of the great unsolveds of crime lore. I believe a large number of people would like to keep it that way because so much is invested in the romance of this mystery.

In my story, however, Beth Short's ghost puts the finger on a Los Angeles surgeon. The genesis of that is the book *Black Dahlia Avenger* by Steve Hodel (Harper). I not only read the book, but have met Mr. Hodel and seen his presentation of the evidence. The surgeon in question was Hodel's own father and Hodel, a retired LAPD detective, found this evidence after his father's death. No less a Los Angeles crime aficionado than James Ellroy (author of the novel *The Black Dahlia*) endorsed Hodel's account. That's good enough for me.

Pat Sajak is, of course, a real game show host. However, I do not believe Pat Sajak is a werewolf. I've only seen him in person once, at Dodger Stadium, and he appeared perfectly normal.

AUTHOR'S NOTE

Thank you for reading *I Ate the Sheriff*. Please take a moment to:

Leave a review on Amazon

For the other books in this trilogy, please go to the Mallory Caine series page.

I mainly write contemporary suspense, both stand-alone books and series. If you'd like to be on my email list you'll be among the first to know when new books come out. You get a free book, too. I won't share your email address with anyone, nor will I stuff your mailbox with spam. It's just a short, to-the-point email from time to time. For your free book, go HERE. (If this is a print version, go to JamesScottBell.com and navigate to the FREE Book page).

Thanks again!

Jim

MORE THRILLERS BY JAMES SCOTT BELL

The Mike Romeo Thriller Series

"Mike Romeo is a terrific hero. He's smart, tough as nails, and fun to hang out with. James Scott Bell is at the top of his game here. There'll be no sleeping till after the story is over." - **John Gilstrap**, New York Times bestselling author of the Jonathan Grave thriller series

The Ty Buchanan Legal Thriller Series

"Part Michael Connelly and part Raymond Chandler, Bell has an excellent ear for dialogue and makes contemporary L.A. come alive. Deftly plotted, flawlessly executed, and compulsively readable. Bell takes his place among the top authors in the crowded suspense genre." - **Sheldon Siegel**, *New York Times* bestselling author

Stand Alone Thrillers

Your Son Is Alive
Long Lost

No More Lies
Blind Justice
Don't Leave Me
Final Witness
Last Call
Framed

The Trials of Kit Shannon Historical Legal Thrillers

Book 1 - City of Angels
Book 2 - Angels Flight
Book 3 - Angel of Mercy
Book 4 - A Greater Glory
Book 5 - A Higher Justice
Book 6 - A Certain Truth

"With her shoulders squared and faith set high, Kit Shannon arrives in 1903 Los Angeles feeling a special calling to practice law ... Packed full of genuine, deep and real characters ... The tension and suspense are in overdrive ... A series that is timeless!" — **In the Library Review**

ABOUT THE AUTHOR

 James Scott Bell is a winner of the International Thriller Writers Award, and the author of many bestselling novels and books on the craft of fiction. He lives and writes in Los Angeles.

Visit JameScottBell.com

www.ingramcontent.com/pod-product-compliance
Lightning Source LLC
Chambersburg PA
CBHW020245180626
46810CB00006B/2370